Nehemiah and the Accountability Of Greed

Sharron C. Dickson

This book is a work of fiction. Names, characters, places and incidents either are products of the author's imagination or are used fictitiously. Any resemblance to actual persons, living or dead, events, or locales is entirely coincidental.

Sharron C. Dickson

Printed in the United States of America

First Printing: May 2018

ISBN-9781982986995

When all else fails……..Breathe!

Chapter One

It was a Tuesday! Nehemiah knew that because he always did the accounts for a company that made wellington boots for dogs, on a Tuesday. They were good accounts, always in the black, paperwork always in order. However, that wasn't the reason for the tightness in Nehemiah's belly, or the pounding in his chest that had been there since he had woken up, nor for the excitement running through his veins. The last time he remembered feeling like this, was when he went to Disneyworld, but then, he was only seven! This morning, the feeling had woken him early and had been present throughout his usual morning ablutions. Breakfast had remained stuck in his throat and even his usual Jasmine tea, on arrival at the office, had failed to calm his pounding heart. Lunch had been impossible and the avoidance of caffeine throughout the day had still left him unable to shake the rising excitement, the feeling that something amazing was about to happen. Yet, here he was at 2:00 in the afternoon; methodically working his way through the accounts of 'Chappy Feet' and nothing was more normal than that!

Nehemiah loved numbers! When Nehemiah Toosh worked with numbers, he felt as if he could see into the secrets of the Universe itself. They fascinated him, enthralled him, drove him out to the very limits of space and brought him home again, at super speed. He only ever truly felt at ease when he was working with numbers, he loved the infinity of them. It didn't matter how much he worked with numbers, he could never have enough! There would always be one that he had not seen before, a new number in front of him, a new calculation to answer a new problem. To Nehemiah it felt like a kind of immortality! As a child, he had been fascinated with Pi – the exact numerical value of Pi, actually. He had found the answer while he was still quite young, 3.14159265359….., but later, as an adult, he had discovered that mathematicians and their computers had extended the decimal representation of Pi, to more than 12 trillion digits. Now, THAT was a number to work with, never repeating, always different.

It was of no surprise then, that Nehemiah chose Accounting as his career. He worked hard throughout school, finally managing to secure a place in Oxford, where late nights at his desk, secured him the Distinction he so badly wanted. His Grade A, student record was not without its downfalls, though. He was unable to describe the inside of the Student Union Bar and to this day, was still blissfully, unaware as to the meaning, of a nightclub VIP list! He was always happy with his own company, but obsession with numbers and his penchant for hard work, had found him very few friends. Friends that would stay the course, that is. He had one good friend from University, who had also been studying Accountancy. His name was Damian and he had taken his Degrees to the City, where he now had a wife, a young son and an apartment worth a couple of million pounds. They kept in touch but even Nehemiah had to admit, that the friendship was dwindling. His life was just not interesting enough for most people to want to stay in regular touch, and after a while, he would fade into the background of their memory and slip unnoticed from their minds. However, he was content. With his numbers.

Upon finishing at Oxford, Nehemiah had managed to secure himself a training contract, with a good family firm that had been in business since 1820, a firm that was well thought of in Financial Circles! Four years later, Nehemiah had gained his CIPFA Professional Qualification and not long after that, he set up in business on his own. His company was known as NT Accountings. He now had two contracted clients, one of which was quite large, and he was making a modest income, without too much fuss and absorbing himself in his numbers, whenever he wished. He had been to a design company and had had a logo created and all the required headers, bits and slips of paper that were necessary, for a young man starting out in business. 'Making You Accountable', was written across every piece of stationary. He liked that! He liked the pun and the reality. A real-life double-entendre!

So engrossed was he, in his numbers, that he had failed to notice the small gentleman of Japanese appearance, who was now standing in front of his desk, until he looked up to, once again, check the clock.

"Excuse me!" Nehemiah said, "I did not hear you come in to the office."

"No!" said the small gentleman, "I was quiet. You were so engrossed in your work that I was reluctant to disturb you. It is good to enjoy one's work."

"How can I be of help?" Nehemiah asked, closing the book of accounts that he was working on, in order to best preserve his client's confidentiality, and pointing to a chair on the opposite side of his desk.

The small gentleman looked around the office and headed towards an austere leather sofa that was placed at the opposite side of the room.

"I think I would rather sit here, if I may and some of that Jasmine tea would be rather splendid. A perfect way to discuss our business."

"Absolutely!" said Nehemiah and headed to the small kitchen at the back of his office, to make some tea. It was only while he was waiting for the kettle to boil that he began to wonder how the gentleman had known about his penchant for Jasmine Tea!

"Ah! This is good tea, Mr. Toosh." Said the man as they settled back to enjoy its aroma and flavour.

"Nehemiah, please." corrected Nehemiah

The Japanese gentleman nodded his acknowledgement

"My mother loved Jasmine tea. It was her favourite beverage." Began the small gentleman. "Let me introduce myself Mr… sorry, Nehemiah. My name is Yoshi Toshimoto and for you to better understand my needs, it is essential that I tell you a little about my story."

"Please, go ahead." Said Nehemiah

"I was born into a very wealthy family and was an only child." Mr. Toshimoto started, "My parents were both older than most, my Mother being 40 when I was born and my Father 62 years old. I think this was one of the reasons that my upbringing was both a calm and quiet experience, but very loving, nonetheless. The warmth of my parents enveloped me, for every second of my time with them. As befitted a wealthy family of some standing, we had a large apartment in Azabu, in Tokyo, and my Father travelled every day to his office in Otemachi, while my Mother stayed at home with me and tried to teach me all she could about beauty and nature and art. She had a fondness for Bonsai trees and used to send a lot of time with her beautiful miniature forest, tending them, and singing to them in a gentle voice, all the time explaining to me how to ensure their continuing health. I never did get it right, I'm afraid. My talents lay in other areas." He shook his head sadly. "My Father invested money. However, he was a very principled man who believed in the necessity of balance in all things. As a result, he would only invest in companies that showed a good ethical grounding. So, you see, he did not spend his time playing with the Big Corporations who bulldoze their way through the hearts of the people and the soul of the earth. Rather, he put his money into the smaller companies who were known for actions that chiseled away at the hard canker that threatened the planet and the people on it. Nevertheless, he made a considerable amount of money to add to his already significant inheritance." Yoshi paused to savour his tea and collect his thoughts.

"You might say I had a privileged life, Nehemiah, and you would be right, but the memories that I treasure are not the ones involving our life in Tokyo, but the times we spent at the family retreat. The house was built on the western shores of Lake Kawaguchi, at the foot of the great Mount Fuji, or Fujiyama, as I knew it. They were beautiful times, Nehemiah in beautiful surroundings. Our house was large with long sloping roofs to protect from the rains during the monsoon season." He chuckled softly. "It was built on stilts, you know? So, that it could be protected during earthquakes, the stilts sitting on foundation stones. It worked too! The house would certainly bounce during those times but was left structurally sound. The gardens were filled with beautiful trees, cherry blossom bounced in the breeze, during spring, falling gently like confetti when it had served its purpose. While in the autumn, the garden was ablaze with the beautiful colours of the Osakazuki maples, looking like the flames of nature. My Father and I would spend a lot of time in these gardens. It is where he taught me to carve Netsuke, which I still do today. My parents went to live in this house, when my Father retired, and it was in this house, that he died. He lived until he was 102 years old, you know, a feat that he attributed to living a good life and I tend to agree with him. My Mother passed away two years before my Father, an event that her beautiful bonsai trees did not survive, I am afraid." A genuine sadness showed in Yoshi's eyes.

"I am very sorry," Nehemiah said, "About your Parents and the bonsai. I have never been very good with plants, which is one of the reasons why I opted to live without a garden, but as you say, my talents lie in other areas."

"I am not very good, myself, which is why it is very fortunate that I am in able to afford to employ excellent gardeners!" replied Yoshi and he started to laugh.

The sound of Yoshi's laughter took Nehemiah's breath away! It sounded like a babbling brook, the water bubbling and frothing over the smooth stones, chuckling as it raced from one rock to the next, splashing as it made its giddy way along to the river. It was a sound that came all the way from Yoshi's shoes and spilled out of his mouth, as if his tiny frame could not contain the happiness within him, as if the joy had to be released into the world, to be shared by all. It was the sound of tinkling bells, of rustling leaves, of daffodils, swaying and bobbing in the breeze, of ferns dancing in the sunlight beneath gently moving branches of majestic trees. It was the sound of true joy and Nehemiah breathed it in deeply and felt his muscles relax in its beautiful warmth.

"Ah well!" Yoshi said, once his laughter had subsided to a mere chuckle of its former self. "To business! I have continued my Father's company, both in practice and principle and now, I have a need to invest in an ethical accountant. I have been looking for one for some time and it was this that alerted me to your presence." Yoshi pointed at the business card in his hand. "Making you Accountable" it says, and that is what I need! I need you to make me accountable!" and he started to laugh again, all the way from his shoes!

Nehemiah looked at My Toshimoto. He had been fascinated by his story and he was beginning to feel a genuine affection for the little man. He was interested in the job, but he felt unsure as to whether he could handle such a huge account. Yoshi sensed his reluctance.

"Let me explain," he said "I have corporate accountants that deal with all of my business investment needs. They are a small firm, but they are very capable, and they do a good job. No! It is my personal accounts that I need you to deal with. You see, I travel all over the world, in my search for ethical companies and adventure and I get involved with all sorts of investments, from billions of pounds paid to large companies, to £50 given to a small business, that is trying to bring something beneficial into the world. These trips often lead to boxes of paperwork, receipts that must be entered into ledgers and balanced, just as business accounts must be. It is, however, a monumental task and only someone with a genuine love of numbers will be up to the task."

Nehemiah knew that he had a genuine love of numbers and he was extremely curious to see all of these receipts. The clients that he had now, where not that challenging.

"How many receipts are we talking about?" Nehemiah asked. "How long do you envisage the job taking?"

"I am not sure." Yoshi replied "I would imagine that at least a year would be required to get things in order, maybe longer. Maybe, we should start with a contract for one year and I think maybe a figure of £1,000,000 if that is acceptable to you. Of course, I will still be taking trips while you are working, so it may take longer than a year. What do you think?"

Nehemiah was astounded! Never in his wildest dreams had he thought that he would ever be offered such a job. It could set him up for life! However, more exciting than that, was the thought of getting his hands on those receipts, the numbers speaking to him of all the adventures that Mr. Toshimoto had had. The lights in the office, which were on sensor, suddenly came to life and it was only then that Nehemiah realised just how much time had passed, since they first sat down with their jasmine tea. He shuffled in his seat, placing the now cold beverage on the coffee table.

"It has become late, Nehemiah. Will you allow me to buy you dinner and we will talk more on the kind of work that I do and the kind of work you do and how we can help each other?"

"Certainly!" said Nehemiah and they left the office just as soon as he had placed the ledgers in the safe, not even washing up the porcelain, which was a first for Nehemiah!

They walked in companionable silence, along the main street towards a very fashionable Italian restaurant, the crepuscular light closing in around them, as the streetlights popped on, as if in alarm at the approaching darkness. Nehemiah walked into the restaurant which had just opened its doors and came to stand before an imposing figure. The Maître De looked at Nehemiah, down his very Roman nose, and after surveying him from head to toe, closed the appointment book, with a look on his face that screamed 'Refusal!'. He was just opening his mouth to speak, when Mr. Toshimoto entered the restaurant door and came to stand beside Nehemiah. The Maître De stopped in his tracks, the closed look on his face changing to surprise, which was quickly converted to a warm welcoming smile.

"Mr. Toshimoto!" he exclaimed, "It is always an immense pleasure to see you here, at our humble restaurant. I will have your table prepared immediately. Please, follow me." With that, the man walked imperiously into the restaurant, snapping his fingers at various waiters, firing commands and instructions like accurately aimed arrows, while people scurried off to deliver or find cover! Nehemiah and Yoshi were directed to two comfortable armchairs.

"If you would be so kind, as to allow me a few minutes to prepare your table, Mr. Toshimoto. The drinks are of course, complimentary"

Nehemiah watched, as the Maître De made double quick time to intercept a waiter who was about to seat a young couple at a table, with outstanding views of the gardens. The couple were duly seated at a different table, which still had a window and offered complimentary drinks to assuage their disappointment.

Crisis averted, the Maître De then proceeded to supervise the table setting and in no time at all, returned to inform them both that their table awaited. En-route to the table, Nehemiah averted his eyes in order to avoid the glares from the young couple at the window!

The evening passed in a sparkling bubble of excellent food, good wine and fascinating conversation and all too soon the meal was over, and it was time for Nehemiah to head home. Yoshi made a quick phone call and just as the bill was paid, right on cue, a liveried gentleman appeared, to inform them that the car was waiting. They were gently but firmly bustled into a car, which purred its way into the stream of traffic.
"This is a DS420!" Nehemiah exclaimed, delightedly "Of all the Daimlers, this has always been my favourite." He stroked the beautiful white leather of the seats and struck up an enthusiastic conversation on the benefits of the Daimler DS420 Limousine which kept them both happily entertained until they arrived outside Nehemiah's apartment. Then Yoshi became serious once more.

"I will leave you to consider my proposal Nehemiah. Will you call me when you have made a decision?"

"I will!" said Nehemiah "Soon!"

He stood on the pavement and watched the beautiful car drive away. A light drizzle had just started, and he turned up his collar and broke into a trot, reaching the doorway without suffering too much dampness. A quick, elevator ride later, he was home and he stood for a minute to catch his breath and just listen to the noises of his apartment; the clock in the living room, the hum of the refrigerator in the kitchen, the 'puff' of the flame igniting in the boiler. It all said, 'welcome home'.

He had bought this flat when he first qualified and had used the small spare room as an office initially. After a while, the paperwork and the lack of appropriate client meeting space, had forced him to look for his own office. The flat was a modest 2-bedroom abode in a relatively fashionable area and was his first home. He had gone for the minimalist look, primarily because he hated shopping and it made it so much easier to tidy up. He had the walls painted light grey, white and magnolia, because he wasn't very good with colour and stuck to blacks and greys accompanied by wood for the fixtures and fittings. Although the kitchen and bathroom sported all the mod cons, they were not very big, but rather sufficient to a young man living on his own. Once he had settled in, he had put his attention on to his work, and that was how he still operated. Occasionally, he would go and sit in the window seat of a café and 'people watch' while he ate, but it didn't really touch him, although he found it interesting to speculate how people's lives played out. He didn't get bored and he didn't regret his life alone. He just got on with things.

After he had been living in his flat for about a year, he had got a little restless. He decided it was time to be a little impetuous and, with a spring in his step, had headed to the DIY store to buy paint, for his bedroom. After a considerable amount of time walking up and down the aisles, he came across a colour called 'Straw Boater'. The name bought images to his mind of punting on the Thames, striped blazers, pretty girls and champagne. He felt frivolous and bought enough to finish his room and headed home to get started. However, when he got home and opened the paint, he discovered that it was just magnolia and no different from the colour that was already on the walls! He donated the paint to a local charity shop, that was trying to do a re-fit on the cheap and took on board the lesson – that you can only be, what you are! There was no point in trying to pretend to be someone else. It didn't work, and something always came along that knocked you back in line, with a thump! Nehemiah felt more content after that and settled into his life, as if it was a comfy pair of slippers; cosy and familiar.

During the night, Nehemiah woke, heart thumping. He felt as though he had been on a giant Ferris wheel, music loud, lights flashing, adrenaline pumping. He lay very still and breathed slowly through his nostrils, noticing every breath as it entered and exited his body. Finally, his heart began to slow and his mind calmed. He lay reviewing the events of the previous evening. The adventures that Mr. Toshimoto had talked about over dinner had seemed so fantastic to him. The places he had been and the people he had met, were all so magical, different and exciting that Nehemiah felt giddy just thinking about them. That life, was so far removed from his own, that it made him feel almost sepia in comparison. He wondered how it would be to work for such a man, every single day and how that would make him feel, how it might impact on his life, how it might change him? He was still thinking as his eyes finally closed and he drifted off into a deep sleep. Sleep that was filled with dreams of Inuits, in the coldest Greenland; Pyramids, rising over mere mortals, in Egypt; glittering ballrooms filled with masked dancers, in Venice and the minarets standing tall, above the buildings of Morocco. He slept deeply, until he was pulled to consciousness by the piercing trill of his alarm.

Chapter Two

Yoshi Toshimoto, sat enveloped by a huge, leather chair. The only sound he could hear, was the spit and crackle of the fire in front of him. He was deep in thought! While he had not expected Nehemiah to give him an immediate answer, he had thought, that he would have given a stronger indication, as to whether the offer would be accepted. Yoshi was convinced that he was the right man, for the job. His references were impeccable, he was hard working and thorough and had a seriousness and maturity that were well ahead of his young years. Yoshi had heard about the tragedy that had made him an orphan, but only in the vaguest terms and he was sure that Nehemiah was the man he was today because of the experiences he had had, sad or otherwise. He wanted this young man beside him in his adventures, what is more, he felt as if he needed him here. Yoshi sighed and shifted in his chair. He didn't deal very well with waiting. He was a man who was used to getting what he needed, when he wanted it, and now he felt a vulnerability that he hadn't felt in many years.

"What if he says, no?" his mind said "What if he doesn't want the job?

"Nonsense!" said Yoshi, out loud, startling the small cat that was stretched out in front of the fire. "Who would NOT want the job?"

Yet, in his heart, Yoshi knew that if the answer was no, there was nothing he could do about it. The whole thing literally, was in the hands of the God's.

"Please say, yes," he muttered under his breath, "Please say, yes!"

Somehow, Nehemiah managed to complete his tasks over the rest of the day, but his heart was not in it. Rather, his head was not in it, and he found himself checking and re-checking his work, just to make sure that there were no errors.

By the time he came to lock up his office, he felt exhausted! He realised, that he would have to make a decision soon. This was not just a contract that he had to sign, this was a new life! He decided to walk home, to better give him time to think. The next 45 minutes, saw him striding out, determinedly, hands in pockets, head bent, staring at the ground in the blind concentration that is only associated with people who are grappling with weighty problems. The 'problem', as he saw, it was two-fold. Firstly, whether he was able to do the job that had been offered him. Secondly, in order to give Mr. Toshimoto his full attention, he would have to find someone to take over his current accounts, so that he had time for all of the receipts. He felt that there would be no space in his life for other clients, once he took on Mr. Toshimoto. So, he had to make sure that someone would be able to take over his present clients. Someone, who he could trust to do a good job and someone, who would understand the client's particular needs. They would, of course, have to honour the present pricing strategy and deliver a high quality of service. He understood the benefit of happy clients, so it was important for him, to do this in a way that would not give cause for offense. By the time he had reached his apartment, he had come up with a plan.

Once he had settled in to his chair, he picked up the phone and dialed the head of accountancy, at the firm he had carried out his training with; Bradford, Bradford and Weekes. They were a good firm and they understood the value of loyalty, in a client/accountant relationship. The conversation lasted an hour and at the end of it Nehemiah had managed to get an agreement that they would take on both clients, on the same terms that had been agreed when he had started the contract. Next, he phoned his clients and arranged for them to come and meet him, in his office, over the next two days. He would have to put in extra hours to wrap everything up, but if he could pull this off, he would be free to take on Mr. Toshimoto's adventures, or rather accounts.

He knew instinctively, that he was meant to do this! His Mother, had had a saying, that she used to use all of the time, when he was a child; "If the train doesn't stop in your station, it is not your train!". So, as he was growing up, he always felt that fate played a part in his life, that some things were meant to happen. He had been quite calm about making big decisions, believing that it if was right for him, it would come together and if it was not, then there was something better waiting for him. However, he had never felt more certain about anything in his life, than he did about working with Yoshi Toshimoto! He KNEW, absolutely, that this was what he was meant to do. It was as if his whole life, had been in preparation for this moment, as if all of the prior events, in his life, had just been a build up to his true purpose and his true purpose revolved around Mr. Toshimoto. Why? He had no idea, but he sure as hell was going to grasp this opportunity with both hands! But, it had to be done properly, ethically.

The next two days were frantic! The first client had completely understood the situation, being a big company, and the changeover had happened very smoothly. However, Mrs. Lamprey, the Sole Proprietor of Chappy Feet, actually burst into tears when Nehemiah told her what he was planning to do with her account. It had taken two cups of Jasmine tea and much hand patting, to get her to stop crying. A meeting had to be hurriedly arranged, with Mr. Bradford, Senior and they travelled there together, by taxi, Mrs. Lamprey occasionally sniffing into her handkerchief, silence predominating. On arrival, Mr. Bradford, Senior, had been nothing short of amazing! He was a portly gentleman with a ready smile and a soft-spoken manner. He oozed reassurance and Mrs. Lamprey loved him immediately! Hi razor sharp wit and astute accounting ability, were gradually revealed as the conversation progressed and by the end of the meeting Mrs. Lamprey was grinning from ear to ear and positively glowing. Her eyes sparkling with humour rather than tears. The ride back to Nehemiah's office was filled with excited chatter and upon their return to the office, she threw her arms around Nehemiah in a bone crushing hug, wishing him much success in his new venture.

She then wandered off, singing to herself, as she searched for her car keys in her enormous handbag, leaving him shaking his head, as a smile slowly appeared on his face.

He slowly sat down in his chair and took a deep breath! It was done! He was ready! He could feel the tightness of excitement, in his belly and breathed a deep breath right into it, to ease it a little. With shaking hands, he lifted the telephone and dialed Mr. Toshimoto's number. The telephone only rang once, when it was answered by Yoshi himself.

"Nehemiah!" he exclaimed "I am so pleased that you called. Have you made your decision yet?"

"Yes, Mr. Toshimoto," he answered, "I have! I have decided to take you up on your offer and handle your personal accounts!"

"Excellent!" Mr. Toshimoto sounded genuinely pleased. "When can you come and start work?"

"Well, if you can arrange to have your accounts transferred to my office, at a time that is convenient to you, I can start working on them straight away. I have decided to work exclusively on your accounts, until they are completed." Nehemiah replied

"That won't work, I am afraid" said Yoshi "I could not possibly bring my accounts to you! There are just too many of them! They will not fit into your little office. You will have to come here to work, I am afraid."

This was something that Nehemiah had not envisaged, and it created a whole new pile of problems for him to deal with. He could not imagine how all of those receipts would look, how many there would be. However, he was determined that he was going to do this. He wanted this job!

"I am sorry," he said, "I had not realised. I am sure we can work something out, though and if I have to travel to your house every day, I am willing to do that. Where is your house, by the way?"

"Why don't you come out to the house and have a look at what is involved, before we officially seal the deal? In fact, why not make a weekend of it?"

"I would love to!" said Nehemiah

"Excellent! Then I shall have the car come and pick you up at 7:00p.m. on Friday evening, if that suits?"

"That would suit me just fine," Nehemiah said, "7:00 p.m. tomorrow evening. I will look forward to it."

After he had hung up the phone, Nehemiah sat back in his chair and tried to picture what Mr. Toshimoto's accounts actually looked like. He could not imagine so many pieces of paper that they could not fit into his office, even with the upstairs storage! Then he realised that he had an office that he no longer had a use for. He would have to deal with that! It was always better to have a building occupied, heated and lit, than empty. Buildings that were empty for any length of time, usually meant trouble! Big Building Trouble!

It was just after he had moved into his flat that he had realised that he would need to find an office. It had taken a few months searching, to find a lovely little place, just off the High Street. It had some beautiful period features, fireplaces, sash windows and cornicing. It was accessed via an alleyway that ran between two shops, but as all of Nehemiah's clients were found by referral and word of mouth, a 'shop front' was not really necessary to his business. The building had originally been a small house, with a small entrance hall, which led onto a comfortable size living room.

A large fireplace dominated one wall, with large windows on the opposite wall, letting in plenty of light. Through the living room was a family size kitchen and access to a stairway that led up to a reasonable size bedroom, with en-suite facilities. It had taken some time to get the Planners to agree to a change of use, from residential to business and once that had been achieved, it had taken even longer for the Architect and designers, to come up with the plans. It was now a modern, warm and comfortable office space, with plenty of storage upstairs, a small office kitchen downstairs and toilets for clients off the main office. A comfortable sofa and coffee table at one end and Nehemiah's beautiful antique desk at the other, finished off the office, where he had been successfully and comfortably working for two years now. The desk had been a gift from his Father, on completion of his CIPFA. He had been overwhelmed by the beautiful lustre of the mahogany, which framed the deep, red, leather top that had been recently restored. His Mother had bought him a deep, red, leather chair of similar style, to match. He had been deeply moved by both gifts. Both his parent, had been tragically killed in a boating accident, not long after and every day, he was grateful for these beautiful, lasting reminders of their support and generosity. Often, while taking his lunch, he would sit back into his chair, feeling it supporting him and run his hands over the warm wood of his desk, feeling his fingers glide smoothly around the edges and he was reminded that he was still supported by his parents, even though they were no longer here. It had taken a long time and a lot of soul searching for him to get over the loss of them both. Even now he felt a void in his heart, where they used to be. He was sure, that they would have been proud of him, though and he knew they would approve of the moves he was now taking in his life.

The next day was Friday, and it went by in a blur of activity. In no time at all, Nehemiah heard the intercom announce the arrival of Mr. Toshimoto's car.

He checked the lights were on automatic and that the heating was turned down to tick-over, then picking up his weekend bag, he let himself out of the flat, locking it securely behind him. On the pavement, a liveried driver was standing beside the passenger door of the red and white Daimler, and on seeing Nehemiah exit the building, opened it for him. Only when he was content that Nehemiah was safely seated, did he walk round to the driver's door and get in the car.

"Thank you very much, for coming to pick me up." Nehemiah said through the open, glass partition.

"You are very welcome, sir." replied the driver, in a crisp English accent.

With that, Nehemiah settled back into his seat and watched the busy city rush by, eventually giving way to lush, slightly swaying, trees and green, rolling hills. He turned his thoughts to the job he was about to assess and the man responsible.

Yoshi Toshimoto was a small man with a huge heart! That he was immensely wealthy, was beyond doubt and yet Nehemiah had never met anyone who was so unaffected, by such wealth. His compassion was obvious and the way that he treated people demonstrated both kindness and respect. He was obviously a happy man, and his laughter bubbled out of his mouth at every opportunity, infecting everyone around him with joy. He was very astute, and his sharp mind was admirably demonstrated, to anyone who engaged him in conversation and yet, he listened intently and had an uncanny knack of reading between the lines, of picking up on the inference and easily making the leap to actuality. In fact, it almost seemed as though he could read people's minds! For a small man, he seemed to take up all of the space that he occupied, but not in a way that made a person feel uncomfortable.

Rather, it was as if he enveloped people into his warmth, brought them in out of the cold, into a safe and comfortable environment, giving people the freedom to express their innermost thoughts. Thoughts, which were held by him, carefully and confidentially. Nehemiah could never imagine him gossiping about anybody, or indeed, making fun of anyone. In fact, he possessed an almost magical quality about him, that had made Nehemiah feel looked after and cared for, when they had sat down together. He wondered if Yoshi's beliefs had anything to do with this and made a mental note to inquire as to His philosophical ideals, whenever he had the opportunity. Nehemiah knew that both Buddhism and Shinto were very popular in Japan and he suspected that as a child, Mr. Toshimoto had benefited from instruction from both belief systems, especially as His Father and Grandfather before him, had been so determined to deal only with ethical companies. Nehemiah, himself, had looked into the Buddhist philosophy while travelling through Asia, after his parents had died. It had given him no small amount of comfort to think that his parents were continuing with their lives in another situation, ever moving towards their goal of spiritual freedom. He had worked hard, since that time, to try and feel kindness towards people, from all areas of society and all walks of life, sometimes going out of his way to try and ease people's suffering, in any way that he could. However, he was aware that there was always room for improvement and that his own attainment of enlightenment, was still quite a long way off!

"Always be kinder than you feel, Nehemiah" he thought to himself, "And, that includes being kinder to yourself!" He smiled.

"We will be arriving in about five minutes, Sir" said the driver.

"Thank you for that." Said Nehemiah, deciding that the enigma that was Mr. Yoshi Toshimoto would have to be figured out over a period of time and was too deep to be resolved in one short car journey. He looked at his watch, it read 8:15.

"One long car journey!" he thought.

Shortly thereafter, the car swept through an old gateway that once must have held impressive gates. To the left of the gateway, surrounded by a beautifully tended garden sat a traditional lodge house. It was very a very 'chocolate box' picture, except for the solar panels on the roof and the small but very busy windmill that seemed to be situated not far behind a substantial, vegetable patch. Nehemiah smiled to himself. Mr. Toshimoto's ethical business model, obviously applied all the way down to his property's electricity supply!

"Good for him!" he thought.

The car continued on along a single-track road, driving through beautiful tree tunnels, where he was astounded to see red squirrels, sitting on the branches. He had never seen a red squirrel in his life before!

"They have always lived here, Sir!" said the driver, meeting his eyes through the rear-view mirror.

Nehemiah remembered, too late, to close his mouth. The journey continued on, past a lake on the right and rich, green, rolling paddocks on the left, the horses calmly chewing grass, tails twitching lazily. In the distance a substantial stable block could be seen alongside, an equally substantial miniature block of similar buildings. Squinting hard, he was able to make out the outline of what looked like large pigs in that area.

"Is that pigs, I can see over by the stables?" he asked the driver.

"Yes, Sir, it is! Mr. Toshimoto has a fondness for Vietnamese Pot-Bellied Pigs. He currently owns sixteen of them." The driver replied.

"Sixteen is an impressive number of pigs." Said Nehemiah

"Thank you, Sir." nodded the driver.

"I look forward to meeting them." said Nehemiah.

Shortly thereafter, the road widened and became as straight as a Roman road. The landscape opened out into formal gardens, revealing a beautiful topiary of fantastical creatures. Nehemiah spotted at least one unicorn and a dragon. Whoever had created them, was very skilled, indeed and they seem to have been caught mid movement, frozen in time, forever green. Behind the topiary stood a very grand house, with an imposing flight of stairs leading to two, enormous doors. A small parapet, ran parallel to the front of the house, protecting the terrace from prying eyes. The windows loomed large, taking up the full height of the rooms within, allowing the light to stream in. The car swept up to the wide stone steps, and the driver opened the door for Nehemiah.

"Mr. Toshimoto will be expecting you, Sir." The driver said, indicating the steps with his arm. "I will bring your belongings in, forthwith."

Nehemiah thanked the man and proceeded towards the two huge doors at the top of the steps. He noticed how detailed everything was, how finely crafted. The two marble lions on either side of the steps, looked as if they had just come to rest and he almost expected to see the rise and fall of their ribcage. On reaching the house, he couldn't help but notice the beautifully carved doors. The carvings were of dragons, flying in and out of cherry trees, the blossom swirling in the air, a casualty of the flight. Every scale of the dragons gleamed and every petal of falling blossom was caught in stasis.

He couldn't help but reach up and touch the beautiful images. It was as if the dragons had paused, in their game, because he had arrived, and that once he stepped inside the house, they would continue their carousing. He watched as one of the dragons started to move and jumped in fright. It was the chuckle, that made him realise that the door was actually being opened, the action giving new life to the carvings.

"They are very lifelike, are they not?" said Mr. Toshimoto, still chuckling.

"They are exquisite!" said Nehemiah "It is good to see you again, Mr. Toshimoto" he continued, extending his hand.

"Yoshi, please." He replied opening the door further to welcome Nehemiah into his home, clasping his hand in a firm, but friendly grip.

He led Nehemiah into the hallway, with its deep, mahogany, floorboards, which glowed with a plum coloured light. A large staircase led upwards, branching into two other staircases, which led to the upper floors. A deep red carpet ran down the centre of the stairs, accentuating the warmly glowing banisters. Nehemiah could almost see the loving caresses of the people that had used it to support them, over the last few hundred years.

"This way, please." instructed Yoshi, leading Nehemiah off to the left of the staircase and down a long hallway, which was filled with beautiful paintings and sculptures. Passing the exquisite works of art, in a dream, Nehemiah walked, mouth open, head turning at every opportunity. Here, was the Samurai armour, bristling with threat, glistening with honour; there was a scene embroidered on silk, capturing a maiden at work, Mount Fuji watching over her as she leaned into her task. He just kept putting one foot in front of the other, unable to take in the aesthetics of it all. Until, that is, he came upon a figure of a crane, that stopped him dead.

It was just about to take flight, poised, ready to lift the foot that connected it to earth and feel the air beneath its wings, beating against it to gain altitude and soar over the rest of the poor, earthbound, creatures. Every strand, of every feather, clearly visible, every muscle clenched, ready for the final leap. The detail was so fine that Nehemiah's hands itched to touch it even as his manners forbade it.

"It is beautiful, is it not?"He heard Yoshi's voice behind his left shoulder.

"It truly is!" he breathed, "Who created it?" he asked in a whisper, reluctant to break the spell that it had woven over him.

"My Mother." Said Yoshi and he turned and continued the walk down the hall.

Nehemiah pulled his eyes away from the crane and looked at Yoshi's back as he proceeded along the corridor. Shaking his head, he trotted to catch him, his mind reeling as to how it must have been, to be raised by such a person. He briefly looked back, to bid farewell to the bird. The corridor ended in large panelled double doors, which were opened for him. Nehemiah, had been amazed at everything he had seen since entering the house but the sight that greeted him now, made him feel truly overwhelmed. The thrill of excitement started in the soles of his feet and slowly, started making its way through his body, as his eyes took in the sight before him. Finally, in awe, he moved and took his first step into his future.

Chapter Three

The numbers were everywhere! There was no place that he could look, that did not fill his eyes with numbers. Slowly, moving into the room, looking all around him, the numbers shouted to him, scrambled for his attention. Each one promising a new story, a new solution, a new path that would lead him into an unknown future. He remembered to breathe. In every available space, was a box or container of some description. Some were beautiful wooden boxes, intricately carved, threatening to spill all of the numbers from their delicate lids. Some were cardboard boxes, crudely painted, the size of small coffins. Some had black lacquered surfaces, the size of shoe boxes. There were leather bound trunks, the black iron strapping, giving them the appearance of pirate treasure. All of it calling to him, making his hands twitch. He shuffled further into the room. A desk was positioned in the middle of the room, the chair vacant, the leather-bound ledger opened at a clean new page, the pen calling to him. He stumbled towards it, sat, lifted the pen and opened the lid of the box closest to the desk, and so it began!

Date: - 01-01-2000 - Expenses for the Egyptian expedition- £1,559,320.25, sailing in the Arctic - $23,475 – Safari Park purchase $7,672,916, Tesco - £23.60, releasing animals into the wild, environmental, humanitarian, building, creating, developing. Each piece of paper, an intricate a part of Yoshi's life, each one telling a story, each one waiting to be 'accounted'. As he wrote, Nehemiah became lost to the real world. He did not hear Yoshi talk to him. He did not see him taper off, realising what was happening to Nehemiah. He did not look up as Yoshi quietly exited the room, closing the doors behind him, leaving him to his new adventure. The numbers sang to him, pulled him into their universe, each one a small galaxy of action and reaction, accumulation and separation, peaks and troughs, losses and gains, all interacting with each other.

All connecting and building a picture, of the life of the little man, creating one giant story. The story explaining the intricacies of the person, who was now quietly walking back along the corridor to sit on his own, in the huge dining room, that sat thirty-six people.

Nehemiah continued for some time. He was unaware of the Liveried Gentlemen that entered the room, to close the curtains and switch on the lights. Unaware of the plate of food, that was placed beside his left elbow, on the desk. Old habits die hard, and his hand sought the food, putting it into his mouth, as he continued to enter the numbers in the columns, page after page. He was unaware that the sun had set with a glorious display of pinks, reds and oranges, each one reflected by the lake, that he had passed on his way to the house. Unaware, of the passage of the moon over the house surrounded by its sparkling jewels in the night. Aware only of the numbers until he heard the words.

"My Honourable Friend!"

He looked up, allowing his eyes to lift from the page in front of him, to take in Yoshi's face. He was shocked at the passage of time. Shocked, that Yoshi was standing in front of him in his dressing gown, carrying a tray containing a steaming teapot and tea cups. He slowly released the pen, letting it rest in the fold between the pages and rubbed the back of his neck, circling his shoulders as he did so.

"What time is it? He asked in a croaky unused voice

"My friend." Yoshi answered, "It is 2:00 a.m. Will you not finish now? I fear my hospitality has been very remiss. After all, you came here to be my guest for the weekend and all you have done since your arrival, is work. You will be well paid for your time and efforts."

Nehemiah stretched his long legs out underneath the desk and sank back into the chair.

“That is ok, Yoshi. After all, we have not yet signed an agreement. This night is on me. I enjoyed it, such numbers and all of them representing such adventures and journeys, each connected to the other. I really have been enjoying myself. You lead an amazing life.”

Yoshi chuckled and set the tea tray on the desk before Nehemiah could lift up the pen, again and began to serve the tea.

“I am sure it looks more glamorous on paper than it is in real life, but I must admit that I am very privileged. Come let us drink tea together, before you catch some sleep. Then we can sit for breakfast and after that, I will show you my most prized pets. My Pot-Bellied Pigs!”

Nehemiah carefully removed the pen and closed the ledger, moving it to a position of safety. He mentally checked in with his body to see how tired he was after working so long into the night, and discovered that actually, he was not tired at all. More invigorated, inspired. He felt alive! He let out a laugh.

“I feel amazing, Yoshi! But I will join you for tea and after a small sleep, breakfast and I will relish a good walk and a few Pot-Bellied greetings.”

The rest of the weekend passed in companionable activity around the rambling estate that was Yoshi’s home. When Sunday morning arrived, after breakfast, Yoshi led Nehemiah into his office and the contract negotiation began in earnest. Nehemiah found himself arguing against a lot of clauses, most of which were for his benefit.

“You cannot possible pay the mortgage on my office, Yoshi!” he stated

“But, if you have to work here I could not let you be out of pocket Nehemiah!” returned the little man.

"Leave that to me! I have an idea as to how I am going to deal with my office. I do, however, have one stipulation. I need to have my own desk and chair, here with me when I work."

"Of course!" said Yoshi, "I will arrange for it to be brought here, on your say so."

In very quick time a contract had been drawn up that pleased them both and a quick phone call to Yoshi's lawyers, saw the production of the said papers. A signature later, and it was decided. Nehemiah had one week to get all of his affairs in order, and then a car would arrive for him at 7:00 a.m. Monday morning. In no time at all Nehemiah was sitting comfortably in the Daimler, speeding his way back to his little apartment, mind racing.

Dorothy Weekes sat looking out of the kitchen window drumming her fingers on the worktop! If she had to listen to Justin, go on and on again, about his lack of space, she thought she would go completely insane! She wondered if it was because he was much younger than the other two, that made it difficult to reason with him. Maybe she was just too old now, too tired. She sighed! Her father, Mr. Bradford (Senior) of Bradford, Bradford and Weekes, had done everything he could to help Justin, after he had completed his Accountancy qualifications, but the truth was that they just did not have any more space in their offices to give Justin the office, that he needed. Her Husband, Geoffrey, a senior partner in the firm, had managed to find him a room toward the back of the building, that used to house the office supplies, but it wasn't really, much bigger than a broom cupboard. It certainly wasn't instilling the confidence in his clients, that he deserved. She put the kettle on and sighed again. Justin was the youngest of her three children. Her eldest son, David, had studied architecture and now had his own firm in the City.

He had recently got married and she was very hopeful at the prospect of becoming a Grandma in the future. Her daughter Jessica, had gone on to become a doctor, specialising in Oncology. She was very dedicated to her work and Dorothy had no delusions about her ever having the time to meet anyone, who would be able to put up with her dizzying schedule. She had been forty when Justin had appeared, rather unexpectedly, though the age gap between the siblings had never been a problem, and they had become very close. It was at this point in her ruminations, that the phone rang.

"Nehemiah!" she exclaimed, "How lovely to hear from you! How are you?"

"Dorothy." Nehemiah said, "I need your help!"

"What is it? What can I do for you?" she said. She had always had a soft spot for Nehemiah, since he had started training with them, all those years ago. As she listened to his problem, her face broke out into a large smile. The she started to laugh.

"My dear boy!" she said, "You have no idea, how happy you have made me! Justin has been desperately looking for an office for months now, but they have all been too small or too expensive! He has been operating out of the old supply cupboard at the back of Daddy's suite! It just isn't working! Call him Nehemiah! Call him now please! He will be delighted."

A few minutes later, it was a different Dorothy Weekes that waltzed her way across the kitchen, to make the tea!

Nehemiah put the phone down and shook his head smiling!
"Some things were just meant to be!" he thought.

The meeting was all arranged with Justin Weekes for the following morning and it looked like his office would be rented out, with little fuss.

That night Nehemiah slept the deepest most relaxed sleep that he had had in years and woke to the sun streaming across his face with a golden, warm caress. The first thing that he noticed, was the feeling of excitement in the pit of his stomach and, not a little fear, for the unknown turns his life had taken. He was suddenly reminded of the Christmas that he had asked Santa, for a bike. Not just any bike but the beautiful shiny red BMX bike, that he had seen in the shop on the High Street. He was eight years old. His heart had almost thumped out of his chest as he had walked, slowly, down the stairs to the living room, on Christmas morning. He had stood with his hand on the door knob hardly daring to open it, in case he should be disappointed. It was, after all, all he wanted. Eventually, he had summoned the courage to turn the door knob and open the door and there, beside the enormous Christmas tree, had been a beautiful shiny red BMX bike, just like the one in the shop window. He could hardly believe his luck and had spent the next half an hour looking over every inch of it, touching the gleaming handle bars, admiring the shiny red paint before he had actually allowed himself to sit on it. Thinking about it now, lying in his comfy bed, he could smell the pine scent from the tree and hear the rustling of paper, as his parents gathered up the torn wrapping, checking every inch of it before stuffing it into black plastic bags, for the recycling bin. He took a deep breath and looked around the room, to shake off the memories, then sprang from his bed and headed to the kitchen.

"Today is the first day, of the rest of my life!" he said.

The next three days were taken up with meetings and arrangements for Justin to take over his office. Contracts had to be prepared and papers signed, and banking arrangements made, but by Wednesday evening, he arrived home feeling more confident. He had just put the key in the door when he heard the phone ringing. It was Yoshi, arranging to have his desk and chair picked up on Friday morning and with that appointment, he was free to enjoy the next few days packing clothes and arranging the things that he was going to take, to his new job on Monday.

He spent the whole of Saturday wandering around London, visiting a gallery, eating in restaurants and finally seeing a show. He didn't know when he would next feel inclined to be in the large city, so thought he would make the best of it, now. Sunday flew by in the hustle and bustle of packing and shutting down the flat and before he knew it, Nehemiah was standing in the hallway, complete with bags, waiting for the intercom to buzz, to announce the arrival of the car. When it finally went off, he jumped and dropped his keys! With a last look around, he left the flat, locked up and headed downstairs to the Daimler.

The journey to Yoshi's house flew by and soon Nehemiah was once again walking up the stone steps to the imposing front doors, where Yoshi was standing smiling, arms open in welcome.

"At last, you are truly here!" said Yoshi "Come, your desk has arrived!"

They headed back along the corridor to the room of boxes and Nehemiah felt the same rush of excitement as he entered the room. The boxes had been moved to the outside of the room and the fireplaces at either end had been cleared in preparation of being laid. In the centre stood Nehemiah's desk and chair, looking small and unimposing in such grand surroundings. The ledger was open on the desk, where he had left off and the box of receipts he had been working on were standing open on the floor beside it.

"I have taken the liberty of putting a small fridge in your office so that you can have refreshments whenever you need them." Yoshi, explained. "I also have installed a small area so that you can avail yourself of your Jasmine tea, whenever you desire."

Nehemiah noticed a small area against the wall that consisted of a beautiful lacquered sideboard on which stood a small urn and a teapot and cups. Several tea caddies stood at one side and he was immediately curious as to what they contained.

Yoshi walked him over to it, and they spent several minutes investigating the contents of the side board and the fridge beside it.

"Thank you, Yoshi." Nehemiah took his hand and shook it earnestly. "I am very grateful. It is such a long journey to your kitchen, I am afraid I would end up doing without!"

Yoshi laughed his beautiful tinkling brook, like laughter and his eyes shone."You are very welcome Nehemiah. Now, I shall leave you to your work. Should you need anything at all, please just ring this bell and someone will be straight here to help." He indicated a ring pull located at the side of each of the fireplaces. With that he turned and headed to the door. "I shall have your things put into your room and will see you at lunch, hopefully." And he left chuckling to himself.

Nehemiah made his way to his desk and sat in his chair. He felt so grateful for this opportunity that had been given to him. He took out his pen, from his inside pocket, unscrewed the top, and lifted the lid on the box of receipts. Then, he disappeared into the universe of numbers, for some hours. Once more, he was unaware of the food that was placed on his desk, though he ate it anyway and continued on, until Yoshi, again, came into the room, to break his attention away from the numbers.

"You have had a busy day!" he said as he looked at the empty boxes beside Nehemiah's desk and the neat piles of receipts stacked in front of him. "Let us retire to the drawing room; I have had a little treat prepared."
Nehemiah stretched and closed the ledger for the day. He found it difficult to comprehend how quickly his day has gone, but the view from the window clearly showed a setting sun. They walked together in companionable silence along the corridor, though the entrance hall and on to another corridor. Large doors on the left led to a light room, with large comfortable sofas on either side of a crackling fireplace.

On the coffee table in front of the sofas, two large mugs of steaming hot chocolate sat, with small bowls of marshmallows to the side. Nehemiah sank into the nearest sofa and lifted the mug with an enormous grin on his face.

"I could get used to this!" he said

"Good!" was the reply and they sat enjoying their treat in silence, neither feeling the necessity of polite, small talk. A short time later and dinner was called so the men made their way through to the dining room, for a light dinner. They talked about the latest environmental work that Yoshi was taking part in and the conversation was lively and stimulating. Still, Nehemiah started to feel the day catching up with him and, over coffee had to stifle a yawn.

"Come, young man," Yoshi said watching him struggle to stay awake. "Let me show you to your room so that you may rest that weary body of yours. I have had your things moved there, so you should be comfortable."

Nehemiah followed Yoshi wearily, unsure of where they were going. They finally arrived at his room.

"Thank you for all of your hard work today. I will see you at breakfast, which is usually served at 8:00 a.m. If you need anything, please just ring." Yoshi indicated a ring pull at the side of the bed and turned to leave. "Goodnight."
"Goodnight." Nehemiah replied, taking a look around the room. He could not see his things anywhere. He saw two doors, one on each side of the enormous bed, so opened one gingerly to see if that was where his possessions were located. The door led into a walk-in wardrobe and he could see that all of his clothes had been unpacked, folded and hung appropriately, his shoes neatly lined up on the shoe racks and, he suspected, polished! He was astounded! Such care was being taken of him and his things, and he felt a little emotional.

He had been on his own for a while now and had forgotten how it felt when people did nice things for you. He re-entered the bedroom and walked around to the other door to investigate. This one led into a very large bathroom and it was at this point that Nehemiah was struck by the theme throughout the rooms. Egyptian! The bathroom had, as a centre piece a large sunken bath in deep blue marble the taps and fittings throughout, glowed warm gold. There was a small antechamber that led to the spa shower on the left and at the back of the room another, that discreetly housed the WC and bidet. He toed the heels of his shoes and slipped them off, bending down to remove his socks and then stepped down into the sunken bath. He sat, trying it out for size. It had always been a problem, to find a bath that was long enough for him to lie down in. Baths were not made for people who were six feet five inches tall! This one was, however, and he lay fully stretched out on the floor of his sunken bath, amazed! He started to feel his eyes heavy and thought that bed, really, was the place to be. He forced himself out of his bath and went to clean his teeth and complete his night time ablutions. Once complete, he found his PJ's and headed for the bed. It was luxurious, with beautiful soft Egyptian cotton sheets and a memory foam mattress, that he had only ever imagined in his dreams. He lay quietly just experiencing the comfort of it all. In no time at all the silence was broken by gentle snoring and then, peace. His dreams, when they came, were comfortable and relaxing and he had a most restful night's sleep.

When Nehemiah started to surface, he became fully awake, quickly. Not the sudden awakening of fright but the instantaneous awareness that comes from a good night's rest and the anticipation of a good day to come. He stretched and lay looking at the new surroundings, taking it all in, with appreciation. Then he heard a light tap on the door.

"Come in." He said cautiously.

The door opened, to admit a Liveried Gentleman carrying a tray, expertly balanced in one hand.

"Mr. Toshimoto thought you might appreciate some tea when you awoke, Sir," he said placing the tray on a golden chest with inlaid colours of turquoise and carnelian. "It is Jasmine tea, Sir."

"Thank you so much," Nehemiah said sitting up, "That is very kind."

"You are welcome, Sir." The Liveried Gentleman replied as he let himself quietly out of the room.

Nehemiah leapt out of bed to stir the tea in the pot and made his way into his bathroom. It was then, that Nehemiah noticed that the flooring was decorated with embedded golden scarabs tastefully placed in random sequences around the sunken bath and along the marble tops next to the sink. He made his way to the antechamber, at the back of the room, looking all around him as he went. As he raised his eyes Nehemiah noticed two golden statues in the shape of cats. Their painted eyes appraised him, frankly, and their Godlike poses, were not a little menacing. Everywhere he looked he saw something Egyptian always beautiful, always tasteful and very imposing. It was while he was washing his hands that he noticed the towels, complete with hieroglyphic monograms. He smiled, and made his way back through to the bedroom, to enjoy his jasmine tea. He poured his tea and sat on the bed, taking in all of the exotic decoration. Above the bed hung a beautiful canopy in blue and gold silk with fine lines of turquoise and coral running through it. Around the edges golden scarabs seemed to scurry along and this continued across the thick rug that lay alongside the bed. Everywhere he looked were beautiful Egyptian art, pictures that hung on the wall displaying images of pyramids at sunset, golden sphinxes poised with a kingly demeanour, cats of all shapes and sizes, each with a different painted face, each displaying their separate, regal, personality. It was then that he noticed the death mask! He placed his cup on the bedside stand and headed over to have a look at it. It was hanging on the wall opposite the door and as he neared it, he could see how exquisite it was.

It looked to him to be solid gold, the eyes painted on it, staring at him with a wide open, almost startled gaze. The enamelling was so fine, the reds and blues of each tiny piece shining brightly. It was ablaze with turquoise and coral. Nehemiah slowly lifted his hand to gently touch the mask, to feel the coolness of the metal, the smoothness of the enamel. He knew he shouldn't touch it, but its beauty called to him. He felt he had to touch it to see if it was indeed real.

"I wouldn't do that if I were you!"

The voice came from behind him and he whipped around to try and find the source of the words.

"That it was not very wise because you see, if you had touched it, I would have to have my guards kill you!"

Standing in front of him was a young man that Nehemiah could only describe as a young Pharaoh. He looked to be between 12 to 14 years old and he was naked down to his waist, with the exception of a large gold and enamel collar. From his waist, he was covered in white cloth and his feet were bare. Standing behind him were two large gentlemen wearing only armbands and a loin cloth, each of them carrying a spear with a large sharp looking head. None of them were smiling!

"Who are you?" asked Nehemiah in a shaking voice "and where did you come from?"

"I am the Pharaoh!" The young man said haughtily, "and I came from of my home to find the man who is going to make me Accountable. I believe that is you?"

Nehemiah nodded but he could feel his stomach sinking.

"Come!" Said the Pharaoh, "I will show you what you will do for me." He turned towards the open door through which was now visible a desert scene, spilling its sand on to the beautiful Egyptian carpet.

"I'm really sorry," said Nehemiah contritely, "I cannot help you at this time. I have a contract with Mr. Toshimoto that will take an entire year to fulfill. I cannot renege on this contract."

The young Pharaoh looked at Nehemiah directly. His face darkened in anger.

"You Will Make Me Accountable!" He said

The Pharaoh's guards moved towards Nehemiah, pointing their spear's menacingly. Nehemiah took a step backwards.

"Well," he said, "I am not going anywhere in my P J's! I need to dress before I leave this room."

"Proceed!" said the young pharaoh crossing his arms.

Nehemiah scooped up the clothes that he had dropped on the floor the night before and had made a hasty exit into the bathroom closing the door behind him. He leaned against the door and breathed a sigh of relief, glad to be out of the presence of the Pharaoh. He realised his hands were shaking. He could not understand what was happening. He dressed quickly then heading towards the antechamber and scooped up his toothbrush and toothpaste, slipping them into his back pocket. Then, he turned to face the door and took a deep breath.

"You always regret the things you don't do, more than the things you do, Nehemiah." He said to himself, then put his hand on the door knob and let himself out of the bathroom, with a sideways, longing glance at the sunken bath. He ignored the Pharaoh and his guards and entered the walk-in wardrobe, heading straight for the shoe rack. He selected a sturdy pair of leather boots that he often used for walking when in the country and headed back to the bedroom to put them on. The silence was palpable as the three men watched Nehemiah prepare for his journey. He reached for his phone, hesitated then picked it up and slipped it into his pocket.

"What is that?" said the Pharaoh.

"A communication device," answered Nehemiah.

"Like a tablet?" asked the young Pharaoh, thinking of the wax tablets that his scribes used.

"Just like a tablet!" said Nehemiah smiling, "it will help me make you Accountable."

"Then you may bring it." said the Pharaoh

"Thank you."

"Can we now proceed?" said the young man sarcastically.

"I think so," said Nehemiah, "Where are we going?"

"Come! I will wait no longer!" said the Pharaoh, heading towards the bedroom door. Nehemiah looked through at the doors and stopped, aghast at the sight before him. He had not noticed the desert flowing into the bedroom or indeed the people standing outside the door, beside a canopied platform.

"Come!" said the Pharaoh, "I will not tell you again."

Nehemiah stumbled after him, remembering just in time to close his mouth. He felt the arid heat of the desert hit him firmly in the face and felt its hot breath in his throat. The sun was so bright, after the cool Egyptian room, that he raised his hand to shade his eyes, squinting to try and see the scenery around him. The Pharaoh clapped his hands.

"Get this man some shade!" he barked from his platform, underneath the canopy. A small boy scurried off in the direction of a massive, white pavilion. The Pharaoh clapped his hands again and then seated himself upon a golden coloured chair. The men standing around his canopied platform rushed forward to lift it upon their shoulders.

It was obviously very heavy, and the men were in very poor condition. They struggled under the weight. Eventually, they got their legs under them and started to move towards the pavilion, slowly. Nehemiah glanced back and looked straight into the Egyptian room in Yoshi's house. He breathed a sigh of relief. If he just turned around now he could get back and slam the door shut and maybe this would go away. As if reading his mind, the two guards trotted back and stood either side of the door, their spears forming an X shaped barrier to re-entry. Nehemiah sighed and moved toward the Pharaohs platform which was now slowly moving away.

"You cannot go back!" the young Pharaoh said, once he caught up with him, "Not until I say so, and I shall not say so until you have made me Accountable!"

"But, Mr. Toshimoto..." Nehemiah started.

"Can wait!" finished the young man and he stared ahead with stubborn determination that gave Nehemiah the distinct impression that the subject was now closed. He watched the procession move out and felt a jab in the small of his back. He whipped his head round to see yet another spear wielding guard.

"It's alright!" he said raising his hands "I am going! I am going!" He had to stride out to catch up with the Pharaoh.

Once inside the pavilion, the temperature dropped. Beautiful brightly coloured rugs lay beneath their feet. The positioning of the openings, allowed for the air to circulate, offering some relief from the heat. The accommodation inside was quite considerable and they passed through several, generously sized rooms before reaching a space that looked to Nehemiah, like a throne room. In the centre of the room was a large golden coloured seat, with carved armrests, decorated with beautiful jewels.

It stood on a raised plinth, with space all around it, so that it could be viewed from all angles and guarded on all four sides. The young Pharaoh walked over to the seat and sat, looking imperiously over the people around him. They fell to their knees, as one, leaving Nehemiah standing, looking at the young man.

“I can’t really see, what it is you need from me.” He said
The Pharaoh tutted, looking irritated.

“I thought you liked working with numbers.” He said.

“I do! Very much so!”

“Then that is what I need from you. That is where you shall help me. You see, I have a numbers problem.”

“What kind of numbers problem?” asked Nehemiah.

“I will show you.” said the Pharaoh rising to his feet.

Just at that point, the little boy who had been dispatched to find some sort of shade for Nehemiah came hurtling into the room. He saw everyone face down on the floor and immediately threw himself to the floor, a piece of cloth in one hand and a small round fan in the other. The fan flew out of his hand as he dropped and went scuttling across the floor. Coming to rest at the young Pharaoh’s feet, as a look of annoyance crossed his face.

“You!” he shouted “Stupid boy! Come here!”

The young boy ran to the golden seat and once again threw himself on the floor. Pharaoh grabbed a stick that was resting against the arm of his chair and raised it in preparation of delivering a beating, to the boy.

“Don’t!” Nehemiah was surprised at the loudness of his own voice. There was a shocked intake of breath all around him.

"If you touch that boy, I will not help you, no matter how long you keep me here. This is a condition, of my making you Accountable and it is NOT negotiable."

A heavy silence hung in the air as everyone waited with baited breath, for the backlash from Nehemiah's protest. The Pharaoh lowered the stick.

"The boy is good for nothing and stupid!" he spat, "I have no use for him and if I am no longer able to gain pleasure from beating him, then he is truly worthless to me. You want to protect him? Then, you can have him! Boy?"

"Yes, master?"

"You belong to him now!" the Pharaoh aimed a kick in his direction which the boy easily dodged as he came to stand behind Nehemiah.

"I do not want a slave." he said.

"Then I shall just kill him." said the Pharaoh, a smile forming at the corners of his mouth.

"But," continued Nehemiah, "I will, no doubt, need a young assistant." He turned and ruffled the boy's think, black hair. He put his hand into his pocket, feeling something appear there, and pulling his hand out discovered two pineapple chunks sitting in the palm of his hand! He gave one to the boy and popped the other into his mouth. The boy followed suit and Nehemiah watched delightedly, as the boy's eyes widened with surprise and his face split into a huge smile. Nehemiah gently lifted the head cloth from the boy's hand and tied it roughly into a form of headdress which was more modern day than ancient Egyptian but did the trick anyway. Once this was accomplished he stood and looked at the Pharaoh. The young Egyptian King looked back at Nehemiah, trying to get his anger under control. Once he was sufficiently composed he said just one word.

"Come!"

They headed out of the room, attendants scurrying after them, trying to keep up after having to scramble off the floor. The heat hit him like a wall, when they exited the pavilion. The Pharaoh just stood tapping his foot in impatience and Nehemiah was unsure as to what he should do next. However, in short order six men came running towards them carrying the canopied seat and bought it to a halt beside the Pharaoh who glared in response. Once he was seated, men hoisted the platform onto their shoulders and set off at a trot, with Nehemiah struggling to keep up with them even with his longlegs, stretching to a wide stride. Every now and again he had to break into a jog to catch up with them and glancing up at the Pharaoh, he saw his face set in a satisfied grin. Nehemiah scowled to himself but carried on regardless. He guessed they had not got off to a good start, but he couldn't change that. Physical violence was not an option in his universe. Ever!

The Pharaoh signalled a halt by raising his hand, as they crested a small hill. The view before them was a long valley, stretching out for miles. Every inch of it seemed to be bustling with movement, as Nehemiah looked in amazement at the gigantic building site. He could see a huge palatial structure, in front of a massive pyramid. Everywhere he looked, people were pulling ropes, scurrying from one place to the next, striking rocks with tools, the noise ricocheting around the hills, that enclosed the site. The construction was certainly grand but the people building it were in a sorry state. They were bone thin and bowed in back and in nature, parched and withered, beaten and bruised. He could see a fat man with a loincloth on, walking up and down the lines, every now and again, he would raise a wicked looking whip and hit one of the people. Sometimes they did not get up and when he saw that, the fat man would pick them up by an arm and fling them out of the way, as if he were removing useless rubbish. As he watched, Nehemiah saw that once the fat man had moved on, people would scurry out of the line and collect up the fallen person and bustle them away.

Nehemiah started to feel his blood boil! That human beings were being treated so badly, was unforgivable. Yet, the people who were suffering such unspeakable cruelty, showed so much kindness and compassion for their fellow man's suffering, at no small risk to their own safety. There was goodness in the people here and a kindness, that belied their situation. That could not be said for the regime! He turned to the Pharaoh.

"I have seen enough!" he said firmly.

"But, you have not even seen it all!" said the Pharaoh, shocked. "You have only had the briefest of overview. Come, we will go down to the buildings so that you can admire my beauty."

"No!" said Nehemiah firmly, "I have seen enough!"

The Pharaoh's eyes widened in shock and his face turned a deathly white. Never in his entire life, had anyone ever spoken that word to him, and he had no idea how to respond. He tried to smile but Nehemiah had already turned and has heading down the hill towards the construction area in long angry strides.

"Come back!" the Pharaoh shouted. "I will arrange a chair for you. We will have refreshments!"

There was no response.

Nehemiah was furious! Although he respected authority there was no way that he was going to stand by and watch such despicable behaviour! He heard the young Pharaoh shouting, but just kept walking. Well, marching actually! When he reached the start of the construction site, he saw that it was much worse than he had anticipated. The guards were using whips on the men, women and children working on the site, but they were also spitting on them, and kicking them, at every opportunity.

He watched as one of the guards kicked a young boy over and raised his hand to lash out with the whip. He raced over and got there just in time to hold the guard's arm up.

"You can't do that!" he shouted at the guard.

"Can't do what?"

"You can't treat people like that!" Nehemiah said holding the guard's arm aloft.

The guard gave a sneer.

"They are not people!" he said and started to laugh.

Over his shoulder Nehemiah could see the Pharaoh approaching and he whipped round, looking him straight in the eye while keeping a firm grip on the guard's arm.

"I will not help you with your Accountability while there is one single person suffering!" he stated loudly, trying to get control of his anger.

The Pharaoh looked at him puzzled."No one is suffering!" he said, "The guards are all well fed and get regular breaks."

"Not the guards! The builders! They are suffering!"

The Pharaoh started to laugh!

"But they are not people!" he exclaimed, "They are slaves! They are born to this life. It is their destiny to be so treated."

"No!" Nehemiah said. "I will not help you under these conditions!"

The Pharaoh sighed and signalled for the platform to be lowered to the ground. He stepped off, and walked over the Nehemiah, who now released the guard's arm so that he could drop to the floor in obeisance. He reached out his hand.

"My friend!" the Pharaoh said, "It is but a difference in culture. This is how we live, it is our way."

Nehemiah pulled his arm back from the Pharaohs reaching hand.

"No! Not while a single person suffers. All men are equal, in my eyes."

The Pharaoh started to laugh, and the guards and entourage joined in.

"But, Nehemiah," reasoned the Pharaoh, "How could I possible afford such grand structures, without slaves to build them? No one, has that much money, except Mr. Toshimoto, of course."

Nehemiah stopped in his tracks. "You know Mr. Toshimoto?"

"Yes! I haven't personally spoken to him or entertained him, of course, but I know of him. My building projects are very important to me, which it is why you must make me accountable in this."

Nehemiah folded his arms across his chest, in a stubborn stance.

"No!" he said and started to stride away from the construction site, back to the pavilion, back to Yoshi's spare bedroom, the little dark-haired boy trotted beside him, grinning like a thing possessed! He didn't get very far, when he became surrounded by the armed guards. Each pointing their spear in his direction! He was furious! He turned to the Pharaoh.

"I will not help you in this, Pharaoh, and I will not be compromised. I cannot and will not condone such cruelty, so if you want me to help you, this will have to change." He stopped to draw breath. "And you can call your dogs off me, or just kill me now and then you will never be accountable!"

The young Pharaoh immediately signalled for the guards to put up their spears.

"I agree! I need to make changes, but I need your help with this. Please accompany me back to my temporary accommodation, and you will tell me what needs to be done."

Nehemiah was still angry but could see that some progress was being made. The fact that the Pharaoh was backing down, showed how much he needed him to continue with his projects. That gave him leeway to negotiate aid, for these poor people. That gave him an idea.

"Stop the building!" he demanded, "And feed and water these people and then I will sit with you and help you. Not before!"

For a moment, Nehemiah thought he had gone too far. He could see the venom in the young Pharaoh's gaze, but he did not look away. He would not back down. Time passed, and it felt like an age to him, but eventually Pharaoh gave a slight nod of his head. He turned to the guards.

"See to it!" he commanded then resumed his seat on his platform and clapped his hands. The men set of towards the pavilion at a trot. The guards watched him disappear, with open mouths.

"You heard him!" shouted Nehemiah, "Get to it!"

They jumped to attention and set off in the opposite direction which left Nehemiah and the little boy standing alone. He let out a big sigh and bent over, hands on his knees.

"Phew! That was close!" turning towards the boy, he asked, "What is your name?"

The little boy shrugged. He looked the boy up and down trying to decide what would be a suitable name. He reminded him a little of the cartoon character Mowgli, from the Jungle Book but shook his head. Then he grinned!

"Then, I shall call you Moses!" He reached into his pocket and pulled out two hard lumps. "Pear drops!" he said handing one to Moses and popping one into his own mouth and they set off at a more leisurely pace towards the Pharaoh's pavilion, in companionable silence.

Chapter Four

Nehemiah and Moses finally made their way back to the Pharaoh's pavilion, but when they entered, they could see that the young King was not happy to be kept waiting. In fact, he was furious!

"Another first!" Nehemiah thought!

It had taken them longer than expected, because on the way he had decided that it would be good fun to teach Moses how to whistle! Then they had to keep stopping so that he could show him how to position his tongue behind his teeth. Once Moses had produced his first whistle they had then worked together to come up with a tune that they could both whistle at the same time. As a result, it really had taken a long time to get back. Nehemiah looked at the Pharaoh's face again. Deference was required!

"Your Highness," he said bowing slightly, "Please excuse my tardiness. I am not used to walking in such temperatures and I was tired from my recent adventures."

He could see that the title and the bow went some way to mollifying the Pharaoh, who now gestured stiffly for him to take a seat beside him, be it all at a lower level. Once he was seated, a hand clap summoned a string of people into the room, each carrying platters laden with food. Nehemiah realised that he was hungry and got stuck in with enthusiasm. The young Pharaoh did not disrupt his eating, so he ate his fill, but not before heaping food onto a plate and passing it back to Moses.

"I order you to taste this for me!" he barked with a wink and Moses, duly ordered, got stuck in too!

The Pharaoh could not hide the look of disgust on his face, but he refrained from comment and politely picked at the various platters arrayed in front of him.

Throughout the meal, Nehemiah made sure that he looked every slave that served him in the eyes and thanked him, or her, for their service and as the meal started coming to a close, he could see that it was making a difference. These people were walking a little straighter and meeting his eye, when he spoke to them. He wanted the Pharaoh to see that if you treat people with respect, they will respond in kind. Their work would be better delivered and of better quality, as the people learned to have pride in what they did. However, looking up at his face, he could see that this was a lesson to be learned another day. The disgust was only thinly veiled and that was slipping fast. Nehemiah just smiled pleasantly up at him, in an attempt to relieve the situation.

After the meal had finished, Nehemiah found that although he was unsure as to the correct protocol, he was getting quite sleepy. He did not know if it was custom for people to retire at his time of the day, so he was very relieved when the Pharaoh issued a curt order to find him a room in the east wing and withdrew. An old man came to stand before him and signalled with his arm, to follow him. Nehemiah was astounded at the size of the pavilion. It just seemed to stretch on and on. Eventually, they turned off into a corridor and then branched off again. He assumed it must be the east wing. They then turned into a large room, which was dominated by a huge bed in the centre. There were storage boxes in gold and small stools to sit on, and chairs with arm rests that were exquisitely carved. The floor was covered in brightly coloured rugs and oil lamps hung from the ceiling.

"Thank you." Nehemiah said turning to the old man. He held out his hand in greeting. "My name is Nehemiah. What is your name?"

"I don't have one." was the reply, "I am usually addressed as 'slave."

"But, you must have been given a name by your parents when you were born."

"I never knew my parents and was usually referred to as 73. You may use this name if you desire." said the slave formally.

Nehemiah took his hand and shook it firmly. "73!" he said, "I am very pleased to make your acquaintance." and he smiled. He looked around the room and noticed that there was only one bed.

"Can we find another bed, to put in this room?" he asked 73.

"Do you not like the sleeping accommodation?"

"Yes, absolutely! But there are two of us." Nehemiah pointed out.

"Slaves sleep on the floor." 73 pointed out.

"That may be true, but you see Moses is not my slave. He is my assistant and assistants have their own beds. He will need a small chair too as this one is far too big to be comfortable for him." The older slave was dumbfounded. He looked at Nehemiah with incomprehension.

"What is an assistant?" he asked

"Someone, who helps another person, in a job that they have to do." Nehemiah said, seeing the lack of understanding plain, on the man's face. "Is it possible to find the bits and pieces that I need for this room, please? Then I will explain everything."

The slave bowed low and left the room speedily, which gave Nehemiah the opportunity to start moving things around, in the room, to better suit his needs. Moses tried very hard to help him move things but actually, got under foot more that he helped, so he was put to work creating a new tune that they could both whistle later. He took this task very seriously sitting on the floor, crossed legged in the corner where he wouldn't be in the way.

A short time later, the old slave was back with several other people in tow. Each carried something that was required by Nehemiah. The most important of which was a canvas bed which was very similar to the camping beds of old. The furniture was placed around the room at Nehemiah's request and soon it look exactly as he needed. Then he looked at the men and women in the room and asked them if they had eaten today. They just looked at him aghast.

"We eat at sundown." said 73.

"Not today!" said Nehemiah and he told the servants and that he was starving and would like to be served with food immediately. They took off at a trot and soon returned with platters of food. He saw that it was simpler fare, than the previous food he had eaten but good, nonetheless. He then instructed all of the people in the room to sit down and eat. It took some doing! In fact, it was only when he 'commanded' them to eat, that they listened to him. There were six people altogether and as they ate we went among them, introducing himself and asking their names. Most did not have names, and this disturbed him. So, he came up with the idea of asking them to think of a name that they would like, that he could use when he was talking to them. This prompted much laughter and some quiet discussion. He watched the people eat and noticed that they ate efficiently, quickly, but not leaving a single scrap behind. He was pleased to be able to do something so simple to help them. He looked over to check on Moses and noticed him quietly snoring, curled up in the corner. A smile crossed his face and he went over to him, gently picking him up. He carried him to the huge bed which was now against one wall and placed him on it, tucking him in gently. The silence in the room was palpable and he turned to see all of the slaves watching him, mouths open. He shook his head, gently.

"Let him sleep," he said, "he has had a busy day." When he met the eyes of 73, he saw tears falling.

"Thank you." The old man said.

"You are welcome," replied Nehemiah and then started to yawn himself. He made the people promise to return before breakfast and made his way over to the canvas bed. He lay down and in no time, was fast asleep and the only sounds in the room were the strangely harmonious, gentle snores of the two tired adventurers.

The old man walked into the room, just before dawn. He took in the scene and stopped in his tracks, amazed. There was Nehemiah, in the camp bed and Moses in the huge bed, both fast asleep and both snoring gently. He had never experienced such kindness from a stranger before. He had no understanding of what it would be like to help someone in the way that He did, when you didn't even know the other person or their circumstances. To have compassion for complete strangers, to understand the basics of humanity so thoroughly, that reacting to them with kindness, became second nature. The old man had suffered his entire life. He had learned to live with cruelty and oppression. Learned to eke out what small relief he could, whenever it was possible. He had seen terrible atrocities, every single day so that had become normal to him. He understood that the slaves needed to stick together, protect each other wherever possible. To keep their heads down and make the best of what they had. Yet here was a man who had been kidnapped and taken away from his life, a stranger in a stranger's land, standing up for what was right. Putting his life on the line, for people that he had never even met, people that he knew nothing about. Nehemiah had instinctively known their pain and their suffering and put himself in the line of fire while ensuring that they lost none of their self-respect, none, of their basic humanity. He shook his head gently. This man deserved the truth more than any other person he had ever met. If they had any chance of improving their lot, it would only come if they worked with this young man and gave him their hearts, minds and muscles. He quietly turned around and headed back to the kitchen to prepare a light breakfast, as requested, thinking as he went.

Nehemiah woke up and lay listening with his eyes closed, to the sounds of the pavilion. That is how he knew that it had not been a dream, that somehow, he was in ancient Egypt, so that he could make the young Pharaoh Accountable.

"So be it!" he thought and sprang out of bed and tripped over Moses, who was lying beside his cot, sprawling on the carpeted floor. He looked around. "What are you doing?" he asked, slightly annoyed.

"Slave not sleep, in bed!" was Moses reply.
"Well that is alright then, because you are not a slave! I free you as of now!" was the reply. The young boy looked horrified and tears started to well in his eyes.

"But, wh... where will I go? What will I do? Ho..how will I live?" he stammered.

Nehemiah took a deep breath. "You will stay here with me and become my assistant. I have need of a good assistant, one who runs fast on good strong legs, one who likes to smile and especially one who whistles cheerfully as they work! For all that work, you will receive wages, money that you can save or spend however you wish. You will have your own bed and your own work space, here beside mine. How do you feel about that?"

Moses just looked at him, thinking about what he had just said, then slowly a huge grin appeared across his face and the tears started falling in earnest. He ran to Nehemiah and grabbed both his legs, wrapping both arms around them and stood for a while sobbing. Once he had calmed a little, he let go and looked up into the man's face.

"Thank you." he said

Nehemiah ruffled his hair and putting his hand into his pocket pulled out two hard yellow sweets. "You are welcome!" he said, "Sherbet Lemons!" he handed one to Moses and popped one into his own mouth.

"Now, as my assistant, your first job is to go and find 73 and tell him that we are ready for him now. Also make sure he brings everyone with him from yesterday."

"But, what about the guards?" Moses asked, "They will beat me! They will not believe that I am your assistant, Nehemiah!"

"They will not beat you and they WILL believe!" he walked over to the doorway and stuck his head out. He called over the guard. "This young man is on errands for me all day. They are of the utmost importance! The Pharaohs Accountability depends upon it. He is not to be molested! Do I make myself clear?"

The guard looked at Nehemiah suspiciously but nodded his head and turned to speak to his fellow guard, who listened and then limbered off in the direction of the guard's quarters, to spread the news.

"Done!" he said to Moses, who grinned and ran off to complete his errands, whistling as he went.

After the boy had gone, he busied himself tidying the room, making beds, making space, planning what he wanted to say and how he was going to say it. He needed to help these people cultivate self-respect and that started with a person's name. Their idea of self. In short order they arrived, bringing put up tables and platters of food and stools to sit on. Then everyone just stood looking at Nehemiah. He grabbed a plate and loaded it with food instructing everyone to do the same and for a while the only noise that could be heard was the noise of people eating. Once that was out of the way, he stood up and started to explain to everyone that the small boy, that was his assistant had been freed and had taken on the name of Moses. He told them about the story of Moses, in the bible, being found in a basket by the Pharaoh's daughter and that as he had found him, the name seemed appropriate. The rest of the people nodded and smiled but the story didn't really have any impact upon then.

That is until 73 stood and cleared his throat."I have been thinking about this and have decided to take a name myself." He said self-consciously. "I rather like the name of Zaph-enath-parn-eah." There was silence while his fellow slaves took in what he said and then someone let out a guffaw! Everybody else started laughing, much to the old man's consternation. One person laughed so hard, that he actually fell off his stool, knocking into the table next to him, causing it to collapse and spill the contents all over the floor. There was a sudden silence then the laughter started again but more raucously! Even Nehemiah, couldn't help but join in. Once the hilarity had calmed a little, people started to clean up the mess, picking up broken crockery and cleaning up spilled honey from the rugs and this is how the guards found them. Everyone froze in terror as the guards walked in to the room. Nehemiah wandered over to them with a grin on his face.

"Sorry!" he said holding out his hands in supplication, "I go a bit over excited and had an accident."

The guards looked at him suspiciously but everyone else was busy cleaning, as they should be, and they could see nothing wrong taking place.

"The Pharaoh will see you in one hour." They said before leaving the room, eyes following every move.

Before discussions could build again, Nehemiah suggested to 73, that if he wanted to be called Zaph-enath-parn-eah that he had every right to be so but that for convenience sake it might be an idea to shorten it to Zaph. The old man agreed and 73 became Zaph! He spent the next hour talking to all of the people, listening to their stories and discovered that they each had many skills. Zaph was in fact a Master Mason who was responsible for all of the fine carving on the palace, until he had fallen out of favour by being too honest and upsetting one of the foremen, who had been making money on the side.

He had been badly beaten and ended up working in the kitchen but also spent a lot of time washing sheets in the river with the women. His story was not unique. All of them had a similar tale to tell and it hurt Nehemiah to think of all that knowledge and talent being wasted. Putting this right would have to become a part of the Pharaoh's Accountability, he decided as he said goodbye to them and headed to the Throne Room, Moses in tow.

The Pharaoh sat on the throne fingers idly tapping the armrest. He smiled when they entered.

"Welcome!" he said to Nehemiah, "I am looking forward to hearing your plans for my Accountability."

"I am looking forward to that too! However, I feel that I must go down and have a look at how your building projects are doing and how to make things much more efficient for you. There is no point at wasting money on inefficiency, is there?"

The young Pharaoh beamed! This was exactly what he wanted to hear. "What do you need?"

Nehemiah paused, he had to be careful in the way he worded things here. It had to feel as if the ideas were all those of the Pharaoh. "In order for me to assess what can be done, in helping your projects grow, I will need to tour the facilities and the local areas. I will need to have a team of people to guide me around and procure anything that is essential to the task and I will need this done as quickly as possible. Now, to do this cheaply, I can use slaves for that, if you agree?"

"Definitely! I shall find you some."

"Actually, Your Highness." Nehemiah artfully inserted the title to broaden the young man's smile and ease the transition of control, "I have gathered a few that didn't seem so busy this morning. I think they will do, if it suits?"

The Pharaoh was delighted that it was working out exactly as he needed without any effort to himself. “Perfect! As long, as it will not affect my projects, and will improve my Accountability, we are at your disposal.”

“I will need to speak with people as I inspect the situation. I wonder if it is possible to change the working schedule for a few days, maybe a week. I understand that this may slow things slightly at first, but it will make things better in the long run and the quality of work should increase, without costing more.”

“That sounds very efficient. As long, as things progress as they should and there are no great delays in my projects, I have no problem. However, I will be watching very carefully, Nehemiah. I will not be overly delayed, and I will be made Accountable!”

“Absolutely, Your Highness!” he bowed low and started to back out of the Throne Room, smiling to himself.

On the way back to his room, he gave instructions to Moses, who took off at pace. He stretched his stride and swung his arms, returning with purpose. Once in his room he took out his mobile and switched it on, making a list was top priority but he couldn’t do that when everyone was here. He sat quietly in the corner laying out his plans, back to the door so he could cover himself if someone caught him by surprise. A few minutes later, plan formulated, he heard Moses whistle getting louder and quickly saved his document, and switched off his phone, slipping it into his pocket. The ten slaves he had started getting to know filed in behind Moses and stood looking at Nehemiah expectantly.

“I have a plan!” he said, “Please have a seat as this could take some time. I need to tour all of the construction site and the surrounding areas, to get a feel of how things work around here. I also need some equipment and a place that I can work, this room will not be enough for all of us when we all start working together.

I will need tables, chairs and a means to record information, whatever that is here?"

Zaph put up his hand, "We use papyrus to write on. It is not cheap but if we are careful in our use, then I am sure the Pharaoh will not object to your supply."

"Splendid! So, I guess the next question is who can read and write?"

All hands went up, with the exception of Moses. He put his head down. Nehemiah went over to him.

"Your talents lay in other areas, your strong legs and your superb whistling which we are going to work on soon." He ruffled the young boy's hair and put his hand into his pocket and pulled out two hard round shapes. "Humbugs!" he said giving one to Moses and popping the other into his own mouth. His gaze returned to the people in the room.

"The other thing that I need is assistants, not slaves! So, if you all agree to become my assistants, you will be treated as such, with respect and kindness. You will receive a wage, although that will probably not be much, and you will eat and drink on a regular basis. You will not be molested in your work, but you will be expected to work! This is going to be the most difficult task that has ever taken place here and I can promise you that nothing will ever be the same again! So, who would like a job?"

All hands shot in the air, Moses included!

"Excellent!" said Nehemiah. He went among them asking names and speaking about abilities and thinking, all of the time, how best he could use these people to achieve his aims. Once he had finished he separated them out into smaller groups and gave them their tasks, with the exception of Moses and Zaph, who he left till last. Finally, when there was just the three of them left, he spoke to Zaph.

"I need to be able to tour the area. I need to be able to see everything, not just the buildings. I want to see where people sleep and eat, where they wash where they heal and where they worship. I need to be able to understand exactly what is happening here and exactly how it works, warts and all!"

"I can do that for you Nehemiah." Said Zaph seriously, "Let me guide you, let me show you everything, good and bad."

"Thank you, Zaph." He said turning to Moses, "Now, you have a very special job! You will be coming with me, but I really need you to work on your whistle! Sometimes, I might want to go somewhere, where the Pharaoh does not want me to go. That means that I might have to sneak off and hide and be careful. If you work on your whistle, we can agree a tune that you will whistle, that can warn me of approaching danger. Do you think you can do that, as well as running my errands?" Moses looked delighted and nodded his head vigorously!

"Excellent!" said Nehemiah, ruffling his hair.

They set off straight away, heading down to the palace construction site. Moses ran on ahead, whistling as he went. It sounded as though he were experimenting with various tunes. Nehemiah smiled to himself.

"I want to see all of the areas that no one sees." He said, turning to Zaph. "The places where the slaves sleep, where they eat, where their food is stored."

"We will need to go to the palace first. The guards will have been instructed to watch where you go, so you will need to put in an appearance, and be suitably impressed before we can sneak off to the darker places. After a while, they will get bored watching you and then we can go explore reality."

"Don't worry Zaph, I will be the most boring tourist there is!"

They continued on, until the building loomed tall above them. Nehemiah felt his heart would break at the plight of the people building the palace. They were hungry and cowed. Many were completely unsuited for the type of work they were being forced to do. There were young children and older women in amongst the able-bodied men and all of them displayed fear, and most showed signs of torture. They walked around the building, looking at the features and admiring the architecture. Nehemiah nodded at the guards and made suitable noises of appreciation, for the stunning work that was being done. He loudly proclaimed the wisdom of a Pharaoh, that would invest so heavily in such wonders and at the patience of the guards, forced to endure such tedious work in such appalling heat. The guards were pleased and eased up their suspicious looks, eventually, feeling relaxed enough to wander away from where he was. He continued on with Zaph, touring, only every now and again, he would stop and help someone who was trying to lift a particularly heavy load, asking for names and smiling. When he saw that the guards had stopped watching him altogether, he turned to Zaph.

"Let's go see some real life." He said.

Zaph put his hand on Nehemiah's elbow and steered him down an open corridor, through the palace, they continued walking briskly until the noise of the whips and the hammering lessened. Moses appeared beside them, tugging at his arm. He stopped and gave the boy his attention. Moses started whistling a simple tune that was not unlike the Humpty Dumpty nursery song.

"Is this your warning tune, Moses?"

Moses nodded, looking very proud of himself.

"Excellent choice!" Nehemiah reached into his pocket and pulled out two lumps, "Chocolate limes!" he handed one to Moses and put one into his own mouth. Moses trailed along behind them, quiet for once while enjoying his treat.

As they continued to walk, the road turned into a path and then into a sandy track. The smells became more difficult to ignore and eventually when he looked around, Nehemiah saw that they had left the construction site well behind. When they finally came to a standstill, Nehemiah could see row upon row of narrow streets. Each, exactly the same, as the other. There was no decoration, no colour, just silence and sand.

"This is where we all live." Explained Zaph, "These houses are where we all sleep. Food is taken as we work so there is no need for dining facilities. We only have need for shelter while we sleep. We have no belongings, or at least very few and those that we do have, have no material worth. This is it, Nehemiah! Our home!"

"Show me!" he croaked

They walked down to the first row of buildings. They were all the same size, oblong, one door at one end and two small windows evenly spaced along the side of the long wall. These were covered with loose sacking, in an attempt to keep flying insects out, but as they entered the room, it was obvious that it was also keeping out the light. It took a while before their eyes adjusted to the darkness after the sunshine outside. The whole building was one large room with support pillars running down the length of it. It was filled with row upon row of beds, or rather tatty rugs covered with clean but tatty sheets. Beside each bed were small heaps of belongings, some more than others. Some had small beds closer to the bigger ones. The space between each bed could be measured in inches, the people being crammed in as closely as possible. The heat was stifling and although it looked unsoiled, the smell of human suffering reeked throughout. Nehemiah let out a soft groan.

"This is despicable! Nothing is important enough to force such cruelty on people. Surely, there must be some other way?"

"This is all there is!"

They left the building and walked on to the next. Everyone was the same, row upon row of poverty and suffering, until Nehemiah could hardly bear to look anymore.

"How can you bear it, Zaph?"

"It is what we have. There is no point in worrying because I cannot change that. I have only me and I have only my life. There is no point in being upset about things I cannot change."

"How many people live in this whole area?" Nehemiah asked, his arm sweeping the complex.

"I do not have that number, but I do know that it was originally built to house half the number of people who live in it now.

Nehemiah whipped round and stood looking intently at Zaph. They stood stock still and his gaze never strayed.

"Half, you say?"

Zaph nodded.

"That's it! A temporary solution, but a solution nonetheless." Nehemiah set out for the construction site, striding along with a determined look on his face. The others had to run to keep up with him but all the time his mind was working, thinking about the numbers of people, about the square footage of the accommodation about the cost, about the amounts. With him, it all came down to numbers!

As he made his way back to the pavilion Nehemiah thought about the task in hand. It was a huge undertaking! The statistics were enormous! Any other person would be overwhelmed by the amount of work that had to be done. But, statistics were just numbers and Nehemiah DID numbers!

He understood them in a way that other people understood simple tasks like setting their alarm clock, or making tea in the morning... They were as natural to him, as breathing, as the gravity that held his feet connected firmly to the ground that he walked on. By the time he had reached his temporary home, he knew exactly what he would do, and he headed immediately to the Pharaoh's audience room, nodding to the guards as he strode purposefully past them.

Entering the audience room, Nehemiah could see that the Pharaoh was already busy with business. There were three well-dressed men in front of him, hands raised in supplication. The young King seemed to be considering their request but the look on his face showed that his heart was not in it. When his eyes met Nehemiah's, they lit up with interest and something resembling relief.

"I will consider your request." He said imperiously, "You are dismissed." He clapped his hands to signal the end of the audience. The three men were escorted from the room by the guards, each of them glancing surreptitiously at Nehemiah as they passed.

"Nehemiah Toosh!" said the Pharaoh, rising to greet him, hands outstretched. "We were concerned for you. You were not in the pavilion and we did not know where to find you. Are you well? Have you eaten? You must be tired. Come and sit with me while you tell me where you have been." He started walking towards the exit that would lead to his private chambers. When he saw that he was not being followed, he stopped and turned looking at him quizzically. Nehemiah really wanted the Pharaoh to be on his side and had decided the best way to achieve this would be through flattery and humility. When it came to Egos, they youngster had the biggest that he had ever seen! He turned to face him and gave a low, slow bow of sheer subservience.

"Your Highness! I am saddened and ashamed that I have given you cause for concern. I merely went to survey your immense building project so that I could better see how to serve you and your Accountability. I must admit that I was overwhelmed by what I saw and took longer than I had planned. Forgive me." He did not look at Pharaoh's reaction but rather, kept his head bowed and his eyes downcast. The youngster was delighted! He clapped his hands with glee, his voice betraying his pleasure.

"There is nothing to forgive! Come I would hear all about your adventures." He said turning towards his chambers, confident that Nehemiah would follow.

Once they were seated, the Pharaoh turned once more to Nehemiah, eyebrow raised in enquiry.

"Well? What have you been up to my honoured guest?"

Nehemiah paused. This was going to be tricky and he needed to make sure that he took the right approach. "Your building project is immense. In fact, I have never seen such a fantastic piece of architecture! The idealism behind it is truly splendid and I am certain that when it is finished it will be a wonder without parallel." The Pharaoh beamed, nodding his head while puffing out his chest in pride and straightening his spine. "However, it is unfortunate that it will never be completed in your lifetime!"

"What? Why would you say such a thing? It is the purpose of my life!" the young man exclaimed, astounded at such brutal honesty, crushed by the cruel dashing of his moment of pleasure. "If this is about your ideas of slavery, I will not tolerate it!"

Nehemiah held up his hands. "No, Your Highness. For once it is not about the condition of the people who make up your workforce, although they are indeed pitiful."

"It is about knowing what tools you have and using the correct tools for the job. For example, how many carpenters are there in your work force? Who are the Master Masons? What are the skills of the people who work for you?"

"I have no idea! They are slaves, what does it matter what they used to do?"

"Let me give you an example," said Nehemiah, turning in his seat so that he could look the young man in the eyes, "If you were to ask me to build you a table, how long would it take, do you think? Would it be worth the wait? Or would the end result be disappointing?"

"Don't be ridiculous! You cannot build a table that would be worth using! You are an accountant! I don't think such a table would have a place in my beautiful palace!"

"Exactly! How much more sensible it would be, to hire a carpenter to build you a beautiful table!"

"Much more expensive, too!" said the Pharaoh squinting suspiciously.

"In the case of a table, maybe it would be, but in the case of your Palace, it would not!"

The young man looked at Nehemiah as if he had lost his mind. "How is this, the case? How could this be?"

"Bingo!" thought Nehemiah. He had his attention! Slowly but surely, he started to outline his plan, keeping all mention of the humanitarian issues out of the conversation, so as not to alienate him at all.

"Within the workforce that you have, there are all sorts of people, men, women, teenagers, children and old people. All of them, working on your palace."

"Each of these people has different skills, right down to the children. Some of them are fast runners, some are sturdily built, some have excellent memories, and some are fast learners. Now, it wouldn't make sense to use a strong lumbering child to carry an urgent message. It wouldn't work if you used a child with a poor memory. No! You would need a fast sprinter with a good memory to carry out such a task. Agreed?"

Pharaoh nodded in agreement, weighing up Nehemiah's argument.

"So, if we knew which child, had which skill, we could be much more efficient in or use of their talents and achieve much more in a shorter amount of time. Now the same applies to all of the men and women that are working on the site. Even the older people have skills that are much needed in your monumental construction."

"That is as may be, but we do not know what these skills are, so how will that help us at all?"

"It will help, because I intend to find out!" said Nehemiah emphatically, "With your permission, I would like to go amongst the workers and talk to them. I would like to find out where their talents lie and re-organise their labour to best capture this skill. That way we will get a much better job done in a much faster time. Efficiency will be prioritised."

"No!" said the Pharaoh. "It cannot be done! Such a task would take a huge amount of time. My building would not be progressing, and I would appear to be weak to my people! They need to be ruled with an iron rod! They need to be told what to do, not allowed to please themselves! That is not true leadership! It would look, to them, as if I had gone soft. They would mock me, not give me the respect that I deserve for providing them with the opportunity to be part of such a fantastic project! Besides, there are so many of them, one man could not possibly talk to so many people. No! It cannot be done!"

Nehemiah took a deep breath and paused as he prepared to reel the Pharaoh in! "What if I was not working alone? What if I could find some among your work force to help me with this task? People who could write? Keep records?"

"You will not find such people in my work force! They are just slaves!"

"Your Highness! I have already located ten people who could help with such a task and I have not even begun looking yet."

The young Pharaoh was genuinely stunned. He sat speechless for a few moments, shocked such a thing! "How is this possible?"

"How, indeed? If I was able to interview people, who knows what skills we would uncover. This would make you appear truly great in the eyes of your people."

"But the building work has to continue! It cannot be stopped so that you may carry out your interviews, as good as they may be."

"I think I may have found a way. What if you called a National Holiday in honour of your magnanimous greatness? It would only have to be for a few days and it would give me the opportunity to get everything set up. You would be able to throw a huge banquet and invite people of great importance to come and see the wonder of their great Pharaoh."

The young man became puzzled and Nehemiah took some time to explain to him the concept of a National Holiday, all of the time emphasising the benefits to his rule. In fact, he managed to make it sound like a thoroughly miserable event for anyone who happened to be part of the Underclass! At the end of his explanation Pharaoh looked somewhat mollified and more than a little thoughtful.

"I will consider your suggestion, Nehemiah Toosh." He clapped his hands, "You are dismissed."

Just like that, Nehemiah found himself ejected from the inner sanctum with no clear indication as to whether he had succeeded in persuading the Pharaoh or not. He wandered back to his room feeling a little glum, head bowed, deep in thought. Moses and Zaph were waiting for him and as he saw Moses hopeful face he put his hand into his pocket, closing it around two lumps.

"Pan Drops!" he gave one to Moses and put one into his own mouth. He shook his head when Zaph looked at him enquiringly.

"Guess we will just have to wait and see." He said.

Chapter Five

The next two days felt like two months. He stayed in his room, pacing the floor, with only Zaph and Moses for company. It was only when he had given Moses a satin cushion sweet, that he realised that he had been walking up and down with his hands in his pockets all day. He realised that he had already given Moses 1, chocolate lime; 1, mint imperial; 1, sweet peanut; 2 pan drops and a sherbet lemon!

"This has to stop!" he said removing his hands from his pockets and turning to face them. "We have too much to do, to be mooching around here! I need to get out there and see how things sit. Zaph, get organised I am going sightseeing again." He nodded and took off to arrange things.

And You!" he said turning to Moses, "Get no more sweets, until I have managed to work out how to get you cleaning your teeth!" he ruffled his hair to lighten the statement.

In no time at all they were ready, and they took off at a pace, heading in a different direction from the building site. As they progressed, Nehemiah noticed that the walking got easier; the path became a road which widened and became neatly cobbled. There was a camber to it so that the animal waste ran off to drainage channels running parallel, keeping the walking area, clean. His attention picked up immediately and he started noticing other improvements, that made the walk, a very pleasant experience. He saw that they were headed to a huge fountain, that was in the middle of a large square. In the middle of the fountain there was an immense sculpture, of the young Pharaoh, riding in a chariot that was being pulled by two beautiful horses. The work was exquisite and so detailed the horses looked like they might shake their manes, at any minute. The Pharaoh's fisted hand was raised in a victorious salute, his face triumphant. Or rather it would have been if someone had not thrown something at the head, which had caused the nose to fall off.

In fact, it looked as though the statue had been the recipient of many pieces of rotten fruit, recently. He couldn't help by wonder, what the Pharaoh's reaction would be if he saw it!

At the fountain, Zaph and Moses stopped. "We cannot go any further." Zaph said "This is the Rich Quadrant. They beat our kind, just to keep the boredom at bay, for a little while. You will have to continue alone but you will not be harmed. They will see to that." He indicated over his shoulder with his thumb, where two burly guards were trying to look as if they were just passing, casually and weren't following at all! Nehemiah thanked them both and asked if they had any advice they could give him.

"You will be ok as long as you don't get drunk!" said Zaph

"Why on earth would I get drunk? I don't drink as a rule and when I do I only drink a little and certainly not before lunchtime!"

Zaph laughed at his response. "It is all anyone here does! There is nothing else to do but eat and drink and stay out of the Pharaoh's sight. You will see. These people are rich! That is all they are, rich! They just have wealth. Their life has no meaning, no purpose. There is nothing for them to do, so they sit and gossip and drink! That is all that is important to them. I think it is better to be a slave, than to live like this." He shook his head sadly.

Nehemiah looked around him in disbelief. Everywhere, there stood beautiful buildings surrounded by walled enclosures. Fig trees and lemon trees reached over the walls their boughs heavy with ripe fruit, as if trying to escape the strictures of the boundaries that had been imposed upon them. Yet, despite the obvious wealth he could see no sign of industry. The streets seemed to be empty, no stalls, vendors, businesses, just houses all closed up, and shut away from the rest of humanity. A man appeared staggering from one side of the street to the other, with a halting gait and a haphazard sense of direction. He stopped to vomit into the gutter, before continuing on his way.

"Thank you Zaph. I will stay away from any drink!"

Zaph and Moses bowed to him respectfully and turned and headed back in the direction from which they had come, raising their hands in farewell as they walked.

Nehemiah started into the rich quadrant walking with purpose, his long legs striding. He noticed the smells of the place, very different to the places where the slaves lived. It had the smell of respectability. No rubbish, here. Just the smell of the fruit hanging off the trees, unpicked, unnecessary. The further into the area he walked, the more he noticed the sounds that were echoing off the empty streets. The noise seemed to travel from every place at once. Shouting made up a good portion of the noise, drunken abusive language thrown at whoever was sober enough to understand it. Singing, but not happy joyous music but rather alcohol induced dirges, phrases repeating over and over, meaninglessly. Fractions of songs, that originally had been beautiful turned into maudlin droning. He started to hear the sound of fists on skin, grunting in pain. He was appalled! The sounds of this place were all negative, all bad. There was nothing normal about this so-called paradise. It may have beauty on the outside but inside it was rotten.

The further in he walked the worse it became, and he started to see people wandering around the streets in a drunken stupor or a drug induced daze. Meaningless and wasteful. Sad and lonely, with all the trappings of wealth. He came across a man sitting on the pavement, propped up against the wall, softly humming to himself and he stood watching him, trying to assess whether he needed help or whether he just couldn't stand up through drink.

"I wouldn't worry about him!" said a voice from behind him and Nehemiah whipped round to see who had spoken. There was no one else on the street apart from two burly guards who were pointedly, not looking at him. "He sits there most days, at this time. He will move along and head home once he has sobered up enough to be able to walk again."

Nehemiah followed the sound of the voice, eventually looking up to see an elderly gentleman sitting on a balcony above him.

"What is wrong with this place?" he asked in astonishment.

The elderly gentleman chuckled quietly, "That would be a question that is best answered over some tea. Would you care to join me?" he indicated a doorway to the side of the wall occupied by the drunk man. Nehemiah nodded and headed through the door and up a cool wide flight of stairs. The elderly gentleman waiting for him at the top of the stairs introduced himself as, Amun. He discovered that Amun had lived in this part of the town all of his life but unlike the rest of the residents, he actually had a job. He was a merchant and traded in all sorts of high value goods, from fine wine and linen, to rare artefacts and object d'art. The business had originally been started by his Grandfather and although the daily grind was now being carried out by his younger and much more able children and grandchildren, it was obvious that Amun still held the reins, dealing with the finances and the contracts. In many ways he was like Nehemiah as he also loved numbers and had an appreciation of how they worked, how important they were and how they related to everyday life. He understood their power.

Their conversation stretched out over many cups of tea and Nehemiah found himself drawn to this man, who had such a warm manner and ready smile. Amun was astonished to hear his story and how he had come to make the Pharaoh Accountable but also sympathised at his untimely removal, from Yoshi's house. It turned out that he knew Yoshi and had, in fact, done quite a lot of business with him. He had actually sold him the death mask that hung in the room that Nehemiah had been sleeping in, along with several other pieces of furniture. Which explained why it had all looked so authentic, because it was! Their discussion was eventually disrupted by the sound of a commotion in the street below.

A chariot careered around the corner tipping onto two wheels at one point, the driver whooping loudly as it weaved dangerously from side to side before clipping the corner of the wall at the end of the street and disappearing from sight.

"So, what is it with this place?" Nehemiah asked again.

"In a word, boredom!" Amun explained, "Everyone has everything they need, fine food, clothes, wine, houses, wives, everything they could ever want. Yet no-one has ever lifted a finger to earn any of it. They just sit and watch everything come to them. Now, they feel as though they deserve it! As though it is theirs, by right. They have no responsibility and take no responsibility. They are not accountable for their actions."

Nehemiah winced, he was beginning to get a little tired of that word!

"I am familiar with the concept!" he said. "This is just a small part of a much bigger problem, as I see it. The whole system is out of kilter and needs to be brought in to balance."

"How do you mean? The whole system?" asked Amun.

"Well the Pharaoh has an ambitious building project that he is trying to complete. In order to be able to fund this project, he has created a situation of slavery. Free labour. However, this goes against the principle of a person's right to do an honest day's work, for an honest day's pay, which would actually restore their respect in themselves and in humanity. Respect, that every human being deserves. Yet, here is a whole area of people who also are not following the principle of a fair day's work for a fair day's pay and therefore, also have no respect in themselves or others, either. I think that the two are connected in this and therefore, the solution is also connected. They all need a purpose in life. They all need something to work towards and achieve."

He was starting to formulate a plan. He was going to solve this and get back to Yoshi's house and to his much more comfortable but not less challenging job of accounting.

Amun smiled at him, "You are a very interesting young man! How can I help you in this mammoth task you have taken on?"

"What if we were to ask the people in this quadrant to help with the building project?"

Amun laughed, "They would never do it! Why would they? What would be their motivation? They have no reason to get out and help, no responsibility to anyone, not even themselves." He shook his head, "No, my friend, if you wanted to get them to do anything, you would have to market it in a way that would appeal to their self-righteous view of themselves. It would have to benefit them, or they wouldn't even listen to you."

"Market it! I am not sure I know how to do that!"

"Well, it is a good job that you have me to help you then." Said Amun smiling.

When he woke the next day, Nehemiah knew exactly what he must do.

"If we are going to do a skills audit on all of the slaves, then we need to have the space to collate all of the data that we accumulate. So, let us assume that we get the go ahead, we should start re-organising the space so that we are ready." He said to Zaph and Moses as they were eating breakfast. "We better get the team together for this as we will need lots of strong arms."

In no time at all everyone was assembled, and they started erecting tables and moving furniture once again, trying to eke out as much space as they could in preparation for the Pharaoh's decision.

They removed the big bed and changed it for another camp bed which made a big improvement on the space. Even so, when they had the tables all set up in rows, there was a pitiful amount of space available for storage of all of the data they would need to collect. Nehemiah slumped into a chair, feeling despair creeping into his bones. He had not truly realised the scale of the task in front of him, but he was starting to feel a little overwhelmed by it all. As he was trying to work out what to do, Amun walked in to the room.

"Why so glum, my friend? You have a team already by your side!"

"Ah Amun! The space is just not up to the size of task that we have ahead of us."

Amun made a survey of the room, "No, this will not do at all. There will be many more tables required and much more space, too." He agreed. "I am sure that your friend Mr. Toshimoto would help if he knew the predicament that you were in."

Nehemiah thought about this and knew that it was true. He thought quietly for a little while, everyone standing, watching him. He realised that he would not be any less a person for asking for help. Help was good when it was needed, enabling not weakening. He stood up and brushed his hands on his trousers.

"What you outflow, you must also inflow! I will do it but in order to do so, I am going to have to ask everyone to leave, except you, Amun." Nobody questioned him but they all filed out of the room until only the two of them stood together. He walked over to the corner where his things had been thrown into a pile and took out a small notebook and pen that had been in his pocket. Amun raised his eyebrow in a query.

“Don’t ask!” Nehemiah said, “Anything about this must be kept secret. You cannot know what I am using to get the message to Yoshi as it is not your time for such things, yet. I am going to ask you to give this to him, though, as you already have a way of contacting him.”

“I will do that for you, my friend, but it will take many days to get a reply, I am afraid. This method of business is not fast.”

“It is ok, Amun. I don’t even know if the plan will go ahead yet. I am still to hear what the Pharaoh has to say.”

“You may want to think about any personal items you might need, too.” Amun said looking at Nehemiah’s grubby trousers. He laughed and sat to write the list for Yoshi, remembering to add a natural resources toothbrush for Moses, too. He wondered whether he should also write a letter of explanation to him, for his mysterious disappearance but decided against it. Paper was a very rare commodity and he didn’t know when he would need it again. He figured that Yoshi would know what had happened, somehow, that he would know what to do. He finished the note, folding it in half and giving it to Amun, who fingered it gently, trying to work out what it was made of. Tucking it away into his belt he left the room smiling.

Everyone trooped back in to the room after Amun’s departure and they all set about trying to re-organise things, once again, eventually getting the room into a semblance of working order. There was much smiling and back patting at their achievement, which is how the guards found them when they entered unannounced. They looked around suspiciously, eyes finally lighting on Nehemiah.

“The Pharaoh commands your attendance in the audience room.” One of them announced and stood to attention waiting for him to follow.

"This is it! Decision time!" he said to Zaph and he followed the guards to the audience chamber with a feeling of trepidation.

The Pharaoh was looking very pleased with himself, which did nothing to ease the nervousness that Nehemiah felt.

"Ah! You are here!" He said in a very self-satisfied manner, "I have reached a decision on your predicament!"

"Thank you, Your Highness, for your time and wisdom, on this matter!"

"It is my job as leader of my people, to display generosity to my servants and guests. I have decided to declare a national holiday to celebrate my greatness. All will be able to take part in honoring me and my magnanimous nature! During this time, you may go amongst the slaves and do with them what you wish."

"Thank you, Your Greatness!" Nehemiah gushed, before being stopped in his tracks by a raised hand.

"But! Said the Pharaoh, "As you know, my funds are very much tied up in my building project. As a result, any expenses incurred by this little venture of your, will have to be met by yourself. This includes any materials you need and any accommodation you will require. The slaves you may have for free, of course. You will have seven days! No more!" With this announcement, he arose from his throne, signalling the end of the audience and exited to his private chambers, his entourage scrambling after him.

Nehemiah stood alone in the hall, a huge grin spreading across his face. "Yes!" he shouted, punching the air.

Once in his room he lifted Zaph off his feet in a rib crunching hug that would not be out of place on a rugby field!

“We have got it! Seven whole days to sort this lot out! Get as many people together Zaph, who can read and write. Get them here as soon as you can. It is going to be all hands-on deck!”

He turned to Moses, “You go get everyone that was here before, together and make sure they bring all of the supplies they have managed to find. Fastest legs, Moses! Fastest Legs!”

Chapter Six

It was of no great surprise to Yoshi Toshimoto, that he received a visit from Amun which happened to coincide with the mysterious disappearance of Nehemiah Toosh. He had gone to see Nehemiah two days previously, to check that he was well rested and ready for the day ahead. He had not arrived for breakfast and Yoshi was worried for him. He knocked on his door, only to be met with silence. Upon quietly entering, he had found it to be vacant of accountants but had found sand in abundance. It was then that he realised that the young man had gone on an Egyptian Adventure! He exited quickly and walked round to the second entrance into the rooms. A more discreet entrance that involved hidden panels and small corridors, inside wide walls. When he got to the right place he pushed a small hand plate on the left-hand side of a panel of blue and gold. With a whoosh, the panel slide to the side and gave Yoshi entrance into the bathroom that adjoined Nehemiah's bedroom. Walking quickly through it, he opened the door and entered the bedroom. From here he could see the door wide open and the desert reaching out onto the horizon. Two burly guards stood outside of the door with spears crossed over the exit.

"So!" he thought, "It is confirmed!" he quietly retraced his steps and made his way to his study to await the communication that he knew would surely come. He was not surprised. Such things happened in his house all of the time. He was also confident of the young man's safety. In fact, Nehemiah had impressed him with his level-headed capability and his sincere wish to 'Do the Right Thing!'. He knew that he would be in need of material assistance though, as he had left with very little to prepare him for the adventure to come.

"Yoshi, my friend!" said Amun, entering the room with a broad smile and extended hands, "It is so good to see you again, and looking so well!"

Yoshi smiled, standing and accepted Amun's hands into his own, "And you, Amun! Please sit! Join me for some tea and you can tell me how I can be of assistance."

"Indian or Chinese Tea?" asked Amun.

"Chai, of course!" they both chuckled settling into comfortable chairs in front of the roaring fire. They watched as a Liveried Gentleman brewed tea for them both.

"Your young friend, is a remarkable man." Said Amun, "He is so very kind and yet determined and maybe even a little bit stubborn, all at the same time. I have never met anyone quite like him."

Yoshi nodded his agreement. "He is indeed! Is he doing alright? Is he achieving everything he wants to do?"

"If it were down to Nehemiah's will power alone, we would all have been turned upside down, put in a bag, rattled around and everything set out perfectly again! Unfortunately, it is not quite so simple. What he is lacking, is supplies for his vision. Things that will help him accomplish his task."

"Yoshi nodded, "So, what is this task?"

"He has to make the Pharaoh, Accountable!"

Yoshi drew in a deep breath, held it and slowly let it out. "That is no mean feat! He has taken on a truly, herculean task. Still, if anyone can do it, Nehemiah can! Am I right in assuming that supplies and even necessities are not readily forthcoming?"

Amun stroked his chin, "Well, our young Pharaoh means well, but if truth be told, his fortune is limited and much of it is tied up in his massive building project. However, that aside, I doubt if he would give Nehemiah what he needs even if he had an abundance of resources! Accountability does not sit well with him!"

"I am sure he is doing the best he can."

"You are very generous! Primarily, the biggest problem is the plight of the slaves. They are in dire need!"

"Slaves?" asked Yoshi, his eyes and voice hardening, "I think you had better tell me all of the details, so that I can fully assess the situation. I do not like to hear talk of slavery. All men, after all, are created equal and should be treated as such!"

"I heartily agree!" said Amun, raising his hands in a placating manner, "And what is more, so does Nehemiah!"

"I expect nothing less. Come, tell me about these slaves, and their plight."

Amun started to explain to Yoshi everything that had happened since Nehemiah had first walked into the desert. He held nothing back and delivered the facts as they were, without embellishment. He didn't bother expressing his opinion or guessing information that he didn't have, he just repeated what he had seen or been told to pass on by Nehemiah. Time passed, and he continued on. Every now and then, Liveried Gentlemen would approach them and leave food on little side tables or refresh tea that that long since gone cold in the pot. Some hours later, the tale was complete. Yoshi looked deeply into the flames of the fire, over steepled fingers.

He lifted his eyes to meet Amun's. "There is much to do, but not too much! I think I may have a plan. What we chiefly need is to get Nehemiah is a facility to work in. Then we need to look at getting good food and shelter for the poor mistreated people."

"Pharaoh will not allow good quality food to be given to slaves! He will keep it all for himself. He was ever a greedy one!"

"What if he doesn't see it?"

"How will he not see it, my friend?" asked Amun, shaking his head, "He will have his guards check everything that arrives. He will see the food immediately."

"What if he only sees cheap food in open sacks?

"I don't understand what you are saying!"

"What if we fill sacks with grain and pulses of the highest quality, but just put a layer of poor grain on the top? Then we fill some sacks with good food and make it a gift for the Pharaoh to keep? He will be fooled I am sure!"

Amun stared at Yoshi with wide eyes. "My friend, it might just work!"

Yoshi laughed, "We will dangle such a bauble in front of the eyes of the Pharaoh, that he will not be able to see anything that is happening around him. That is how we will get everything to Nehemiah, right under his very nose!"

Later that night, after Amun had gone home with strict instructions not to tell Nehemiah anything about the plan, Yoshi sat quietly at his desk. Pen and paper at the ready, he started to list all of the things that would be needed. It was a long and complicated list. It was important that nothing should be allowed to travel through that would affect their future development. However, in order for Nehemiah to be successful he would need the aid of some technology that was well in advance of their current development. Not least of which was a toothbrush for little Moses. Yoshi chuckled to himself.

"Good job bamboo toothbrushes are back in fashion. With natural bristles of course!" he thought.

After he had completed his list, Yoshi wandered towards the Egyptian room, through the secret passages, carrying a rucksack in his hand. It contained lots of things that he thought would be useful to Nehemiah personally. A change of clothes, all cotton and silk, material readily available at the time; some light sandals and a spare pair of sturdy boots; some toiletries including Moses' toothbrush and an alum crystal deodorant stone that he would certainly need in the desert heat. The most important thing was right in the bottom of the bag, wrapped in a cotton shirt. It was a small electronic notebook and solar charger. Yoshi knew that he could rely on Nehemiah to be discreet and he also knew that the storage and processing capacity of the device would be invaluable to him in his audit. When he arrived at the blue and gold panel, he pressed his hand to the plate and entered the bathroom. The bedroom looked the same as always except for the fresh sand on the floor. He placed the bag on the bottom of the bed as he had agreed with Amun, so that it would reach Nehemiah as quickly as possible. He wished he could join him, but he knew that this was not his adventure to have. He sighed and turned back to the bathroom. "One day, I must remember to show Nehemiah the secret exit to this room!" he thought chuckling.

The next morning Yoshi slept late but after breakfast he launched himself into the day with vigour. There was so much to accomplish, and the logistics alone were staggering. Getting everything to his house in a timely fashion was taking up a huge amount of energy. There always seemed to be someone at the other end of a telephone or computer screen, telling him why things could NOT be done; why things would NOT be able to arrive on time!

"Being positive is probably the most important thing that I will do today!" he thought.

When he had experienced as much negativity as he could bear, he started to rephrase his questions, so that only a positive answer would do. He kept being told, by one lady, that the wooden crates he needed would never be delivered in line with his time schedule. So, he changed the question.

"Madam! What CAN you deliver to me within the timescale?" The woman stumbled on the question and asked him, politely to hold the line. Shortly she was back telling him that she could deliver barrels but not crates.

"Barrels will do nicely!" he said

And so, as the day progressed, the task seemed to get easier, the people seemed to be more pleasant and the jobs seemed to complete much quicker. At 20:00 he sat down to dinner. It was with some surprise, then that his port and cheese was disturbed by a Liveried Gentleman leading Amun into the room. Yoshi rose from his chair immediately.

"My friend! Is everything alright? Is Nehemiah well?" he asked.

Amun raised both hands, "Do not worry! Nehemiah is fine. It is a personal matter I wish to speak with you about... I would like to do some business with you."

"It is always a great pleasure to do business with you! Please sit and partake with me and we will get straight to discussions."

So, over port and cheese, Amun enlightened Yoshi about his intentions, which involved him buying a considerable number of bolts of cloth.

"The people who are being held in slavery will feel considerably better about themselves if they are suitably clothed. I have many seamstresses and tailors on standby to complete the task, but I just do not have enough cloth the make clothes for 1,000 people."

"I do!" said Yoshi, "Or at least I will have in a few days!"

There followed much haggling and bargaining, and it was well into the night before hands were shaken on a deal.

Yoshi managed to secure some finest Egyptian cotton for himself as part of the deal, before bidding his friend farewell and turning in for the night.

The next morning, Yoshi woke with excitement. Today was the day that he intended to organise the 'bauble' that was to distract the Pharaoh and enable Nehemiah to put his plan into action. After a hearty breakfast, he entered his office and put in a video call to his friend, Jasper Goodman. He was the young designer who had worked on the Egyptian room and, indeed many other rooms in his house.

"Yoshi!" said Jasper with a big smile on his face! What is the job this time? More exquisite themed rooms in your beautiful home?"

"Not this time, my young friend. This time I have a very challenging proposition with an extremely tight deadline. This job may best even your abundant skills, I am afraid!"

"Never! However, now I am really intrigued! Do spill!" Jasper said moving closer to the camera, "Come on Yoshi, I haven't had a job I can really get my teeth into for ages! What do you need?"

"What I need is a pavilion!"

"A pavilion? Is that it!" the disappointment was evident in the designer's face.

"Ah but this pavilion has to be fit for a King!"

"Can do that with my eyes shut!"

"Jasper! It really has to be fit for a King! A real King!" I have friends in very high places!" Yoshi said watching his words sink in with the designer.

"You mean a pavilion FOR a King, not fit for a King! Well, that is something I can really go to town on! What is your budget Yoshi?"

"What is a budget?" was the reply.

Jasper laughed out loud and rubbed his hands with glee. "Theme then? What is it to look like?"

"I have only two criteria. It has to be Egyptian, of the style seen in ancient Egypt. No modern-day materials, all-natural cotton and silk, the sort of material that would have been available in that time period. Secondly, it must be huge and of the sort of quality to dazzle even the most materialistic Pharaoh who ever existed. It must be the most luxuriously huge folly that has ever been invented!"

"Wow!" exclaimed Jasper, "This sounds like the kind of job I have been waiting my whole life for! What is it being used for? A film set? Theme park?"

"No Jasper! Do not think along those lines! I do not want you to just design this pavilion. I want you to make it! To bring it to fruition! To make it real! It cannot be remotely fake. It has to be suitable to actually be lived in by a King, along with all his entourage and possessions!"

"Yoshi, the cost will outweigh the end result, if everything has to be original! You are talking gold, jewels, silks and materials that are so rare in modern day society that the price would be crazy. This will cost millions! The size would be massive, unwieldy!"

"Does that mean you are not able to create this for me?" asked Yoshi.

"You are insane! However, I can create you the most extravagant pavilion about half the size of a football pitch! I can't wait!"

"Good! Then it is agreed! How long will it take you?"

Jasper thought hard, "About six months if I really push it."

Yoshi looked at his picture on the screen and smiled broadly. "Make it the exact size of a football pitch! And Jasper? You have one month!" and with that parting comment, he cut the connection.

Chapter Seven

Nehemiah lay awake, thinking. The task ahead was truly herculean, but he felt that today would mark the beginning of the end. He had been hurriedly summoned to the Pharaoh's audience chamber the night before. Pharaoh had been looking very pleased with himself, when he had entered. He was beginning to realise that this never boded well for him.

"I have made a decision!" he had said imperiously. "It will take some time for me to get all of the arrangements in place for my holiday in honour of my Greatness. However, there is no reason for you to be idle during this time. You must start work immediately on my Accountability! Too much time has been lost."

Nehemiah had been told that he had complete control over the slaves but that the building must continue apace. In fact, the Pharaoh had intimated that he expected an increase in the work being carried out! So, he had immediately gone to see Amun and had managed to procure a large warehouse to start using for interviews and data recording. It was a ramshackle building but it was covered space so that was all that mattered. Zaph had been asked to get together all of the people who could read and write and it had turned out that more that 120 of the slaves were well suited to recording interviews and data. A further 60 were ideally placed to deal with the filing and organisation. So, he had his work force!

"So, it begins!" he thought bounding out of bed.

He quickly dressed and ate a small breakfast making sure that Moses ate heartily, which never seemed to be a problem. When they were ready, they headed off in the direction of the warehouse, where Zaph was going to be meeting them, with the workforce. He glanced at Moses as they walked and noticed how healthy he was starting to look.

He was sure he had grown a couple of inches, in the last couple of weeks. He was glad! It was good to see something positive happen, even if it was only the increasing health of a little boy! They had to pass the construction site to get to the warehouse and Nehemiah's good mood deflated rapidly. These people desperately needed food and rest. They needed care and attention and healing, but they also needed respect and kindness, in equal measures. He lengthened his stride so as to speed up his arrival, speed up his plan.

The first thing he noticed when he walked in to the warehouse was the smell! It was the stench of human slavery. Unwashed bodies in an enclosed space, was a new experience to him. However, he went among the people and shook hands introducing himself to his new team mates. He had never seen such sorry looking people in his life; they were literally skin and bone and looked downtrodden and so exhausted that some looked as if they might collapse on the spot. So, after tables had been set up and stools put in to place, the first order of the day was food and water. He spoke to Zaph who immediately got everyone moving on food gathering and preparation. Nehemiah had already agreed with the Pharaoh that his instructions must be carried out without question from the guards, so it was not long before the food started to arrive. Soon, all of the new team of people were eating at the tables and Nehemiah took Zaph to one side, where they discussed the possibility of getting people to bathe and dress in real clothes. It was decided that it wouldn't be a good idea if everyone headed off for a bath at the same time, as it would surely be commented on by the guards, but a shift system would be set up. People could then start on building up their own respect, which would be an essential part of the healing process.

It was not long after this that Amun arrived carrying a rucksack. He asked Amun how the meeting with Yoshi had gone but found him strangely tight lipped.

"Yoshi is an expert in this area, my friend. I think we have to trust that he knows what to do." Amun said, putting his hand on Nehemiah's shoulder, "Do not worry. All will be well! Here, he sent you a gift."

Nehemiah took the rucksack from Amun, thanking him. "I guess there is no point in worrying about things that I have no control over! It is just wasted energy and I need all of the energy I have to deal with the adventure we are creating!" he said, while looking into the bag. When he saw some of the contents he was thoroughly delighted at the gift from Yoshi and decided to take his own advice and head down to the river for a bath!

The river was busy with women pounding clothes on the rocks and they all smiled and raised their hand in greeting, when he arrived. He shouted a greeting and left them to their work, as he made his way along the river to a quieter spot. He had a quick rummage in the bag and looked at the clothes that Yoshi had sent him. It was splendid to have a change of clothes and of such quality and lightness. He was going to feel much cooler and have much more freedom of movement. He stripped of his clothes and dived into the water, much to the amusement of the ladies who were washing the clothes. Using handfuls of sand, he scrubbed his body clean and then swam for a little. It was good to get some exercise and he put his heart into it for a little while. He came out of the water dripping and breathing hard. It was only when grabbed the towel to dry off and cover his modesty, that he discovered the electronic notebook, by dropping it on the ground. He hastily threw his clothes on top of it and looked around furtively to see if anyone had seen it. Everyone else seemed busy with their own tasks, so he scooped it up along with his dirty clothes and stuffed it into the bag. He hoped beyond hope that he had not damaged it. He draped the wet towel across his neck and waving to the ladies on the bank headed back to the warehouse, sharply.

The warehouse was a hive of activity when he got back. His idea of finding a quiet corner was blown right out of the window, as the minute he walked through the doorway people began asking him questions. He was surrounded in a very short time, every request an urgent one. He looked up, floundering and caught Amun's eye.

"That is enough!" boomed Amun, "Please form orderly queues! Any questions about equipment can be directed to Zaph." He pointed in his direction and several people headed off towards him. "Any questions about filing can come to me, please wait at my desk over in the back of the warehouse. The rest of you will need to wait until we have this young man set up, in his own space."

"Thank you, Amun!" What is happening? How is it going so far?"

"Well I divided the team into sections, some for recording, some for filing and some for interviewing. We have tables set up and enough equipment in place to start but no people to interview yet. I think you will need to sort that out as soon as possible. There are still many questions as to how it is going to work, but I think we are more or less ready to start and we can work things out as we get going."

"That is great, Amun! Thank you so much for your help. Now I need a space to work in. Somewhere relatively quiet and with just a little privacy, would be good."

"Follow me, Nehemiah! I have just the spot!"

They headed towards the back of the warehouse, a glare from Amun being all that was needed to keep them being inundated again! Right at the back there was a wall of crates, neatly stacked, about two metres in height. It was only when they were right beside them that Nehemiah saw that, actually, they had been placed as a sort of wall and when he walked behind them; he saw a desk and chair set up at the back, facing the makeshift entrance.

"If you have tools, that you want to keep private, it might be an idea to place your young friend Moses out the front. That at least will give you some warning." Amun pointed to a little stool discreetly placed at the entrance to the makeshift room.

"Thank you, my dear friend! You have much foresight!"

"You are welcome, Nehemiah!" he said walking away to the people crowded around his desk with papers in their hands.

Nehemiah sat on the chair and emptied out the things that were in his rucksack, onto the table. He folded up his dirty clothes and put them at the bottom then one by one went through everything that Yoshi had sent him, keeping the notebook hidden at all times. He was delighted with the alum crystal and used it straight away. He found the toothbrush for Moses and smiled to himself. That was tonight's job sorted! One by one he packed away the things in such a way that he could find them again, easily. Until, there was just the electronic notebook on the table, currently under a pile of papyrus. Propping up some of them, to create a barrier to any curious eyes, he pushed the power button, hoping that the sound was disabled. Nothing happened!

"No! No! No! Please!" he muttered as he tried again, this time remembering to press and hold the power button. When he saw the little blue light appear in the top corner of the screen, he knew it would be alright. He breathed a sigh of relief. There were not many apps on the screen but then as he had no internet or phone connection, he didn't really need that many. There was a fantastic spreadsheet programme, database app, word processor and the best accounting package that he had ever seen, although he had never used this, particular, programme. However, most important of all was a message from Yoshi. It read: -

"My Dear Friend, Nehemiah,

I hear that you have stumbled into an adventure of your own and what an adventure it seems to be! Please be assured that I will do anything in my power to help you in your mission to make the Pharaoh Accountable. It sounds as though he seriously needs your help in this. I need you to know that anything that you need from me, I am more than happy to provide. You must not feel guilty about asking for help. I really wouldn't offer, if I did not mean this. Just remember to have fun and be true to yourself! All will be well!

Your friend,

Yoshi.

Nehemiah smiled to himself. I was so nice to know that he had a friend on his side, someone to watch his back. It made him feel as though the task just got much easier. He heard the loud cough of someone approaching and quickly shut down the device and slipped it into his bag.

"You have a guest, Nehemiah!" said Amun smiling, "At least we hope he will become one! It is the Master of the slaves. He is here to discuss something about rotations"

"Thank you. Yes, we need to look at splitting the shifts so that we can do the interviews. I am coming." He stood and headed out into the main area. The Master of the Slaves was standing near the entrance, looking very uncomfortable at the number of slaves in the enclosed space. He was the only guard around and yet here were lots of slaves busy with things and no one shouting at them. No one was cracking a whip.

He was very disturbed. What disturbed him more, however, is that many of the slaves looked almost happy to be doing the work. That worried him immensely. He saw Nehemiah approaching and headed out of the entranceway, into the open air. This was a conversation to be had on his ground.

"Thank you for coming. I am Nehemiah." He said, holding out his hand in greeting.

"I know who you are!" said the Guard, looking suspiciously at the outstretched hand and pointedly not taking it.

"What should I call you?" asked Nehemiah politely.

"You can call me Master!"

"I am not going to do that! I would like your name, please. Unless I have to go to the Pharaoh and have a conversation with him about who I will, or will not work with?"

"Rachid!" the guard said reluctantly, "You can call me Rachid! But only you! I am not having those filthy slaves calling me anything except Master!"

Nehemiah took in a breath and held it for a second before releasing it. This was going to be a long process and he had to get the measure of this man and, more importantly, his agreement for them to work together if his plans were to succeed.

"I am pleased to meet you, Rachid and I am very grateful that you have agreed to work with me."

"Meet with you!" said Rachid distrustfully, "I never said I would work with you. I said I would meet with you."

"That is true! My apologies for that assumption. Please will you join me in some tea?" Nehemiah pointed to a small table and two stools that had been placed outside of the warehouse, to the left of the exit.

They seated themselves and Amun appeared with a pot of tea and two cups which he placed on the table. He nodded to the Master of Slaves and headed off back inside the Warehouse.

"How do you know Him?" Rachid asked Nehemiah.

"Amun is a friend of mine, who is helping me on this project." Rachid grunted and watched as the tea was poured into the cups.

"I know that this is all very different from the way things are normally done, here. It is disconcerting, to say the least, when there are such changes suddenly put upon us." Nehemiah began, "However, let me ask you one thing. Do YOU know how to make the Pharaoh Accountable?"

Rachid looked at Nehemiah and shook his head frowning. "I am not stupid, you know! Don't you dare call me stupid!"

"You are certainly not stupid! I would never say such a thing. Let me put it this way. I have no idea at how to be the Master of Slaves. I could not do the job if the Pharaoh himself, offered me all of the money in his Kingdom. I just do not have the information or the experience to do it. You, however, most certainly do! That is beyond dispute. Would you agree?"

The guard pulled himself up a little straighter in his seat, displaying his pride at his job. "It has taken me a long time to get to this position. I know all about the stinking slaves!"

"Exactly!" said Nehemiah, earnestly, "Now, all I know is about Accountability. That is, it! Just that! Yet I now have to know about the slaves, too. Now, who in the whole Kingdom knows the most about slaves?"

"Me!" said Rachid poking himself in the chest with his thumb.

"Exactly! So, it makes sense that the two of us, being experts in our own field, would work together, to ensure that the Pharaoh gets what he needs as quickly and as smoothly as possible. Don't you agree?"

Rachid nodded vigorously, delighted at being referred to as an 'expert in his field'!

"Fantastic! Now, I believe the Pharaoh has spoken to you about the fact that I will need to change things a little, with regard to the working patterns of the slaves. Is that right?"

"He said you could do what you like as long as the building work continues and doesn't slow down."

"That is right. So maybe if I tell you what I need to do, in my area of expertise, you can give me your advice, based on your long experience and history in your field and we can come up with a solution?"

"Explain on!" said Rachid, leaning forward, elbows on knees, an eager expression on his face.

Nehemiah was delighted at this change in attitude. He needed the help of this man, if not his belief system! He explained briefly, his idea of splitting the slaves into three different shifts. The idea was that one shift would be working at any one time and one would be interviewed and taking part in the Skills Audit. The third group of people would be resting, eating, bathing and getting help with healing. He knew that this would be unacceptable to the master, so he put it in slightly different terms.

"The third shift of slaves will have the hardest job of all, but in order to prevent total exhaustion and ensure that the building continues at a pace, we will rotate all of the three shifts. That way my job will be done and so will yours." He explained.

"What will the third shift be doing?" Rachid asked, "They must be working hard, or it is not going to happen!"

“Absolutely! The third shift, have to take part in a gruelling improvement programme that is going to make their work more efficient and much faster. The slaves that are working must be able to cover for the ones that are helping me in my program, and this cannot happen unless they improve, immensely.”

Rachid liked the idea that the slaves had to improve and grinned from ear to ear. “I can give them an improvement program, that will make then jump to it!” he fingered the handle of the whip that hung at his side.

“Unfortunately,” Nehemiah said without showing a single emotion on his face, “The beatings will have to stop immediately! I need people to be able to think and talk when they come in to the warehouse or else I will not be able to collect their data. Also, they will have to have more water on a regular basis so that they can operate on the site more efficiently.”

“How is that going to happen, with fewer slaves on the site and the same amount of work needed? It isn’t possible! There just aren’t enough slaves to do the water run as well.”

“This is where I really need your help, Rachid.” Nehemiah leaned in conspiratorially. “Some of the guards are getting a little unfit themselves, and dare I say it, lazy, when you are not around to keep them on their toes. Maybe they need a self-improvement programme, to get them back into shape, too? It wouldn’t do them any harm to take on a bit of weightlifting and jogging, would it? Your team would look amazing if they toned up a little, and I cannot believe that the result would go unnoticed by the Pharaoh. That would only bring you even higher in his estimation, if such a thing is possible.”

The guard sat back on his stool, leaning against the wall and looked Nehemiah straight in the eyes, thinking.

“You are not trying to trick me, are you?”

"My, friend, I could not trick you if I wanted to. You are too smart for that."

Rachid straightened his spine. "It is about time I shook them up a bit! They are not as fit as they used to be, it is true. They won't like it, but it is not about liking, it is about working! Let's do it!" and he put out his hand to shake on the agreement. Now it was Nehemiah's turn to grin from ear to ear. He took Rachid's hand firmly in his. "Done!" he said triumphantly.

And so, it began! The first few days saw only small teething problems of a logistical nature and they were easily put out of their misery by Amun. Every day the shifts changed with one third at the building site, working; one third resting and one third taking part in the skills audit. The skills audit, could not take everyone at the same time, with only a hundred-people working on it, so the rest of the third shift spent their time preparing food for everyone else, in makeshift kitchens outside of the sleeping huts. It was not an ideal situation, but people started to be fed regularly. After about a week, the pattern was starting to run smoothly. The people who were on rest days started to turn up at the kitchens to help out in the afternoon and some came to the warehouse to help with the filing, and movement of people.

Nehemiah spent most of his time sitting in his makeshift office, putting all of the information onto a database, on his notebook. Moses sat just outside the entrance, whistling to himself. The tune changed, whenever anyone approached and so he was able to cover the tablet with papyrus and pick up a writing implement, making it look like he was working the same as everyone else. Only Amun knew of how he was working with the data, as he had seen such things in Yoshi's house before. After a week, he asked Amun into his office.

"I have a brief overview of the information we have collected so far. Would you like to look at it?" Nehemiah asked Amun. He handed over the tablet and watched Amun's face grow more serious as he looked over the numbers. After he had seen enough, he lifted his eyes to meet Nehemiah's.

"You have the right people." He said, "But the people are not the problem, my friend."

"What do you mean?"

"The facilities are the problem, or should I say lack of facilities!" he shifted forward on his seat, "Look, you have cooks, chefs, bakers, even brewers, so there are plenty to feed all of the workers, but as we are finding out, there is nowhere to prepare the food, nowhere to cook and serve so many people. You have tailors and dressmakers, so you have people to clothe everyone but nowhere to carry out the task of sewing, you have healers to help the injured and the sick but no hospitals or clinics, nowhere that the sick can be while they recover. There are just not enough buildings to facilitate the help!"

Nehemiah scratched his chin in thought. "What if we created a place? What if we made a worker's sector which would allow all of these activities to take place?"

Amun snorted, "And the Pharaoh is going to allow that to happen? The people are kept in those huts when they are not working, as you have seen. There is nothing! No proper ventilation, sanitation, it is just walls and a roof! How will that help?"

Nehemiah stood and put out his hand to receive the tablet back from Amun. He slipped it into his rucksack and put the bag on his back. "Come on!" he said, "Let's go see!" and with that he headed out of his workspace and across the busy warehouse, tailed by Amun and a whistling Moses!

Once they arrived at the buildings that housed the slaves, Nehemiah marched straight in to the first one in the block. Pulling out a handkerchief to wipe his nose, he surreptitiously blocked the smell, while pacing along one wall with measured steps. He continued until he had measured each wall and then made for the exit. Once outside he turned to Amun with a big smile on his face. "Perfect!" he said.

Amun looked at him in horror. "How can you say that! This is anything but perfect!"

Nehemiah raised his hands in order to cut off the tirade. "Hear me out!" he said. "Of course, it is not at all suitable for human habitation and certainly not to house so many people. No, that is not what I meant. It IS a perfect size and space for food preparation, though!" he turned and headed for the next building, talking to Amun over his shoulder as he went. "And this would be ideal for food service. We could put benches and tables in rows and as long as people left the building when they had finished eating, it would be perfect, along with the next two buildings."

Amun's eyes opened wide as he started to see what Nehemiah had envisioned. "In fact, my friend, this entire area would make perfect work buildings! Food preparation, clinics, hospitals, even school rooms for the children. It is wonderful! It is all here already! We would not have to ask the Pharaoh for anything! Except...." he raised his finger at Nehemiah, "living areas!"

They looked at each other in silence. "I am working on it!" Nehemiah said as they turned to head back to the warehouse, deep in thought.

Once he was seated back at his desk, Nehemiah and Amun started throwing ideas around as to how to implement their plans. The discussion was upbeat and included much laughter and this was how the messenger found them both, an hour later. Moses had brought him into Nehemiah's working space, after whistling a warning, and then went back to sitting on his seat at the entrance after procuring a cola cube from Nehemiah's pocket! The messenger looked down at them both, disapproval written all over his face.

"Such levity is not conducive to constructive business!" he said, looking down his nose at Nehemiah. "I am sure that his Greatness would not approve."

"On the contrary," Nehemiah smiled up at the man, "This is exactly what we needed to free up our attention and stop us getting dragged down by detail. What can I do for you?"

"His Greatness has sent me to remind you that your week is now complete, and he is expecting you in his Throne Room tomorrow afternoon with a full report of all of your investigations."

With that, the messenger sniffed disapprovingly, turned and headed back to the Pharaoh, in the pavilion. Nehemiah and Amun looked at each other with open mouths. "I had forgotten about that!" Nehemiah said, "I was getting ahead of myself. Drat! Things have been progressing really well! I can hardly believe that I have to go back to the Pharaoh and argue with him again! Drat!" he thumped the table as he stood and started to pace up and down his tiny work space.

"Calm down, my friend. All will be well. What we need is a distraction. One that is large enough that it will make your meeting seem unimportant. One that will keep the Pharaoh occupied until we can get this situation settled."

"What kind of distraction?" asked Nehemiah.

"Ah! My friend! I have no idea!"

That started them both laughing, again!

Chapter Eight

Nehemiah was dreaming. In his dream the Pharaoh had a huge stick which he kept thumping on the floor to emphasise what he was saying. He was shouting, his face screwed up in rage, his hands clenched into fists. Then he started poking him with the stick.

"You have got to wake up and get on with the job! There is no time left for your laziness! WAKE UP!"

Nehemiah slowly realised that the pokes with the stick where hurting and then realised that they were not actually part of his dream but were real.

"Wass up?" he mumbled.

"Nehemiah! Quickly! You must wake up!" It was Moses shouting at him and poking him, "Something is happening up at the pavilion and the Pharaoh is calling for you. Quickly!"

"What time is it?"

"It is nearly dawn. Hurry!!"

Nehemiah swung his legs over the bed and located his trousers, shaking them to make sure they were free of any small creatures that might have crawled into them during the night. After shoving his legs into them he located a shirt, still fastened from the day before and pulled it over his head. After slipping on his socks and boots he hurried after Moses, who was dancing from foot to foot with impatience.

He had worked late into the night and had ended up sleeping on a put me up bed at the back of his office in the warehouse. That had only been a couple of hours ago, he realised as he looked up at the sky, the sun just starting to wink at the horizon. He finger-combed his hair into some sort of order as they walked. Well, he walked, and Moses trotted alongside him.

He slowly came to realise that there were lots of people all headed in the same direction. All around him, people were running up the hill. He lengthened his stride. Something really important must have happened, and maybe this was exactly what they needed. As he crested the hill, he saw the Pharaoh standing not far from the door that led to the Egyptian room in Yoshi's house. He had his arms crossed and his foot was tapping with impatience.

"At last!" he said crossly, glaring at Nehemiah, "We have been waiting for you and I do not like to be kept waiting!"

Nehemiah struggled to take in what was happening. He bowed low. "My very humble apologies, Your Majesty. How can I be of help?"

"This person, would not explain to me what was going on but instead, insisted that you be here. He says that you have to be the one to take delivery. What does he mean?"

Nehemiah looked in the direction of the pointing finger. Standing just inside the room was a tall Liveried Gentleman. He was holding a small silver tray upon which sat a sealed envelope. He could see that behind the Liveried Gentleman was a whole stream of people with parcels and trunks and crates that went out of the room and as far down the hallway as he could see.

"I will go and find out what is happening, straight away, Your Majesty." He said and hurried over to the doorway.

The Liveried Gentleman gave a crisp bow, when Nehemiah approached. "It is good to see you Sir. You are looking very well, indeed!" he said. "The name is Mortimer, Sir."

"Pleased to meet you Mortimer and thank you!" replied Nehemiah, "May I say it is good to see you, too. Now, what is this all about? How can I help?"

"Well, firstly, My Toshimoto asked me to deliver this letter personally into your hands. He said that the contents are sensitive and should not be allowed to fall into anyone else's hands." He handed the letter to Nehemiah, who surreptitiously slipped it into his pocket. "Secondly, we are instructed to follow any instructions you may have. We are here to deliver goods to the Pharaoh. I believe that this will continue for some time, on and off but the letter explains everything. I would suggest you find the time and place to read it as soon as possible, Sir."

"Thank you! I will read it shortly. I have to say that Yoshi's timing is perfect, as always. If you wouldn't mind waiting here for a minute, I will go and explain to the Pharaoh what is happening and see what he wants to do, although I should imagine that deliveries are definitely in order!"

"Certainly Sir." Said Mortimer.

Nehemiah headed back to the young King, the letter burning a hole in his pocket. He had no idea what Yoshi was up to, but the timing certainly seemed immaculate! This might buy him an extra day, at least, depending on how big the delivery was and on how personally the Pharaoh was involved.

"Your Majesty," he said, once he was stood in front of the Pharaoh, again. "It appears as though my friend, My Toshimoto, has many gifts he would like to send to you. The gentleman at the door has asked if he could start the delivery, straight away. He intimated that there were many gifts and that the delivery could take some time. I am afraid that is all of the information that I have."

At the news of gifts being presented to him, the Pharaoh's eyes lit up and a broad smile crossed his face. He clapped his hands to his personal attendants. "Fetch me my covered throne, immediately, so that I may sit comfortably, and, in a manner, that befits my status while I receive the gifts that will be presented to me."

A flurry of activity followed, and Nehemiah slowly edged back to the doorway as the Pharaoh's orders were being carried out.

"How is Yoshi doing?" he asked Mortimer.

"Very well, Sir. I do believe that it would not be inappropriate to say that He may have a few tricks up his sleeve, that he feels may help you in your quest."

Nehemiah burst out laughing! "I hadn't thought of it as a quest, but I guess you are right. I am also not at all surprised that Yoshi has the perfect solution at the perfect time!"

"He excels in that, Sir!"

Once again, Nehemiah laughed. "I miss him! Please tell him that I was asking after him."

"I believe that you may be able to tell him yourself, soon enough. But I am ahead of myself! The letter will explain everything!"

The sounds of activity suddenly ceased, and Nehemiah turned around to see the Pharaoh sitting on his covered throne, settling Himself in great expectation.

"I think that is your cue to start the presentation of gifts." He said to the Liveried Gentleman.

"I will be honoured, Sir" replied Mortimer.

Nehemiah stood for a while beside the Pharaoh's canopied throne, watching as the gifts started to come out of Yoshi's Egyptian room. He was as fascinated as the young King to see what kind of things, were being presented, in front of the throne. The first gift, presented by Mortimer himself, was a hand sized cat shaped statue made of solid gold. The features of its elegant face were made up of precious stones, the eyes emeralds and the markings diamonds and rubies.

It had a collar of turquoise around its neck and it sat upright and godlike. The Pharaoh's eye lit up with greed and he could not stop himself taking the statue from Mortimer's own hands.

"Your Majesty!" Mortimer said, "Mr. Toshimoto has asked for me to deliver this into your hands personally as a mark of his friendship and respect for the work that you have taken on, with Mr. Toosh. He admires your quest for Accountability and will do anything he can to help it run smoothly..." He paused to add emphasis to his next words. "Mr. Toshimoto, would also like to pass on to your Majesty, that as long as this work continues, and Mr. Toosh is allowed to continue his work unmolested, he will continue to show his gratitude in this fashion." He bowed low but did not miss the narrowing of the Pharaoh's eyes as Yoshi's message sank in. It was a fleeting expression, quickly covered by a polite smile.

"Of course!" he replied, "Please pass on my thanks to My Toshimoto for this beautiful gift and the other forms of acknowledgement, for my great magnanimity. In response to his generosity, I would like to announce that Nehemiah's new programme has been extended to another month! I do not have the time, now, to devote my entire attention to it, so have extended my trust and authorisation to him, to complete this important work." The trusted retinue and various sycophants eyeing up the door to the room, cheered at these words and the Pharaoh waved his hand at them in acknowledgement of his great wisdom.

"Thank you, Your majesty!" said Nehemiah with a bow. "I shall immediately go and inform everyone who is working with me and leave you to your very important matters of State." And he turned and headed back to the warehouse, grinning all of the way. Moses appeared at his side and he tousled his hair, reaching into his pockets and finding two hard lumps there, he took them out and handed one to Moses and put one in his own mouth. "Liquorice comfits!" he said.

When Nehemiah arrived back at the warehouse, all of the workers descended on him, desperate to know what had happened, each shouting out different questions. He held up his hands.

"Wait!" he shouted, "I will tell you everything, but I have to be able to breathe and I have to be able to hear your questions!" he saw Amun elbowing his way to the front of the mob! "Come let us all go in to the warehouse and I will stand on a table so that everyone can hear me and answer your questions."

With that the crowd parted and he walked in to the warehouse with Amun and Moses on either side. Once inside, he walked to the front and pulled a sturdy looking desk into place. He nimbly jumped on it and everyone gathered round, questions still being shouted from all directions. He held up his hands. "Please! Let me tell you what occurred and then I will answer any questions."

He told them everything that had happened, omitting the part about the letter and his conversations with Mortimer. When he got to the part about the Pharaoh extending their project for a month, the whole place erupted into a huge cheer. He looked around at all the people with a large grin on his face! People were jumping round and round, hugging each other, thumping each other on the back and generally celebrating what was, in effect another chance at freedom. Once the noise started to subside, he patiently answered their questions, but he soon realised, that he had been over keen to get away from the scene taking place near the pavilion and he didn't really have that much information as to what kind of things were being delivered or how they would affect the people. Amun came to rescue by offering to go up to the Pharaoh and see what was happening. He also said that he would make sure that any goods coming through, that were intended for the people, would be diverted straight to the warehouse. This satisfied everyone, Nehemiah included and in short order, a semblance of normality settled on the place.

Runners had been sent to the other shifts to tell them what was going on and Nehemiah had sent Moses personally, to explain to Rachid, what had been happening and what it would mean for him and his workers. He invited Rachid to a meeting at his earliest convenience, to discuss the situation.

It was, in fact another hour before Nehemiah had to opportunity to slip quietly into his office and take the letter out of his pocket. His hands shook slightly with excitement, as he opened the envelope and spread the letter out on his desk. It read: -

"My Dear friend, Nehemiah,

I hope this letter finds you well. May I first say that the work you are putting in to your quest, is splendid! The Pharaoh could not want for a better person to help him become Accountable. However, I understand that the Pharaoh may not have the same intentions in this task of Accountability and I feel as though this may be causing you some problems.

I know you would not complain Nehemiah, and I know that you will always do your best to work within your means, but I hope you will not mind if I interfere a little. This is something that I am able to do to help you, if it is agreeable to you.

I have arranged for a little diversion to happen. Something that should keep the Pharaoh occupied for some time. I am hoping that this will leave you free to continue the excellent work that you have started. This diversion should continue, on and off, for at least the next month. It is my hope that the conclusion of this act, will then enable you to finish off everything that needs to be done and maybe you will be able to return to us shortly after this. Maybe? We shall see what happens.

I heard about the problems that you have been having with the facilities that you have been trying to establish. Can I ask, have you considered concrete tents? Easily disguised and a limited life span but long enough to establish a precedent, I think.

Keep up the good work my friend, we are very proud of all the things that we are hearing about you.

With much love,

Yoshi

> *PS: I have sent a programme to your tablet that I think will enable us to communicate more frequently. I hope it will work where you are. If you are able to sit near the door to my Egyptian room, I think that the Wi-Fi will work as I have had it boosted there. Unfortunately, I do not have an answer as to how you will accomplish such a task. I will leave that in your capable hands! YT"*

Nehemiah felt very moved that Yoshi would so kindly 'interfere'. He felt so very grateful that he had such a kind and generous mentor who enabled him to just get on with the job without having to constantly worry about the logistical problems, that kept cropping up. He read the letter again, stopping at the part where Yoshi wrote about concrete tents. "Concrete tents." He mouthed. He heard, just in time, Moses whistling tune change to warn him or the imminent arrival of one of the workers and he hurriedly picked up the letter and shoved it in his pocket. The young man who came up to his desk had a question about one of the questions in the survey, which was not challenging but it did open the flood gates to a whole line of people who were waiting to see him in order to clarify points that they were unsure about. As a result, he did not have chance to read the letter again for the rest of the day, let alone discuss the contents with Amun, who was still occupied with the Pharaoh. However, if anyone had been watching him closely as he went about his work, they would have seen him get a faraway look in his eye, every now and again and see him silently say the words 'concrete tents' at the same time, while frowning in concentration.

Amun walked as fast as his legs would carry him, up to the pavilion. He felt an urgency in his bones, to get to the goods being delivered before the Pharaoh made any major decisions. Although he considered himself to be a loyal citizen, he knew in his heart the kind of avarice that simmered beneath the cool exterior of the Young King. All of Nehemiah's plans would be in jeopardy if the Pharaoh decided not to release any of the goods gifted from Yoshi. The situation called for diplomatic handling, which just so happened to be one of Amun's areas of expertise!

When he arrived at the Pharaoh's covered throne, he bowed low and quickly took stock of the situation that was unfolding. His worse fears had been put in place and he would need to work fast to remedy the problem. Beside the throne was a growing pile of sacks containing grain. The grain was of poor quality and was slowly spilling out onto the ground. In the sack that was at the bottom of the pile, the good grain that had been hidden underneath the dross was starting to be revealed. Amun needed to act and fast to get that grain to Nehemiah.

"Your Greatness!" I heard the good news of your wonderful gifts. This acknowledgement of your high status is only right and proper!" he said in a loud voice, pulling the Pharaoh's attention away from the deliveries that continued to pour from Yoshi's Egyptian room.

"I agree, Amun."

"May I ask what will happen to the rubbish? What will happen to the gifts that so obviously are not of a high enough quality to be worthy of your attention?" he asked, waving his hand vaguely in the direction of the discarded grain sacks.

"I don't have time for such menial decisions now! Look, here is another gift for me." And the Young Pharaoh stood up to look closer at an exquisite bolt of turquoise and gold silk, just emerging from the doorway.

"Shall I deal with it, Your Greatness?" Amun asked obsequiously. "You have many burdens on your mind and this rubbish can be fed to the animals that pull our carts." He moved slowly towards the sacks.

The Pharaoh's head whipped round, and his eyes met Amun's, who stopped in his tracks and lowered his head in subservience.

"You may give the grain to whichever animals belong to me, apart from my Chariot racers, who only get the best! You will not sell it or make money from this! Not a single piece! These are My gifts and they will not be used for the benefit of anyone else. Especially you!" The Pharaoh waited for an acknowledgment of His command.

"Not a single piece of grain will go anywhere but, on the animals, you own, Your Greatness and not a single grain will be sold. In this you have my word." He said bowing low.

"In this you have my word!" mimicked the Pharaoh. "If you lie to me Amun, I will have your life!"

"I swear, Your Graciousness. Oh, King of Generosity and Kindness to all creatures fortunate enough to be under your watchful gaze."

"Get on with it then!" the Young King said, dismissing him as he turned to continue accepting his gifts.

Amun stepped to the sacks of grain and snapped his fingers at two slaves standing behind the covered throne. His heart was pounding so hard in his chest that he was sure that the Pharaoh could hear it. He looked over his shoulder to check that the deliveries were resuming. The Young King had already forgotten he was there in his desire to get to the gifts that were arriving. He breathed a sigh of relief and wiped his sweating brow with his handkerchief.

"Come!" he said quietly to the slaves, in order not to draw attention to himself." Please will you run down to the warehouse and ask for some people to help me with this grain. Not too many and one's with string backs. Tell them not to bring a cart. We don't want any attentions right now." He needed to get the sacks away in case there was any last-minute change of heart.

While he waited, he turned and watched the goods arriving in front of the covered throne. It seemed to him that they were perfectly timed to be the distraction that was needed. A gift of great worth and beauty would be presented to the Pharaoh and while he was examining it, or taking it in his hands, some mundane deliveries would occur. This was not by chance, as he could see a Liveried Gentleman just inside the doorway, directing the flow of gifts and choosing which gifts would arrive and when. He looked at the Young King who was in his element, not only receiving so many gifts but also so much attention. Another Liveried Gentleman was standing to one side of his throne, talking to him on the arrival of the expensive gifts, explaining where they came from, why they had been chosen or how they could be of benefit to him. This ensured that all attention was kept away from the essential, humanitarian supplies that were brought through immediately afterwards. Amun smiled to himself at such adroit diplomacy, yet another example of the quality of people that Mr. Toshimoto employed.

Two more sacks were carried over to the pile but before they could be deposited, he signalled for them to be placed further back from the ones already awaiting uplift. In this way, a new pile of grain was created but a few meters further away from the area of focus.

"Inch at a time, Amun!" he muttered to himself, "Inch at a time!"

A short while later, three young men arrived, all eager to begin the removal of the food sacks. He put his finger to his lips, to indicate that he did not want any attention drawn to their presence. They quickly pulled the sacks onto their back, one sack each, and headed off, at pace, back to the warehouse. In very short order, not only had the original sacks been removed but the pile of sacks that were being delivered had been relocated ten meters away from the centre of activity. Not all food sacks were allowed to be given to Amun. Some were presented to the Pharaoh himself and were quite obviously of the highest quality. These were sent immediately, to his kitchens and personal store rooms, as expediently as possible, in case any of the obviously hungry slaves noticed them. Amun shifted from foot to foot in the hot sand, as he supervised the discreet removal of the supposed poor grain and wondered if it would be politic to arrange to have a covered seat brought for him. Watching the Pharaoh, in his element, lording it over everyone in sight, he decided against drawing any more attention to himself. He sighed and continued with his task.

"Maybe tomorrow will be cooler." He thought, with little conviction.

Chapter Nine

Nehemiah sat with his face to the early morning sun, feeling the warmth seeping into his skin, drawing him into its embrace. He had risen early and set off while it was still dark in order to reach this place and watch the sun rise. He had walked about an hour into the hills surrounding the slaves, living quarters, the way lit by an oil lamp until he could be sure that he was completely alone. After that he had used the torch on his mobile and the going had been much better. He had seen many creatures and insects scuttle out of his way on his walk, and had been delighted to do so, watching the lizards and scorpions escaping into the dark, away from his light. He had finally stopped at a rock shelf and had settled himself down to wait for the dawn, a huge slab of cool, rock at his back. Once he had settled himself, he sat quietly and cleared his mind, feeling the rock beneath him, the pressure of his legs on its hard surface. Feeling his heart's beat, calm and his breath, lengthen. He needed this quiet time to focus, once again. The past two days had been hectic and noisy, with so many things clamouring for his attention, that he had become distracted, unable to think past the clutter, that was constantly demanding that he look at it. Now, he was out of reach of the physical issues requiring his expertise, he intended to clear his mind and meditate a little. He breathed in through his nose and felt the cool air enter his nostrils, drawing it deep into his lungs, feeling his chest expand. Then he expelled the air, feeling the tingle on his upper lip, as it made its way out of his nose. Then, a breath in through his nostrils, expanding his lungs. And so, he continued, until in short order he started thinking about Yoshi's note, again.

"Thinking." He said to himself, as he brought his attention back to his breath. It wasn't long until he found himself working out the cubic measurements of the current sleeping quarters of the slaves.

"Planning." He said to himself and brought his mind back to his breath.

He found himself pulling his attention back to his breath many times, over the next half an hour but by the time the sun was rising above the horizon he felt more focused, more centred and his mind had a clarity about it, that had been missing for a few days.

He watched the sky lighten and the sun rise over the horizon, creating a beautiful show of reds and oranges in the surrounding sky. Once its rays started to touch the rock he was sitting on, he opened his backpack and took out his solar charging pack, placing it in the sunlight, checking that the charging light was on. Then he started thinking!

The logistics needed fine handling in this situation. It was obvious that the accommodation was woeful for the people and that they needed better facilities in every area. The Pharaoh had made it clear that he did not intend to spend a single coin for the benefit of his people, but Yoshi's generosity had obliterated that problem. So, they now had the means to change the entire complex and make the people's life better, in every way. However, Nehemiah was not convinced that the Pharaoh wanted this. He wondered how the King would react to the betterment of people that he only viewed as His Property. He felt that it would be seen as a threat to his superiority and that this would anger the Pharaoh enough, for him to stop all progress. So! The way he saw it, they had to be discreet, and act surreptitiously, making sure that they disguised equipment and buildings that they erected. They had to trust Yoshi to keep the Young Man's eyes diverted away from what they were doing, and once they had got the new facilities into place, it was essential for them to camouflage them in such a way that they would not be seen from the pavilion or its surrounding areas. As far he could tell, Nehemiah had not heard of the ruler coming anywhere near the slave s living quarters, leaving any requirements to the guards, which brought him, to the next problem. Rachid!

He would almost certainly have to pass on some sort of benefit for the guards and their Supervisor and it would have to be an act of such largesse that it would win Rachid over to their side, once and for all. He had been doing some research into the man, finding out about his background and his present situation and had been very surprised at what he had discovered. Although his early life had been very chequered and, by necessity, violent, the last few years had seen a shift in the Head Guard's focus. He had found himself a wife and had, it seemed fallen in love with her. Hook, line and sinker! She had given birth to a daughter a year later and a son, the year after that and it was here that Nehemiah had found Rachid's weak spot. He absolutely doted on his children and would not only compromise everything that he stood for, in order to benefit them, he would also kill anyone that threatened them, in any way. Such was his passion for their wellbeing. So, he had come up with a plan. He had decided to offer Rachid not only material benefit, money for himself and his family, but also the offer to teach his children. A way to help them become more than their father, to open up opportunities for them, that Rachid could only dream of. He wouldn't be able to resist! Of course, that then meant that Nehemiah would somehow have to schedule lessons into his already busy day, but he thought that once the guard started to see the benefit of those lessons on his children, he would already be sold to the idea and on his side. Then he would be able to pass the teaching on to one of the other people, that he planned to use for his training scheme. It might well be that he could integrate them into the classes that he planned to set up for the other slave children, after a while. He nodded to himself! Now he just had to set up the meeting and convince Rachid.

The 'Concrete Tents Issue' was another matter entirely! While the idea had a lot of merit, Nehemiah was unsure as to how they would be able to set them up in the first place. While it was true that all they really needed was water, any kind of water, they would also need a power supply to blow them up in the first place.

Plus, two thousand litres per building would require some serious strategy in a culture that was so lacking in industrial strength. On the other hand, each structure could sleep fifteen people, so that could easily contain a family unit providing privacy and hygienic comfort. They would be erected within a day and ready to move into, so to speak, with no need for foundations and planning. They would be safe against the weather and domestic dangers, such as fire, so that would be another bonus and would last at least ten years. Concrete canvas would be easy to disguise in an area that contained nothing but sand! The colour was perfect and if they built the doors facing away from the Pharaoh's area, they could bury the backs of the buildings in sand, easily enough. The only problem that he could see was the scale of the project. It would require over two hundred tents to be put up, in order for everyone to be properly housed. Nehemiah sighed and stretched, letting his gaze wander over the land below him. He watched the river running through the area, strong and wide and noticed the way the land came down to it, gently, allowing the women to do the washing, the men to fish and the children to swim. He had not noticed just how huge it was before but from this vantage point he could see that it ran for many miles. He sat up, looking harder. There was a water source that everyone used. It was available to all and was easily accessible. What if they built alongside the river? Not immediately on the river banks but set back from it. The structures could easily be placed there, and the people could relocate to this area and would be well away from the pavilion, while still within easy reach of the construction site. He stood up and started to pace up and down the rock shelf. The water would be easily available but that did not answer the question about the source of power for the pumps. He thought about a way round the problem but came up with no solution, until, that is, he was preparing to make his way back to the compound. He bent to retrieve his battery pack and bag and stopped half way through the action.

"Solar panels!" he said, "Solar panels!" he started to laugh.

He was still laughing by the time he had made his way back to the warehouse, where a very worried Moses ran out to greet him, followed by a string of people, questions ready on their lips. Nehemiah ruffled the small boy's hair and reached into his pockets, pulling out two hard lumps. He gave one to Moses and put one into his own mouth.

"Aniseed balls!" he said.

He did not stop to answer questions but headed straight into his office area, asking Moses on the way to keep people out. It was becoming very obvious to him, that he seriously needed help in the administration of the Accountability of the Pharaoh. Most of his time was taken up answering people's questions and he really needed to be working on the planning and meetings and organising. He no longer had time to be bogged down with mundane issues, however important they may be. He needed help and for that he needed Amun. Hitching his bag higher onto his shoulders he decided to go and find him and see what could be done to ease the problem.

He set off towards the pavilion at pace, head down in an effort to discourage people from stopping him in their quest for answers and direction. He was beginning to realise that many people would ask him things that they were perfectly capable of answering themselves, but they had little confidence in their own abilities and so used him as a crutch. He knew very well, that time and results would give them the confidence and that if they were left with the problem, they would come up with their own solution which would help with that. He also knew that you could never really help people in matters of confidence and personal growth. They could only help themselves and the most he could hope for, was to give them the inspiration they needed to grow. The people following him started to drop off as they realised he was not going to answer any questions and by the time he saw Amun in the distance, he was alone. Alone, that is apart from his young shadow, Moses!

"Nehemiah! My friend!" Amun greeted him with a hug. "It is so good to see you."

“Hi Amun! How are things going here?”

“Very well, My Friend! We are siphoning off the food stuff that Yoshi sent for us and making sure that we get what we should. But I have to say that the pace is brutal! I don’t think that even the Pharaoh is going to be able to keep up with the pace of deliveries. Is there some way that we can stagger things? Maybe just receive things every other day?”

Nehemiah thought for a moment. “I will speak to the Pharaoh and Mortimer and see what I can do. But then I need to sit and speak with you about some things. It is urgent Amun.”

“Certainly, I will arrange for someone I trust to take over for me and we will go to my home and drink tea. Agreed?”

“Agreed!” said Nehemiah and jogged over to the covered throne to speak with the young King.

“Your Majesty!” he said as he bowed low. “What an immense accolade, to receive so many fine gifts. Have you had chance to stop and enjoy them all yet?”

The Pharaoh smiled at him, tiredly. “Unfortunately, I have not. The gifts have been arriving for four days now! It is indeed wonderful to know that someone appreciates me so much!”

“Absolutely!” agreed Nehemiah, diplomatically, “But, I wonder if you would enjoy them more if you had time to appreciate them, look at them and feel them. You are looking tired today, your Highness.”

The Pharaoh gave a sideways glance to Mortimer, “I would not like to interrupt the receiving of such gifts, but I am a little tired.”

Mortimer stepped closer to the throne. “Your Majesty, I had no idea that you were a little tired. May I make a suggestion?”

The Pharaoh nodded at him and Mortimer turned to look at Nehemiah, who could have sworn that he winked at him, subtly of course! "I think we can come up with a kind of schedule that will make it easier for everyone. Have no fear, Your Highness, the gifts will keep coming for many, many days yet, but I think we could arrange for the less sumptuous and high value gifts, to be dealt with by Nehemiah, here. That way you would not have to sit in the heat looking at vegetables and grain."

The Pharaoh narrowed his eyes and looked at Nehemiah, who quickly stepped forward. "Your Majesty, I would be honoured to help you in this matter. I know I have your trust and that will not be betrayed in this."

"We could actually spread the deliveries slightly. Bring them through every other day? That way everyone will be able to handle the things coming through, both the highly esteemed Pharaoh and the workers who are carting sacks around." Mortimer chipped in.

The Young King tried to look as if he was considering the proposal, but Nehemiah could see the relief around his eyes. "It is agreed but I think three days a week would be better!"

"As you wish, Your Majesty." Said Mortimer bowing, "We are yours to command." At that he headed off to the doorway, walking past Nehemiah and snagging his arm as he went. Once they were out of earshot he turned to him. "Thank you, Sir! If I had had to stand another day with that spoiled brat, be it all a Royal Spoiled Brat, I think I would have had to start screaming! I don't know how you do it!"

Nehemiah chuckled, "He is an acquired taste, that is for sure." His face turned serious. "Look, Mortimer, I have to attend to some important stuff here but please tell Yoshi that I am working on getting in touch with him. Now that people are not going to be here every day, I may have a chance."

"Don't worry Sir, I will pass on your message." Mortimer replied and then headed off quickly, to the doorway to stop the flow of goods that were pouring through.

Nehemiah made his way back to Amun and they both headed slowly towards Amun's house, in the Rich Quarter. The conversation along the way was light and amusing. Amun was the master of the anecdote and by the time they had reached his house, they were both relaxed and at ease, spirits lifted and ready for the discussions that would now take place over tea. Seated on Amun's balcony, overlooking the quiet street, Nehemiah started the discussion as tea was poured.

"I have to tell you that the work load is becoming quite heavy." Amun nodded but kept listening.

"It is not the things that I need to do that are causing a burden, however, but the fact that so much of my time is taken up answering routine questions and showing people how to do the basic tasks. It is not as if they are doing the wrong job. The fact is, that they know how to do what we have asked them to do, it is just that they are used to taking orders and not to working on their own initiative, they don't know how to do it. It is almost as if the idea of slavery has become so entrenched, that they have forgotten how to think for themselves, any more. Or to do a job, without someone watching over their shoulder, correcting them." He took a deep breath and released it slowly, then continued. "I understand that it is going to take time for these people to gain confidence in their own abilities and that it must be frightening to do something so different, but I just don't have the time or attention to spend nursing them through their own development. Walking them through their own metamorphosis, into individuals who can make decisions and take responsibility for their own actions. What I need is someone who is smart and kind and patient to work with them. To encourage them, when they get it right as they so often do, and gently guide them into thinking how to do things differently, when they get it wrong. Where can I find such a person, Amun?"

Amun lifted his tea cup and sipped his tea, thinking. Nehemiah thought that was a good idea and joined him. The silence was comfortable and peaceful.

"I think I may know of just such a person, my friend. She is a teacher of children but also works for me, managing my accounts and such like. She is very patient and gentle, unless you get on her wrong side, of course, then you better watch out!" Amun chuckled knowingly, "I have been there a few times and never managed to come out of it unscathed!"

"She sounds perfect! Who is she and where can we find her?"

"Not so fast, my friend! This lady is not one to be 'managed'! She has her own mind and is very independent and if she does not want to do the job, then there is nothing on earth that will get her to help you. This needs to be handled carefully!"

"Who is this person?" Nehemiah asked again, "I am intrigued!"

Amun laughed! "It is my own Granddaughter Abha. She will be here later, and you can meet her yourself, but I warn you, do not assume she will jump aboard your ship. She has a mind of her own, that one."

"I was going to get back and see how things were going in the warehouse, actually."

"Nonsense, my friend! Even you have to eat! Stay, eat with us and you can meet her at supper. I think you will like her!" Amun said with twinkling eyes.

"Seeing as you put it so nicely, I will stay to eat with you. I will enjoy your company and look forward to meeting Abha, too. Will the rest of your family be here?"

"Sadly, no. My sons are busy with their own family and business, but you will meet them soon, I am sure. Believe me, Abha is enough to handle for one day." And he sat back laughing.

Chapter Ten

Rachid sat outside his door looking out onto the courtyard behind his simple home. He was watching his children playing. Rania, his daughter was nearly three and was walking around with a little wooden carving of a dog, tucked securely under her arm. She chattered to it in her childish language, known only to herself and her little wooden dog. His son, Gamal was eighteen months old, now. He sat playing with a ball that Rashid had made him, from reeds and leather. He had learned to throw it, after a fashion and would then either crawl or totter to reach it. Rachid thought his children were the most beautiful things that he had ever seen. That such wonderful little people had been produced by one such as him, took his breath away. His wife, Kamilah, was a good woman. She was a kind woman and an excellent mother to his children. She had a quiet way with her and would move around the house, getting on with her work, with an air of confident capability. His home was peaceful and calm and although she would never be known for her beauty, he loved her with all his heart. He was always grateful and surprised that she had thought him worthy enough to be her husband. The last few years had been the happiest of his life and now, tonight, she had told him that she was pregnant and that another child would soon bless their lives. He was overjoyed. And yet, in the back of his mind, he was also worried. Things were changing here and if that man, Nehemiah had his way, he would soon be out of a job. That worried him greatly, as this job was the only one he had ever had. It was the only thing he knew how to do. If it was to become obsolete, he would be homeless and his children hungry. He shuffled in his seat, uncomfortable at the thoughts running through his mind. Yet, he knew in his heart of hearts, that the changes that were happening were good, they were right! The most surprising element of the changes so far, had been the changes to the guards under his supervision.

Most of his working life had been taken up with dealing with the petty squabbles and fighting, that took place between them. A side effect of having a fat, lazy and demoralised work force, he knew. However, now they had real responsibility the change had been huge! For a start they were starting to get in shape, all of the running up and down fetching water for the workers was training their bodies. The weight of the buckets and the hill they had to climb to deliver it, was using up their energy and burning off their fat. More surprising than that, though was how seriously they had begun taking their responsibilities. Now, they were not just delivering water, but were bringing food and supplies sometimes, when needed. If they saw someone in difficulty, Rachid had actually seen them go in and give a hand, until the problem was solved. They had competitions, as to how quickly they could deliver what was needed and how many times they helped one of their team throughout the day. But, the most surprising thing yet, was the fact that people were smiling. He had never seen any of the guards smiling at work before, in his life, but now they were smiling! It was almost as if the fact that they had to produce something now, deal with some responsibility, help someone, had lifted the morale of his whole team of guards. It wasn't just that Rachid had told them that if they didn't carry out their orders, they would be made part of the slave work force. He used to say that to them all of the time and it had never made a difference before, but now they were actually doing something that had a purpose to it and something that was genuinely helping someone else, it had boosted the morale of everyone. There was no denying it, that Nehemiah had got something, here! Something good, but that was actually very bad for him and his family and also, possibly, for the Pharaoh. He had no idea how the Young King would react to seeing his guards behaving the way they were now, but he felt deep in his belly that it would not bode well for anyone! Not the slaves, not the guards and certainly not for him! The way he saw it, he was stuck between a rock and a hard place! He couldn't ignore the implications to himself and his family. That would not fix anything! So, the only thing that he could do was to go and talk to someone and figure it out, before calamity struck. Now, he could go and talk to the Pharaoh, but he was never very comfortable discussing things with him. He usually came out worse off after those talks, he usually ended up being the person responsible for the problems and he felt that in this instant, that could be a very dangerous place to be. On the other hand, he could go and discuss it with Nehemiah. He had had a hard life and his childhood had seen him staggering from one fight to the next, but the fight to survive had been the hardest. Food was very scarce and clothing practically non-existent. His parents were slaves themselves and it had almost broken Rachid's heart to see them treated so badly. They were beaten to death when he was eight and he had learned the hard way that soft hearted people did not live very long in this land. He had no choice but to harden up if he wanted to eat and to run fast if he wanted to live. As he got older he found himself hating the people he grew up with, blaming them for their own situation. He got into fights all the time and earned a reputation of being a bully. This, then, continued on into his early manhood, until he was noticed by the then Supervisor of the Guards and offered a position. That did not help his anger or his bullying. In fact, he became much worse as the feelings inside him battled for superiority. One the one hand he could feel compassion for the plight of the people, having been brought up to be one of them, having endured their suffering himself, but on the other hand he hated everything that they symbolised. It brought back the pain too sharply; the loss of his own parents and their love. They had loved him truly and he had basked in their warmth, for too short a time, as a child. So, he continued in his bullying ways, beating slaves when the hurt became too much, beating fellow guards when he could cope with it.

His wife had changed all of that. She had seen him for who he was, straight away and had protected him against the guard's wives fiercely. In her quiet way, she had seen that the answer to his dilemma was love. Just that! So, she loved him with a strength that took his breath away and as the years went on, he found himself less divided; less angry and less likely to have to hit out at someone, for peace of mind.

When his daughter came along, that sealed it for him. His guards were never allowed into his home, into his sacred sanctuary, so they never had the chance to see this Rachid.
So, at work, he was his gruff self. He was not working alongside the slaves anymore and had earned a reputation among the guards, that his words were enough to ensure the job was done and discipline was tight.

“Good job!” he thought, “Don’t have it in me to fight every day, anymore.”

He stood and stretched, decision made. He would go and see Nehemiah first thing in the morning.

“No getting away from it!” he said to himself, “Time to go make myself Accountable!”

Chapter Eleven

Amun really was the most entertaining host! Nehemiah had not laughed so much since he had been brought into this land. The tales of Amun's adventures as a young man were hilarious and demonstrated admirably how he had developed his picaresque nature. How he had survived so many near misses was, in itself, miraculous and Nehemiah suspected that a little exaggeration may have been used in the telling! Time passed quickly, and the sun was about to set when they were called in from the balcony, to enjoy their evening meal. They entered the dining room, still laughing and sat at the table waiting for their first course to arrive. Each of them had a finger bowl to their left and Nehemiah took the opportunity to dip his fingers in and give his hands a cursory wash before eating.

"Ah, My Friend!" said Amun, "What strange customs you must have in your world."

"You have no idea how strange!"

"Abha!" Amun shouted, "Is there any food to feed us hungry men or must we pass away right now through our starvation?"

A voice came out of the kitchen, "That would take a very long time Grandfather!" the curtain was swept aside, and a young woman came into the room backwards, in order to keep the food away from the curtain. She was carrying a very large bowl of stew in her left hand and an even larger bowl containing bread in her right. As she turned to lay the bowls on the table, Nehemiah gasped! He couldn't help it! Abha was the most beautiful woman he had ever seen! They both turned their eyes toward him, at the sound.

"Are you well, My Friend?" Amun asked in a concerned voice.

He nodded his head while trying to cover his blushing cheeks. His voice had just disappeared, and he had no answer to give. He would just embarrass himself further if he tried to speak.

Abha smiled at him and he thought his heart would explode out of his chest! Surely, they could both hear the noise it was making? The pounding in his ears made him deaf to all other sounds.

"He is probably dying of starvation, as you said, Grandfather. He does not have your adequate resources in that area!" Abha said, giving him time to try and collect himself. She headed back to the kitchen as Amun laughed at her cheeky comment.

"Come, my friend! Eat while the food is hot. Abha is very skilled in the kitchen and you will not find better food anywhere in the land!" Amun said smiling, his hands already dipping bread into the large bowl of stew.

Nehemiah picked up a piece of bread robotically, his eyes never leaving the curtain that separated the kitchen from the dining area. He dipped it into the large bowl in the centre of the table. It WAS very good, and he hungrily got stuck in, his heart still pounding in his ears.

"Abha has already eaten so we will just be on our own, but don't worry my friend, I will speak with her later."

Nehemiah was so pleased about that because he was sure that if he had to say one word to that beautiful woman, he would stumble and stutter like a school boy. He didn't know what was wrong with him! He had never had that happen before and he had seen some beautiful women in London. He concentrated on eating the food. He was truly hungry, and the food was very good, so it was not too difficult. However, there were two other courses that he had to get through, with Abha serving them both. By the time the last course was brought to the table, he was sure that she was just toying with him, asking him questions knowing that he just couldn't get the words out. He just kept his head down and ate, not even paying much attention to Amun and his stories. He was so flustered that he just wanted this whole event to finish so that he could go home. The end of the meal couldn't come quick enough.

As he saw him to the top of the stairs, at the end of the evening Amun suggested bringing Abha to the warehouse tomorrow so that they could meet properly.

"NO!" Nehemiah almost shouted and his friend stepped back in alarm. "I am sorry, what I mean is that I have meetings to deal with tomorrow that are really important. Maybe in a week or so?"

Amun smiled and agreed, shaking Nehemiah's hand as he departed. Once on the street, he started for the warehouse striding out his discomfort. He was so annoyed with himself, but he had been taken aback with her and her beautiful dark almond shaped eyes. He caught himself sighing. "For goodness sake!" he muttered under his breath, lengthening his stride and hurrying to get back to his desk.

On his return to the warehouse he realised that his personally enforced frog-march back from Amun's house had done little to calm his heart or get his head straight. He wondered if this was how it felt to be swept of your feet? He just couldn't stop thinking about Abha, about how beautiful she was, about how very capable she was and about the twinkle she had in her eye as she teased him during dinner. He dropped into his chair and sat at his desk for a while, trying to clear his mind and settle for the evening but after half an hour of restlessness he stood up and started pacing again. He was going to have to work this out and that meant he was going to have to see her again. The very thought made his heart quicken. What was more he had a very strong suspicion that she would be the perfect person for the job that he needed doing which meant he would have to see her on a daily basis. That thought made him feel dizzy with anxiety and excitement. He took a few deep breaths to calm his heart and still his thinking. He needed to get his head straight, get some work done. He picked up his backpack and started out towards the door of Yoshi's Egyptian room, picking up a lantern on his way out of the warehouse. It was not too late, and he might find it quiet enough now to get a message to him and find out what was happening on his side of the doorway.

The night was warm and quiet apart from the sounds of the crickets surrounding him as he walked across the sand. Occasionally, he would swat away a bug that flew too close to his face but apart from that he walked unmolested. He was not sure about how things stood at the doorway during the night. When he first arrived, it had been guarded at all times so that he could not escape but since the gifts had been arriving, he wondered if that had changed. Sure enough, as he approached he saw that the door had closed, signalling that no deliveries would be arriving that day. In front of it sat a guard, spear across his knee, snoring softly. Nehemiah quietly walked past him, so as not to wake him and sat with his back to a nearby tree, so that he could see if the situation changed with the guard or if anyone approached. He sat for a little while to make sure that he was alone before removing the tablet from his bag and switching it on. Once it was up and running he sent his message to Yoshi.

"Is anyone there?"

The answering message came almost immediately.
"*Yes. I am so pleased you are able to get in touch! How are things with you?*"

"Fine thanks! I have not had the opportunity to sit near the Wi-Fi until now. We are very grateful for your distractions of the Pharaoh! It really has helped us immensely!"

"*I thought you would like that! We have slowed down the deliveries a little as the pace was too fast to maintain. I think the deliveries will only be three times a week now, but I will ensure that there are enough goods, of sufficient quality to keep the Pharaoh occupied so that you can continue your work.*"

"Thank you, Yoshi. I have been thinking about the concrete tents. Logistically it is difficult. The idea is great, but I am not sure how to pull it off."

"I have an idea! Solar panels will be the answer for the pumps, I think, and I know just how to disguise them, if you will trust me on that?"

"Absolutely" We are thinking alike on the idea of solar panels I just have no idea how to get them in under the nose of the Pharaoh."

"You leave that to me Nehemiah! I have been thinking about the water issue too. What do you know about the 'Archimedes Screw?"

"Never heard of it! I will see if I can get any info.... I have to go!"

The guard stirred and started to stretch his arms. Nehemiah shut the tablet down quickly and slipped it into his bag, trying to put an innocent expression on his face. He sat patiently waiting for the guard to notice him. He didn't want to give him any excuse to poke at him with that wicked looking spear. The guards finished his stretch and looked around to see if anyone had noticed him napping. It was then he caught sight of Nehemiah and his brows came together in suspicion.

"What are you doing here?" he asked gruffly, picking up his spear and pointing it in his direction.

"I am waiting for the deliveries to start. I wanted to get here early, before anyone else so I could see it all happening. I haven't had the opportunity to see it yet." He said with an innocent expression on his face and a pleasant smile on his lips. The guard did not look convinced. "Nothing happening today!" he said from under his brows.

"Oh well. Never mind. I will come back another day then." Nehemiah rose, shouldered his bag and started to move off.

"Wait!" ordered the guard, "You better not tell anyone that I was sleeping! It would turn out very bad for you if you did!"

"Sleeping? Were you sleeping? I thought you were thinking!" the innocent look remained.

"That's all right then! Go on now. Get!"

Nehemiah, turned his back on the guard and headed back to the warehouse. He was starting to tire now, it had been a long day and as usual, the solving of one problem just led to many more questions. He was glad that Yoshi had taken on the solar panel issue and was intrigued as to how he was going to solve it. However, now he had to learn about the Archimedes screw, whatever that was. He yawned and stretched out his stride. "Bed!" he thought, hurrying back to the warehouse.

One of the things that Yoshi loved about having money, was being able to give it away! He sponsored various good causes but one of his favourites was a scholarship that he had set up for the local art school. He loved art and was so pleased to be able to help others in their creative development and expression. It was also fortunate, for him, that his setting up of the scholarship had put him in touch with the Principal of the Collage of Art, Professor Timothy Bartholemew. He was a fine upstanding man in his sixties, a quiet and thoughtful gentleman whose area of expertise was sculpture. So, he had spoken with the Professor two weeks ago and arranged for a competition to be run for the final year students. The First prize was for £5,000 and an exhibition slot in one of the leading art museums in London. The Second prize was for £2,000 and an article in Art Monthly, about the artist and their work. The Third prize was for £1,000 and a weekend tour of galleries in London. The title of the competition was, 'Impressions of Ancient Egypt' and the style was completely open to the individual artists. They could use any type of paint they desired but it had to be of a certain size and on silicon sheets. They had one week to complete and submit the paintings, so it was a tight deadline, but Yoshi hoped that the prizes would help the students with their motivation. He had arranged for some prestigious artists to judge the competition, the following weekend.

Although Yoshi loved the Arts and was very proud to be a patron of them, he had an ulterior motive in setting up this particular competition. Nehemiah needed his help with his housing problem! Namely, the concrete tents!

Yoshi saw the concrete tents as being the ideal solution to the housing situation of the Pharaoh's slaves. The buildings were not dissimilar to the Nissan Huts used to house the Prisoners of War in World War II. They were the same shape and were design to sleep fifteen people comfortably. They were made of a canvas that had concrete embedded into it. They came ready folded in a cube shaped bag and were pumped up to the right size, with air and then saturated with water. This set within twenty-four hours to a concrete building, completely sterile and ready to use. It could then be buried under sand or ice, depending on the circumstances of use. They had a life of around ten years and would be a much more hygienic and humane way of housing the people that Nehemiah was trying to help. Family units would be able to stay together, and it would afford them much more privacy than the present situation. However, it required electricity for the pumps to erect the buildings in the first place and for this, solar energy would be perfect. The one thing at Nehemiah's disposal was sunshine! They could get the panels set up without too much difficulty and get them out again once they were no longer needed. So, Yoshi had come up with the idea to disguise the solar panels as artwork to be presented to the Pharaoh, as gifts. It was, of course a bit of a gamble because it all depended on what mood the young Pharaoh was in that day but if things continued the way they had been going, he would discard the ones of poorer quality to Amun and keep the better paintings for himself. This was what Yoshi was counting on. The higher quality artwork that he intended to send through, would be on canvas and was part of his own person collection but the student's artwork would be on solar panels, framed to look like paintings. He also had Mortimer on his side, of course.

"Mortimer could persuade even the most stubborn of donkeys!" he thought chuckling, "He could also talk his hind legs off in the process!"

A gentle tapping at his office door brought him out of his reverie.

"Tea Sir." said Mortimer, carrying a tray in his right hand.

"Thank you, Mortimer. I think the saying goes 'Think of the Devil…'!" Yoshi replied smiling up at the liveried gentleman. "Pleasant thoughts, I hope, Sir?"

"Always! Any news from our designer friend, Jasper?" Yoshi asked, accepting the tray of green chai.

"Not yet, Sir, but he does like cutting things finely." Mortimer replied, "Will that be all, Sir?"

"Thank you, Mortimer, that will be all."

As the door closed quietly Yoshi reached for the phone. He still had a pavilion to obtain and time was of the essence if Nehemiah was to ever make it home again.

The conversation took up half an hour of his time, but it left Yoshi feeling at peace. It was all coming together, and the new pavilion would indeed arrive on time. In fact, if Jasper's descriptions were correct, it would be even better that Yoshi had himself imagined and he could imagine quite a lot! It would of course cost twice what Yoshi had originally said was in his budget, but then he had budgeted for that, too! It would be worth it. There was not enough money in the whole world to balance the cost of one human life and the suffering that Nehemiah was trying to eradicate, was an anathema to everything that Yoshi believed in. While it was undeniably true that he was an extremely wealthy man, this did not make him uncompassionate. He was well travelled himself, and had had many adventures, among all sorts of people. He had witnessed many times, Man's inhumanity to Man and had fought hard to help whoever he could, in whatever capacity he could. Sometimes, it was just a kind word, sometimes advice and sometimes practical help, which cost him money.

It did not matter to Yoshi! It was all energy given to others, that helped. Whatever form that took. He had only one rule about the way that he helped others. He never gave anything that would make someone become dependent. He was about making the 'Able more Able'! It was all about quality of life. People needed to be able to accomplish their own purpose and if he could help them to do that, then his purpose was accomplished! He remembered his Father trying to explain this concept to him when he was just a young man. He had been a very foolish young man and had tried to be of assistance to anyone who came along. He soon discovered that his followers, although sycophantic, were thirstier than all the deserts on earth. He did not have what they needed. He had what they greedily, wanted, but it was of no use to them fulfilling their own purpose, their own destiny. Moreover, he discovered that it is the very difficult and trying times, that teach people the lessons they need, to succeed. He had been a very popular man at University but also a very lonely one and when he left, he found that the only real friends that he had, could be counted on one hand. This had taught him much about his own perception and needs, and that had, in turn, taught him much about the ethics of helping people. He was indeed grateful to his Father for his kind patience in helping him through that time, but he was also grateful for the hurt that he had experienced, at the hands of those so called sycophantic friends. It had taught him a valuable lesson. The value of love. So, when he had met Nehemiah, for the first time, he had instinctively known, that he was the right man for the job. He could recognise in him, the urge to help others in a way that made them more able. He had not predicted his sudden departure, nor the task that He now faced, but deep in his heart he was not surprised by any of it. If anyone was capable of sorting out the situation, it was Nehemiah, who had more than enough kindness in his heart and more than enough intelligence in his head to deal with it all.

Chapter Twelve

Nehemiah woke bleary eyed. His sleep had been disturbed by very vivid dreams, most of them featuring Abha! He had so much to do in such a short amount of time, that he could not allow himself to become distracted by this wonderful woman. He sighed. What a beautiful woman, though! So capable and so beautiful and tall and slim and such eyes......! They took his breath away just thinking about them, and…

His daydreams were interrupted by Moses whistling.

"Behave yourself, Nehemiah!" he said to himself, "Work!"

He got out of the camp bed that was at the back of his office area and finger combed his hair. He really needed to wash and change before he started the day's activities. It had been three days and he was definitely not smelling his best, he noticed, nose pointing towards his oxters! He grabbed his backpack, making sure there was a change of clothes in it and headed out of his office to head to the river. As he entered the warehouse, the usual people started talking to him, each one shouting to try and be heard over the other. He stopped and raised his hands.

"I am NOT doing anything until I have bathed!" he said emphatically, "Where is Zaph?"

The old man dodged around the crowd of people and came to rest in front of Nehemiah.

"Zaph, can you please find out what all of these people need? Divert anything that can be diverted to someone else. For example, if it is just a request for supplies, food etc, that can go to Amun. The if you can make a list and prioritise what is the most important, I will look at it when I get back. Can you do that, for me?"

"Of course!" said Zaph heading off to the far corner of the warehouse, "Follow me everyone and we will get things moving."

Nehemiah watched the crowd disperse and follow the old man and breathed a sigh of relief. Moses was standing next to him, looking up expectantly.

"I suspect that I will need a crafty messenger while I am taking a bath." He said, "Preferably one that likes to swim!"

He reached into his pockets and drew out two boiled sweets, handing one to Moses and putting one into his own mouth. "Mint Imperials!" he said, as they set off for the river.

They found a spot some way away from the women washing the clothes and behind clump of rushes, Nehemiah stripped off, and after making sure that his backpack was in a safe dry place, he dived in. Moses was not far behind, laughing and there ensued a fierce game of splashing and diving before the serious business of washing could begin. Moses was not so good at the washing part, but Nehemiah reasoned that if he was in the water long enough, the dirt was bound to come off and kept him entertained and playing long enough to get somewhat clean. After using the fine sand to scrub himself clean, he relaxed into the warm water. He had so much to do but the floating eased his stress and, he had to admit, gave him more time to think about Abha!

While there was no doubt that She would be a really, capable help in the tasks that he had to accomplish, he was not sure that he would be able to pay attention to the job in hand if she were with him. It was always possible that Amun could find something else for her to do but then, secretly, he really wanted to see her again. He really did! He was amazed that for the last week or so, he had seen her every day in one capacity or another. Whenever he had looked up she had been there, working away quietly, always with a ready smile and a wave. Sometimes she would come over and speak to him, if he looked as if he were not too busy and ask after his health.

He loved the way that she would always look him in the eyes and listen carefully to what he was saying, even if it was just mundane things. He really wanted to be able to find some time to talk to her, about herself instead of just working on the project with her. He lay there relaxing in the water, imagining that conversation. That date! He thought about what he would ask her and how she would reply, how her voice would sound. Maybe, he would hold her hand, while they chatted. A noise distracted his daydream and for the second time that morning his reverie was disturbed by Moses urgent whistling and he lazily looked up to see what the fuss was. There She was, standing on the bank, watching him float in the water, stark naked. His heart dropped into his stomach and flipped over a couple of times as he tried to recover himself without displaying those parts of his anatomy that were seriously responding to the sight of her!

"You would think a man of your importance would have a bath brought to him rather than washing in the river with the dirty clothes!" she said smiling down at him, her eyebrow arched.
He blushed furiously but could not come out of the water in his condition.

"I enjoy the river." He said his discomfort coming across gruffly, "and I am not important! I am just me!" He was gesturing furiously to Moses to bring him his towel. Moses, for some obscure reason seemed to have lost all knowledge of anything that Nehemiah might need and was standing grinning at him, in an imbecilic kind of way!

"I think you are looking for this?" Abha held up his towel with her finger and thumb, "You will have to come and get it I think!" Her eyes twinkled, with thinly veiled mischief.

Nehemiah's predicament was getting worse! She was just so lovely and when she teased him like that, she was absolutely irresistible!

"Maybe I am not ready to get out yet!" he said lowering himself even deeper into the water.

"I can wait!" she said.

And there it was! The impasse! Nehemiah could see that he was not going to come out of this with his dignity intact! He steeled himself for the moment when he would have to stand up, trying very hard to think of work and other difficult problems in order to deal with his state of arousal.

"Abha!"

He heard Amun's voice approaching and breathed a sigh of relief! Rescue had come!

"Abha! What are you doing?" Amun exclaimed, astounded. "Give the man his dignity and wait over there!"

Abha winked at Nehemiah before dropping the towel and withdrawing from the water's edge.

"Grandfather, you are such a spoil sport!"

"Please let me apologise for the cheekiness of my Granddaughter!" Amun said as he came to stand behind the rushes, "She gets it from her Mother I am sure. Please finish your ablutions we will wait over there and escort you back to the warehouse." He pointed to a large rock some distance away and left with Abha, taking her elbow firmly.

Nehemiah ducked under the water once more, his ardour much dampened by the arrival of Amun. Happy that his modesty was once again intact, he exited the water and dried himself of with the towel, shielded from view by the bushes. Once dressed and deodorised he glared at Moses, who sniggered, and they headed over to the waiting friends.

As they walked back to the warehouse, Amun started outlining all the supplies they had accumulated so far, from the rejects of the Pharaoh.

As usual, storage space was a problem and so Nehemiah started to explain all about the concrete tents and how they were going to provide living accommodation for the majority of the people. Amun was astounded! He stood stock still while listening about the amazing invention, only starting to walk again once Nehemiah had finished.

"But this is amazing, my friend! It will mean that we can use all of the huts where people are now holed up sleeping every night."

"Exactly!" agreed Nehemiah, "We are going to start as soon as the tents come through. Some of the present accommodations will be used for storage and some for kitchens to prepare food. Others will be dining spaces for people to eat and I have a plan to turn one into school facilities for the children!"

"Actually, talking about teaching, I have been up to some mischief my friend!"

"What do you mean?"

Amun chuckled, "Well I was speaking to Mr. Toshimoto and I asked him for some supplies of my own. The idea you had about trying to get the people in the rich sector to help is a good idea. However, they will never respect slaves! The only way that we could get anything done with them, is if they think the people who are helping them are also rich. We must make it look like it is a good thing to do for the rich people to learn, to train, to change! As I said, we need to sell it to them! So, I purchased some very fine cloth in order to have clothes made for the slaves, who will be instructing them. They must look the part if the deception is to work."

"That won't work, though, Amun! The very same people who will be dressed up are the slaves that have always been here. They will be recognised! Besides, they are in such poor condition that it will be obvious that they are not healthy and not part of that community. The Rich Quadrant will never buy it!"

Amun laughed out loud! "Do you think that the people in the Rich Quadrant ever look at the poor people that the Pharaoh uses for his construction site! They no more look at their face, than they do the bricks that are used for the walls. They have no worth to the drunk, spoilt, people of the wealthy areas. And as for their condition, I think you are living in the past my friend! Look again at these people and see what they have become!"

Nehemiah raised his eyes and appraised the people working all around him. He was amazed by what he saw! The people were indeed in a much better condition than when he had first arrived. They were still thin, that was true, but they now had muscles and a glow of health about them. They had an energy when they worked but most of all they worked with their heads held high and many had smiles upon their faces. He widened his gaze to take in the whole picture, and noticed the guards also looking better, trimmer and brighter and they too were not without their smiles.

"Amun, this is amazing!" he said, "And terrible! If the Pharaoh were to notice how well everyone is doing, he will surely put a stop to everything! We must keep his attention elsewhere, but I am not sure how to monitor a Pharaoh. How will we know if his attention starts to wander back to the construction site?"

"I hadn't thought of that, my Friend! However, that is a worry for another time. The gifts coming through the doors will keep him occupied for a long time that will enable us to carry out our plan."

"Amun, you are right, but I fear it will fall on you to watch the Young King and discern whether his attention is wandering. The cloth is a wonderful gift for us though and I thank you very much Amun. Do you know how we can get them made up and who should be kitted out?"

"The audit has revealed quite a number of tailors and dressmakers and I have a very capable volunteer who will oversee the project. One who is much respected by the Rich Quadrant and is very aware of the fashions of the day."

"Who, Amun?"

"Why, Abha, of course!" Amun said, indicating his Granddaughter with his hand. She smiled at Nehemiah coyly and once again, in his mind, all talk of business was extinguished.

"I am able to confer with the people who are collating the data to find out who are the Masters in their trades. These people will be gathered, measured and fitted with the finest clothes that we can make, in the time that we have available." Abha said, "Then we can turn them over to you for the next phase. What is the next phase?"

Nehemiah looked at her and took a deep breath to steady his heart, "You really are a wonder, you know!"

Now it was Abha's turn to blush and lower her head in modesty.

"I mean…very capable and professional! You must get it from your Grandfather, here! Amun, we need to organise a gathering. A very grand affair it must be, with all the glitz and glamour of the finest ball that has ever been seen in the Rich Sector."

"You cannot just organise a ball!" Amun said, "No one would come if there was not a reason to celebrate! It would not be in their interests! Besides, once they were there, they would become so drunk there would be no way that you could sell them anything, for the falling over and the vomiting and passing out! You have not seen these sort of events, My Friend! It just wouldn't work!"

"Amun, you worry, too much!" said Nehemiah, touching his arm, "There are parts of my world that are about as hedonistic as you can get! I think they would give even the Rich Quadrant a run for their money! We will be celebrating the Accountability of the Pharaoh and the Nation! The event will run over three days and the only thing that will be happening to the people as they eat, and drink is that they will be sobering up! We will be serving the most delicious 'Mocktails' that we can find!"

"What, my Friend, is a 'Mocktail?"

So, Nehemiah explained to his friends the whole idea behind a Mocktail, to the uproarious laughter of Amun!

"You are surely one of the most ingenious people I have ever had the privilege to meet, my Friend!" Amun said when he had recovered his breath. "But surely they will not just drink Mocktails! When you tell them they have no alcohol they will refuse point blank!"

"What they don't know, won't hurt them!" Nehemiah said, winking at Abha, his heart skipping a beat at her blush. That started Amun laughing again and that is exactly how Rachid found them, approaching the warehouse.

"I hadn't realised that Accountability was such a light-hearted past time." He said, looking at Nehemiah disapprovingly beneath lowered brows.

"Rachid!" Nehemiah said, extending his hand in welcome, "There is always something to laugh about if you look hard enough! What can I help you with today? Does the Pharaoh need me to speak to him about his Accountability?"

Rachid shifted awkwardly from foot to foot. "Not exactly, Nehemiah. It is a matter of much confidentiality, I must approach with you today."

Amun took hold of Abha's elbow and put his hand on Moses back. "We will leave you to it." He said moving towards the entrance of the warehouse.

Nehemiah looked into Rachid's eyes and saw a troubled man. "I think we should find somewhere to sit and talk in private." he said. "How about we take a walk away from all the hustle and bustle?"

Rachid's eyes brightened and they headed off away from the warehouse towards the hills. They walked for some time in silence, Nehemiah allowing Rachid to gather his thoughts and decide on the tack he wished to take. When they were far enough away from any prying ears, Rachid turned to the young man.

"I cannot lie to you, Nehemiah!" he started, "I see what you are doing! I see how things are changing. I know what is going to happen and I am frightened!"

Nehemiah put up his hands to stop the flow of Rachid's words. "What do you see, Rachid?"

"Well, I see how people's lives are improving! I am starting to see slaves smiling. Imagine! Slaves! Smiling! I am starting to see my guards, smiling and that is even more unbelievable!"

Nehemiah smiled. "And how is that frightening, Rachid?"

"Well, it is not!" he stumbled, "Of itself, it is not. The frightening part is the repercussions to me and my family. To the guards and their family! I don't know what to do about it!"

"About what, Rachid?"

"Well! The only thing I know how to do is this job! I have been the Supervisor of Guards for years now. Before that I was a guard myself! But that only works if there is something to guard! What happens next, Nehemiah?'

‘What happens when there are no more slaves? What will become of me and my family? I came to you before going to the Pharaoh because he doesn’t know yet, but I can see what you are doing Nehemiah! I can see how it is going to be!”

Nehemiah indicated a flat rock and they both sat down, side by side. He took a deep breath before he started, knowing that this may well be the trickiest conversation that he had had to have, to date.

“Would it be so bad, Rachid, if everyone was treated the same? If everyone was respected?”

“No!” Rachid stated, “I am not saying that! I was born a slave! I know how that feels! My parents were both killed as slaves, never knowing how it felt to be treated as a human being! That is not the problem! The problem is that I have a young family and another on the way.”

“Congratulations!”

“Thank you! How am I supposed to feed them Nehemiah? How am I supposed to keep a roof over their head if I have no job? And how am I going to have a job, if there is no reason for us to have guards, that I can supervise? My children will be destitute! There is little enough prospect for them now! My wife teaches them as she can, but they have no chance of ever bettering their situations and it pains me greatly to think that they will end up with nothing! Unable to work and provide for their families. How can I be a party to something that will harm my own children and family?”

Nehemiah spoke his name softly, until Rachid looked into his eyes.

“I understand your worry. I can see how scary that would feel for a man who is only trying to protect his family. However, you have only seen with your eyes, Rachid. You need to also see with your heart! You need to understand the implications with your heart and then judge the situation.”

"I don't understand!"

"No, you don't! But you will! Allow me to tell you about my dream! If after you have heard about it, if you still feel worried, then go to the Pharaoh! Straight away! But if after you have heard about my plans, you can also see the way it could become, I would very much appreciate working with someone with such a capacity for honesty and loyalty, as you show to your family and land."

Rachid stopped and just looked at Nehemiah, astounded. He had lost all the wind out of his sails, in just that one short statement!

"I believe," began Nehemiah, "That every person should have to right to earn an honest day's pay for an honest day's work! That means Every person."

"But..." started Rachid.

Nehemiah raised a finger to forestall him.

"Now, that cannot happen when you have a system where people are treated without respect. Where people are treated with inequality. Where expectations are put upon people is such a way, that they cannot deliver them. People should be allowed to give their very best, in whatever it is that they are doing. In order to do this, they need to have rest, food and also appreciation of the work that they are giving. They need to be able to appreciate the very task that they are taking part in, not be forced to do something against their will because they are so desperate or so afraid.

Now sometimes, it may well be that someone has aspirations to do the kind of work that they are not yet able to do. Maybe someone would like to be tailor or a blacksmith but because they have been born into a system where they have no choice and no respect, they will never have the opportunity to learn the skills required to do the work, they want to do. Do you understand?"

Rachid nodded, looking at Nehemiah from underneath lowered brows, open but suspicious.

"So, imagine if it were then possible to take these poor people, with aspirations, and change their circumstances so that they could train to do the jobs they really wanted to do?"

Rachid snorted. "How would that work?! The Pharaoh must have his constructions! If everyone was off following their dreams that would never happen!"

"Believe it or not, Rachid, some people actually like construction work! They actually want to do this type of building work and take pride in their skills! In my world, there are people whose job it is to lay bricks! They are hired just to do that job and paid according to the skill they have. They take great pride in the amount of bricks they can lay in a day and how straight and sure the laying is!"

Rachid's jaw dropped! "Really?" he said aghast. "You mean they come willingly? Without a beating? And do a good job, just because they can?"

"And because they are well paid and appreciated for their work and skill." Nehemiah added.

Rachid shook his head in disbelief! "Who would have thought it! Laying bricks because you want to!"

"Exactly!" emphasised Nehemiah. "Is there not something you wished you could do?"

"Well, I always wished I could do numbers. I mean read and add and understand numbers and use them. I like numbers."
Nehemiah burst out laughing, clapping the other man on the back!

"That is exactly what I do, in my world!" he said warmly.

Now Rachid really was astounded. "You mean you get paid for that!"

"Very well, as it happens!" Nehemiah answered to the perplexed look on Rachid's face. "There are lots of things that you can do with numbers, that help in everyday life, Rachid. For example, say you want to re-arrange your home to accommodate the new baby. It helps to know exactly how much space you have in your room and that is just working with numbers."

Rachid still looked a little confused so Nehemiah sat with him, right there and then, and showed him how to work out the area of a square room, by using a stick in the sandy soil. Once they had finished Rachid's face was beaming with a broad smile.

"I have just learned numbers!" he stated proudly, and Nehemiah could do no more than clap him on the back, once again and join him in his big smile!

"I want everyone to be able to learn whatever they need, Rachid. That includes the children, your children, I want them to be able to accomplish anything that they want to accomplish, to succeed in any way they see fit, all the time working together and helping each other. I promise you, Rachid, that there will be plenty of work for you and everyone else and what is more, the Pharaoh will get his building project completed. In fact, it will be splendid, and much admired for hundreds of years to come."

"He is not going to like it!"

"No! I know that, but maybe this is also about learning. Maybe this is his lesson to learn. To look after the people who are in his care and have their best interests at heart. That requires thinking about other people and not just yourself. That requires giving up greed."

"You do know, Nehemiah, that that sort of talk can get you executed by the very Pharaoh that you are trying to help?" Rachid said, a warning in his voice.

"Would you report me for this kind of talk, Rachid?"

The Supervisor of the Guards sat very quietly and thought. He knew that in his position of responsibility it was his job to report all forms of sedition to the Pharaoh and that if it was discovered that he had reneged on his responsibility, it may well be himself at the executioner's block. However, he could see exactly where Nehemiah was coming from! He understood that what this young man was trying to achieve, would save the entire nation. It would help his children and their children and would create a much better world to live in. What was more, it might just work! He had never met anyone like Nehemiah and his determination, kindness and compassion knew no limits. It was time to decide if he was going to throw in with him and help him in his gigantic task or stop it dead. He pictured the faces of his small children and realised that he could not live with himself, if he had a part in destroying any chance they had, of a happy life, before it had even got off the ground. That was when he realised that he was in for the long haul! Turning to Nehemiah he held out his hand.

"Let us shake on this, that I will not report any activities that you are taking part in to the Pharaoh, as long as they are part of your plan and are for the good of all." They shook hands solemnly. "I like you Nehemiah, and if anyone can pull this off, it is you. You have an uphill battle on your hands but if I can help at all, and it is within my capabilities, I will. For my children, I could do no less. However, I must warn you to be careful. Not everyone can understand what is happening here and some will try and jump on the back of anything that changes their own plans for their future."

"Thank you for your support Rachid. It means a lot to me. What you have done with the guards has been amazing. They are looking so much happier and fitter. A fact that the Pharaoh will not fail to notice. You must also be careful my friend."

Rachid laughed. “Don’t you worry about me! I have the guards well in hand and he can hardly complain if they are doing a better job than they were before, for the same money! We will work together. It will be better.” He stood brushing the dust off his trousers, “You must come and meet my beautiful family one day, Nehemiah. I think they will like you!”

“I would like that very much.” He smiled, “If you need anything, just come and see me.”

With a nod of his head, Rachid turned and headed back down towards the construction site and his work. Nehemiah stood for a moment watching his back.

“People are indeed good!” he thought, “And never ceased to amaze me, with their resilience!”

His attention was caught by the sight of Zaph waving his arms furiously in the distance.

“Onwards and Upwards, Nehemiah!” he muttered to himself, as he started to head down towards the warehouse, “Onwards and Upwards!”

Chapter Thirteen

The Pharaoh woke slowly and rolled over in his bed sighing. Today was a delivery day and gifts would start pouring through the door that Nehemiah had come through. He should be excited, but it was so very tiring to be sat there all day, having to pay attention all of the time and he was absolutely sure that nobody understood how hard he worked at accepting the gifts in the manner befitting a Pharaoh! Some of the gifts were quite exquisite and he was certain that they must be worth a large amount of gold but some of them were rubbish and fit only for the slaves. He couldn't understand the disparity in it! Surely the person sending the gifts knew how Great he was and how he did not need paltry presents, as if he were an ordinary person! What did the slaves need with gifts anyway? It is not as if he didn't have enough of them. He didn't really even have to feed them and throw cloth in their direction. If they died, there were plenty more to take their place! He sighed again! It was only because he was so magnanimous that they were treated so kindly, in the first place. They should be grateful!

He heard the scuffling of feet and realised that his wakened state had been noticed by the servants.

"Get me food!" he said in a croaky voice, "And water! I need water!"

He swung his feet over the side of the bed and waited impatiently while some fumbling idiot slipped sandals onto them. He stumbled over to a stool that was next to a table which was already becoming laden with food and water, plonked himself down on the seat and started to pick at the food before him.

His life was so hard! He was surrounded by idiots that had no idea what he had to suffer on their behalf. He was going to have to be nice to everyone all day! He hated being nice to people! He looked up and noticed all of the slaves prostrated on their hands and knees before him, foreheads touching the floor.

"Get out!" he said, "Just get out and leave me in peace!"

The servants ran for the door, as fast as they could without tripping over each other and the Pharaoh was left alone to break his fast.

Chewing sloppily, because he could, the Young King pondered what he would wear today. He did enjoy displaying his finery and loved the clothes he got to wear. He also enjoyed how impressed that man, Mortimer was with him.

"Now, THAT is a proper servant!" he thought, "No snivelling! Just proper respect! Always attentive and ready with good sensible advice, which is exactly what you needed as a ruler of a nation."

Mortimer really was wasted living in his own world. Maybe he should be captured? The Pharaoh sighed and shook his head. That would not do! He would surely turn just like the rest of the stupid slaves, if he were forced to be here. He fancied that Mortimer were more like a friendly advisor, than a servant. In fact, he maybe could be classed as a friend, if Pharaoh's were allowed to have friends, that is.

He finished off his breakfast a little more cheery and headed off towards his dressing room to choose the outfit he would wear for today.

"Maybe today would not be so bad, after all!" he thought.

Amun stood outside the audience chamber and took a deep breath. He turned to Zaph, who stood beside him, smiling.

"I think we need to look a little more downtrodden, my friend!" he said, "It wouldn't do to go in there as if we were anything but humble servants. It is going to be a long day and if we start off on the wrong foot, it will feel even longer!"

Zaph grunted his agreement and let the smile fall from his face. He hunched his shoulders and rounded his back and suddenly became a downtrodden slave again. Amun let out a quiet chuckle!

"Your talents are wasted here, my friend." He said quietly, "You should have been on the stage!" With that he led the way into the Audience Chamber, falling to his knees and prostrating himself as he caught sight of the Pharaoh.

"About time!" Pharaoh said with a frown. "Do you realise how long I have been awaiting your arrival? Me! The greatest man on earth! Kept waiting by the likes of you! I should have you whipped!"

"You Greatness!" Amun said in his most obsequious voice. "I am but your lowly servant and it is my greatest wish to make you happy. However, I am but a poor old man who is without the regal transport that you, deservedly, use. My legs do not work as well as they used to, not having the benefit of your robust youth. Please whip me if it will make you happy." His forehead stayed pressed to the floor and he crossed his fingers that the Pharaoh's impatience would win out and he would be saved a beating.

"Oh, get up, you snivelling idiot! I don't have time for this and I need you working, not lying on the floor. We must get to the door and meet Mortimer and you had better not make me any later, or my patience will finally be exhausted! The Young King stood from his throne and set off at pace towards his waiting canopied chair and string of servants just waiting to be ordered about.

Amun caught Zaph's eye and winked as they followed along behind. "It is going to be a good day, my friend." He muttered quietly as they struggled to keep pace with the entourage.

By the time they had followed everyone outside, the Young King was already seated on his canopied chair and the carriers were hoisting it up onto their shoulders. They set off at pace towards the door and Amun, accompanied by Zaph, headed towards the area where he would have to deal with the poorer quality, diverted goods. There, out of sight was a couple of stools underneath an awning to create shade and he knew that there would also be sweetmeats and cool water, to make their day more comfortable. They had erected some rough walls to stack goods against, until they could be removed and to give them some privacy, from the Pharaoh's prying eyes.

"I wonder what delights will be coming through the door today, Zaph?"

"I don't know, Amun but I do know that Nehemiah was pretty excited about it and is heading to the door himself." Zaph replied.

Amun stopped in his tracks. "Really? Maybe we should go there too?"

"No, it is ok. He told me to carry on as normal but to expect some surprises! I think he will come and see us a little later."

Amun sighed. "I hate it when I don't know what is going on. Come then, Zaph! Let us go and seek some shade and await events as they unfold."

The Pharaoh beamed as they approached the door and he saw Mortimer waiting next to it.

"Good Morning!" he said to the Liveried Gentleman and lifted his hand in greeting.

Mortimer gave a low bow. "Your Majesty! It is so good to see you, and may I say you look resplendent today!" The Young King grinned from ear to ear.

"If you will forgive me, Your Graciousness, I must keep you waiting for just a little while longer. We have a special treat for you that has been organised by none other than Mr. Nehemiah Toosh, himself. He asked me to wait until he could present it to you personally. I have, however, prepared some small dainties from my world, that I think may delight and entertain you, until he arrives." Mortimer bowed again and then ushered some of his colleagues forward, each carrying a sliver tray with small samples of food on it, in their right hands.

The Pharaoh was so pleased that he seemed to have forgotten that he was, once again, being kept waiting. He clapped his hands with delight and waved the Liveried Gentlemen forward with anticipation.

"Only you, could have been so thoughtful, Mortimer!" he said smiling.

"Thank you, Your Highness!" Over the Pharaoh's shoulder he could see Nehemiah in the distance, striding towards them, Moses in tow and he smiled to himself. "I think Your Majesty will particularly like these ones." He said, lifting a tray from the many surrounding him and holding it towards the young man. "I prepared these myself."

"You really should come and stay here, with me, Mortimer." He said as he helped himself to a small delicacy.

"What a delightful idea, Majesty, but I fear My Toshimoto would never agree to such a thing." He replied, "He simply would not be able to manage without me."

The Pharaoh nodded, agreeing with every word but unable to voice his opinion while chewing the wonderfully tasty food. By the time the young man had cleared the platter of dainties, Nehemiah was just arriving. He approached the canopied chair and bowed low to the Pharaoh, then upon straightening he shook hands with Mortimer and clapped him on the shoulder with the other hand.

"Your Gracious Majesty!" he said to the Pharaoh, "It is a pleasure to see you again. We have been very busy working on your accountability and I am pleased to report that all is progressing smoothly and speedily."

The Young King scowled, not because he was displeased with the news but was envious of Nehemiah's easy familiarity with Mortimer.

"What a pity you didn't think to report this to me earlier!" he said. "So, what is this momentous occasion that drags you away from your work and brings you into our midst?"

Nehemiah showed none of the confusion that he felt. He couldn't understand the Pharaoh's displeasure towards him and he met eyes with the Liveried Gentleman at his side, raising an eyebrow in question as to the strange behaviour being displayed by the young man. Mortimer gave a very discreet shake of his head and smiled at the King, once more.

"I apologise for being remiss in my attendance of Your Majesty." Nehemiah began, "I am, however, hoping that the next gift that is brought out to you, will make up for any of my inconsideration. It is a very large gift and will take many days to arrive in its entirety. We have arranged for its continued delivery day and night until its arrival is complete. In order for you to be able to see the gift before this happens, paintings of the finished product have been made, so that you may look upon its beauty and appreciate the scale of the offering, until its arrival and construction is complete." Several Liveried Gentlemen exited the doorway, each pair carrying large canvases, with artist's impressions of the most amazing pavilion. Each picture showed a different room, from many angles, complete with the most beautiful furnishings and luxurious decorations. The Young King gasped as he looked at each picture being carried past him and taken towards his existing quarters.

"As this gift is to take many days to be delivered, it was decided to bring all of the pictures to your accommodation so that you may take the time to look upon each one and see the detail, that has gone into the creation, of what will be you new home for some time to come." Nehemiah said, fingers crossed behind his back. He needn't have worried though, as the Pharaoh was already signalling the chair carriers to follow the string of paintings back to his Pavilion, waving his hand at Nehemiah, dismissively. He was already some distance away before the string of paintings stopped coming through the door and both the Young Accountant and the Liveried gentleman beside him let out a breath of relief.

"What was all that about?" Nehemiah asked turning to Mortimer, "What have I done now? Or rather, what has he found out?"

"It is alright, Sir. He has discovered nothing about any of your plans, but I fear that the Pharaoh thinks he has found a new Best Friend, in me and is more than a little jealous if I speak to anyone else, while he is here." Mortimer shifted onto his other foot, uncomfortably. "You may have noticed that he doesn't have many friends and your greeting upset him a little."

"For Goodness sake!" Nehemiah tutted in disapproval, "I am not really very good at walking on eggshells. Well Done, Mortimer for handling him so well!"

"Thank you, Sir! It is just part of my job!"

"I got word from Yoshi early this morning about the pavilion. Maybe you can fill me in on the full plan?"

"Certainly, Sir! Shall we take a seat in the shade and away from any prying ears? I do believe that Amun has a little den set up for himself, just over there, where we will be able to converse in privacy. It will also save you having to tell him everything later and while we are talking, deliveries can commence." Mortimer starting walking in the direction of Amun's little shelter, Nehemiah following closely behind.

"Excellent idea! Lead the way!"

As they walked they chatted amiably about this and that, catching up on the things that had been happening with Yoshi Toshimoto. Nehemiah was astounded at how busy they had been, in helping his dream become a reality. He was not surprised, however, and was extremely grateful that he had such a caring and compassionate friend to help him.

Amun came out of the shade to greet them both and would hear nothing until they were comfortably seated and holding a refreshing drink.

"Now, my friend!" he said turning to Mortimer, "Tell me the great plan that has been concocted by Mr. Toshimoto. I would hear all of the details, so that I can understand everything and help in any way that I can."

"Well, I think, the first thing to say, is that there is going to be a lot of disruption for the next week! Yoshi has asked me to apologise in advance but to explain that it is necessary in order for you to take delivery of the concrete tents and to erect them without drawing undue attention, of the Pharaoh. Even with all of the disruption and noise, it is going to be a very tricky proposition and may well not be enough to cover your plan." He drew a deep breath. "Mr. Toshimoto has ordered the construction of a new pavilion for the Pharaoh. This pavilion has been built on a massive scale and consists of many different areas that are all joined together, in the final construction. It has been designed using only materials that are readily available here and it will be used as a new palace for the Young King, until such times as his own construction has been completed. It will be filled with many fine pieces that will keep the attention of the Pharaoh for quite some time."

Nehemiah and Amun looked at each other aghast, while Zaph chuckled quietly to himself.

"The reasoning behind this venture is manifold." Mortimer continued, "Firstly, the attention of the Pharaoh must be kept away from the work you are doing and the humanitarian efforts that you are organising. Your work, is at a critical stage and a lot hinges on the next few weeks."

"Few weeks?" questioned Nehemiah, "I thought our time was almost up."

"So, it should have been, however, I have been instructed to suggest to the Pharaoh, that his National Holiday should be postponed until his new accommodations are fully established and I have no reason to believe that he will not follow this suggestion. It would make sense that he should want to display himself in his very best surroundings, after all."

"Ingenious!" muttered Amun.

"As part of diverting the Pharaoh's attention, it was decided that he was located too close to the place where you intend to erect the concrete tents. He would have no possibility of avoiding the site and would almost certainly have come down to investigate. We are going to have to move him much further away from the place where he is now. Much closer to the Rich Quadrant, which does not overlook anything to do with the poor people that you are trying to help. It is also quite a distance away from the construction site, so as not to cause noise disruption. This will also work in your favour as the pumps will create a lot of noise, even if you are only using them a few at a time. Moreover, the noise will be foreign and will certainly bring unwanted attention down on you. You will also have to create your own diversion to cover the noise and Mr. Toshimoto thought you were better placed to decide how this should be done."

"I have been thinking about this problem for a little while, but I have to admit that a solution had completely escaped me. The fact that the Pharaoh will be much further away makes it much easier to deal with. I will put my thinking cap on!" Nehemiah said.

"Excellent!" Mortimer continued, "I will report back to Mr. Toshimoto on that. To continue; Secondly, it was decided that you would need a facility in order to develop your training program. One, that was large enough but also one that would live up to the expectations of those taking part, namely the people in the Rich Quadrant. It was felt that they would be unlikely to take part in any sort of programme that was housed inside servant's shelters. And, it was decided that you really should have some space of your own! Mr. Toshimoto felt that you should not be sleeping on a camp bed at the back of your office. You will need to communicate with him more often and also use the electronic facilities that he has provided. The present pavilion will be able to connect to his Wi-Fi and therefore you will be able to accomplish all of these things, in relative comfort."

Nehemiah was speechless. He felt that the kindness of Yoshi was beyond compare. It was true that he had missed the opportunity to be alone sometimes and was missing his meditation, more and more. The idea of being able to sleep in a bed again also sounded amazing. However, another thought had occurred to him lately and it had to do with Abha. He really wanted to ask her for dinner and had had no idea how he could do that when he was constantly working. Now there was hope that he could do that. His heart skipped a beat at the thought.

"I am both humbled by and grateful to Yoshi for everything that he is doing for us. He has truly thought of everything! That he has taken such an active interest in my little adventure, leaves me feeling lost for words. He is so kind and generous." Nehemiah felt very emotional and he could feel tears of gratitude forming in his eyes. "Will you please pass on my words to him, Mortimer? I could not have done this without him."

"Of course, Sir!" Mortimer nodded, "He also asked me to convey his gratitude for all of the help that you are giving to these poor people, and for the future that you are helping them create. He said to tell you that it is without price."

A tear rolled down Nehemiah's cheek. "It is no more than any of them deserve." He said quietly.

"Very true, my friend!" agreed Amun, patting his arm gently.

Mortimer cleared his throat, "Just so! Now if your gentlemen don't mind, I must finish with the business at hand here. There is a lot to do!"

They nodded agreement.

"The new pavilion will take a week to arrive, in sections and people will start erecting it at the new site, shortly thereafter. We intend to keep the Pharaoh indoors throughout this time by delivering the interior goods to him in person. This will make delivery of the concrete tents and the equipment needed to erect them much simpler. They are large and weighty, and it would not do to have to show each one to the Pharaoh. If we can keep him inside, we will just deliver them straight down to the area you have indicated near the river and work can begin as soon as possible. Because of the noise problem, the actual tents will be the last things to be delivered. Then you can erect them at the same time as work on the new pavilion is being carried out. The rest I leave to you!" He stood as he finished the instructions. "One last thing, Sir! Mr. Toshimoto asked me to stress that you must be very careful. He said that he understands how important it is to see the good in people, but this Young Pharaoh, is without principle or discipline. If he feels threatened in any way, he will turn on you and there is no knowing what will become of you, then."

Nehemiah stood and took Mortimer's hand in both of his, shaking it firmly.

"I will be cautious! I promise. I have made an agreement with the Supervisor of the guards and he is working with us, now. He has promised not to report our activities and to keep control of the guards, in this matter."

"Thank goodness for that, Sir! Mr. Toshimoto will be very pleased to hear that."

"As am I!" said Amun, "I don't know how you managed that, Nehemiah! He was always a bully and a scoundrel, right from childhood. I don't know what you said to him to make him become so reasonable, but it is welcome news!"

Nehemiah laughed, "It must be the association of my silver-tongued friends, rubbing off on me!"

With that they all headed back to the doorway laughing.

Walking back to the warehouse, later that evening, watching the sunset as he went, Nehemiah tried to absorb all that had happened that day. He had sent Moses on ahead to let everyone know that he was on his way and to see if there was any hot food still available and was enjoying the solitude. There was so much to do but he could not doubt that the actions of Yoshi had made it all more possible and more simplistic. The Pharaoh was still a worry, though. He was just so unpredictable, and Nehemiah had never been very good at trying to manipulate people. He preferred to let people be who they were, and direct his own actions to accommodate them, or not, as the case may be. He heard footsteps behind him and aware that he was quite alone, swung round quickly to face the person following him. His stomach flipped as he saw Abha trying to catch up with him, her long legs not quite enabling her to match his stride. He put that thought right out of his head… or tried to!

"I did not mean to startle you, Nehemiah!" she said as she tried to catch her breath. "I did call out to you, but you were deep in thought!"

"I am sorry, Abha." He said, tasting the sound of her name in his mouth, "I did not hear you as I was indeed, deep in thought. "How can I help you?" He could have kicked himself for the formality of his words.

"I just wondered if it was alright to walk with you, back to the warehouse?" she said looking into his eyes and making his heart start thumping loudly. "It will be getting dark soon and I do not like to walk alone in the dark."

"Of course!" he said, "It will be my pleasure to walk with you." They started off again, walking side by side. Nehemiah noticed that her head was just above the level of his shoulders and he liked that. His height was one of the first things that people noticed about him and it was not often that he met a woman that was of comparable height. He took deep breaths to try and steady his pounding heart. He was sure that she must be able to hear it, beating out of his chest. After a little while, he felt steady enough to start a conversation with her.

"So, tell me about yourself, Abha." He said in a pleasant and he hoped neutral voice.

"Oh, there is nothing interesting about me. I don't do much, just work, look after Grandfather and now, help your project. As I said, nothing interesting."

"I don't believe that for a second!" Nehemiah said, looking down into her eyes, "What sorts of things do you like? Enjoy?"

She smiled to herself, "A man of your stature could not possibly be interested in the fascinations of a young woman like me."

Nehemiah stopped and looked at her, seriously, "What stature?! I am genuinely interested in you, Abha! Please, tell me all about yourself."

Abha blushed and started walking again, giving Nehemiah no choice but to start walking again.

"Well then." She started, "I grew up in my Grandfather's home, mostly. My mother died when I was a little girl, some kind of fever it was. My Grandfather tried everything to find some medicine that would help her, even talking to Mr. Toshimoto, but there was no help to be found. She was not a robust woman and just did not have the strength in her, to shake off the ague. After that, my Grandfather made sure that he kept me close to him, as a way of reminding him of his only daughter. He made sure that I had good teachers, and he kept me busy enough. I think it would be fair to say that I wanted for nothing, yet I was taught the meaning of responsibility and sharing. He is a kind man, My Grandfather, but not overly indulgent, I think."

"I am sorry to hear about your Mother." Nehemiah said quietly, "I too, am in this world without my Parents."

"I am sorry for you, too. However, I am not without parents. My Father still lives, and I see him every day. He remarried some time ago and his new wife is very nice. I like her a lot and she is very kind and helpful to me. In fact, she is also helping you in your project, as she is an excellent seamstress. I also have two siblings, a brother and a sister, aged five and three, respectively. I often look after them for my Father, when he takes my new Mother away for weekends. They are lovely. Beautiful to look at and very mischievous! What about you? Do you have brothers? Sisters?"

"No! There is just me, I am afraid."

"Abha frowned. "Is that not lonely? Just being on your own? Do you have no Grandparents? Cousins?"

"Some people think it must be lonely and I suspect that it would be hard to understand if you were surrounded by family, but I am not lonely. I am very busy, often and I do love my work very much."

"I do not think this sounds like fun! When did your parents die?"

"I was grown up and working, when they died." Nehemiah began, "It was not long after I had graduated from University and I was working with a firm, as an intern."

"What is University? And what is this firm? And Intern? What is that?"

There was nothing for it but to stop talking about his life and to explain the workings of his world, when it came to employment. Abha was quiet as he explained things, just occasionally interrupting with brief questions to clarify her understanding. By the time he had finished, she understood what he meant, and they had arrived back at the warehouse. They stood at the entrance, Nehemiah going quiet.

"Where do you need to be Abha? Can I take you somewhere?"

"I cannot go anywhere until I have heard your story, Nehemiah! You cannot tease a girl so, with just part of a story. You must continue to the end! Besides, My Grandfather is meeting me here and will take me home himself. Come, let us find somewhere to sit and you can tell me about what happened to your parents." Abha stood with her hands on her hips looking as if she intended to stand there all night, if necessary! He smiled at her and shook his head. "Come then, my office awaits but I am not sure you will find the tale very interesting!" They headed into the warehouse.

Once seated, Abha prompted him again, "Come then! Let me hear your story!"

"Ok! So, I was an Intern at an accountancy firm. I had been there about six months and was really enjoying it. My parents were so proud of me and never a day went by when they didn't tell me that. Anyway, they went away for a long weekend with friend of theirs, who owned a yacht that was moored in the South of France. They got into difficulties when they were hit by a storm and were too far away from shore.'

'The mast snapped and although they were all accomplished sailors, they never managed to regain control of the boat. The boat sank, and the bodies ended up washed up on the shore, just off Monaco, four days later."

"I do not understand this, Nehemiah! What is yacht? And South of France? And Who are sailors?"

Nehemiah burst out laughing. "I can see that it will take some time to tell you my story! I am not sure I have that much time, to spare!"

"Hello?" They heard Amun's voice in the warehouse, getting louder as he approached Nehemiah's office. "What story is that then, my friend?" Amun rounded the makeshift wall protecting the work space, "And have you seen an aggravating young woman who never stops asking questions? Goes by the name of Abha?"

"Grandfather!" She jumped out of her seat and met him with a warm embrace. "I was learning all about Nehemiah's story but every time I learned something, it just ended up that I had to learn more. His story is very confusing, indeed!"

The men laughed at Abha and she scowled at them. "It is time to go home my beautiful Granddaughter. Tomorrow, is time enough to hear more about our intrepid adventurer." Amun turned to the young man seated behind the desk. "Goodnight my friend. Tomorrow is another day." He took Abha's elbow and they started exiting the warehouse while she was still protesting.

"Indeed!" Nehemiah said, raising his hand in a farewell.

Abha and Amun started walking slowly towards their home. Amun carried a lantern to light the way. It had been a long day and he was tired, so he was happy to let Abha chatter away to him.

He was looking forward to getting home and resting his tired legs and he was getting hungry, so he wasn't really paying attention to what she was saying. It was the only when he heard the word 'internship' that his ears pricked up. It was such a foreign word and had no place in the day's events.

"I'm sorry! What were you saying?" He said

"Oh Grandfather! You never pay attention to what I'm telling you! I was saying that it learned all about internships today. Nehemiah explained to me all about his internship which he started when he finished university. Yes Grandfather! I learned all about university too."

"You learned about university?"

"Yes Grandfather! Do you listen to nothing? I have been telling you that Nehemiah and I spent a long time talking today. He was asking me about my mother, well, he was asking me about my story actually." She said.

"Your Story?" Amun asked. "I am really confused! What do you mean, your story?"

"He asked me what my story is! He wanted to know about me Grandfather. He was interested to find out more about me. It was lovely! It was so nice to be able to share the story of my mother, with someone else who was genuinely interested in hearing what I had to say. There is a very kind man, that Nehemiah and quite handsome too."

Amun stopped walking and looked at Abha with a shocked expression.

"What do you mean, quite handsome?" He asked suspiciously.

"I mean, he is very pleasing to look at Grandfather! Surely you know the meaning of the word handsome!"

"Don't be cheeky with me, young lady! Of course, I know what the word handsome means! I want to know, why you would think Nehemiah was handsome. He is not for you, Abha. You cannot have this man!"

"Grandfather! How can you say that? It is not for you to say who Nehemiah is interested in! I am a grown woman! I am I allowed to make up my own mind! I did not say I wanted this man, I just said he was handsome. What are you thinking? And anyway, if I decide to have Nehemiah, I shall have Nehemiah! It has nothing to do with you, Grandfather."

"In this I disagree! You cannot have this man, Abha! It is not possible. You both live in different worlds. Nehemiah does not belong here, and you do not belong there. It cannot be. Do not to be cross with me, it is not my fault. It is just the way things are. It is like the story of the fish and the bird. They may well love each other but they can never be together. If the bird were to live with the fish it would drown and die! If the fish were to live with the bird, it would suffocate and die! There is no place for them to be together regardless of how much they love each other. It is the same with you and Nehemiah. You cannot have this man, Abha!"

Abha looked at her Grandfather in horror. She could not believe what she was hearing. It had never occurred to her that such a situation could exist, she just hadn't thought about it and now that her Grandfather had pointed it out she realized he was right and she couldn't bear it. She stood stock still and looked at him, tears filling her eyes.

"But Grandfather, it's just not fair! He is such a kind man and so smart! Why should I not want the best of men? He is so perfect, exactly what I have been looking for. Surely, there is a way to work things out? Surely, there is a solution? Nehemiah will come up with an answer! I know he will! I just have to talk to him, I just have to ask him!"

By the time Abha had finished and speaking to Amun, the tears were rolling down her cheek. There was nothing that he could do to make her feel better. He gently lowered the lantern to the ground and enfolded her in his arms to try and bring some comfort to his heartbroken Granddaughter. She struggled against him and, so he released her, and she turned and ran into the night, towards home. Amun sighed to himself and picked up the lantern, slowly walking in the same direction. He felt even more tired and heavy after their conversation.

"No, my darling Granddaughter! Life is not fair!" He thought, "Not fair at all!"

Nehemiah sat back in his chair and stretched his legs out under the desk. What an amazing woman she was! Not only beautiful, but smart, witty and oh, so, charming! He could spend all day explaining things to her, telling her his life story helping her to understand his world. She was so curious, so interested in everything he had to say. The time they had spent together had gone so quickly and couldn't remember exactly what they had talked about just that he had not had the opportunity to finished telling her his story.

"That's Good!" He thought, "That means that we will have to meet again so that I can finish my story!"
He couldn't wait! Suddenly, he grew serious. There was so much to accomplish over the next few weeks he couldn't see how he would be able to spend time with Abha. She had taken on board the job of organizing clothes for the poor people who are going to be instructing the students from the Rich Quadrant. That in itself was a monumental task and had to be given her full attention. She would have no time for polite conversation with Nehemiah. He had the order of the concrete tents to organise and the lands to prepare, the Pharaoh to watch and placate and new areas to prepare for food serving and cooking. On top of this, he had a Gala event to prepare and needed his full attention on the job, in order for it to be successful. There would be no pulling the wool over the eyes of the people in the Rich Quadrant!

They were not stupid by any means, just uneducated and if he was to put that right, he really had to sell the idea to them. He hadn't yet formed the basis of a plan, as to how that would happen. He was going to be relying heavily upon Amun, for the information he needed to make it a success. Amun and Zaph were both going to have to educate him, as to what was needed and how he should behave. It was going to be tricky. Ah but, if he was able to find some time to spend with Abha, it would be wonderful! She really was very beautiful and so clever. He sighed, if only it were possible to see her every single day. That would be the most amazing thing of all. He had never met anyone before that he really would like to see, every single day. She had asked him if he was lonely and he had answered honestly that he was not however, when she was not with him, he truly was lonely and that it never happened to him before, in his entire life. That worried him. It was frightening to suddenly start feeling so lonely, when surrounded by so many friendly people. He was not sure how he would be able to cope without seeing her every day. But he could dream! With that he stood up and stretched.

"Time for bed, Nehemiah!" He said to himself, "And sweet dreams!"

Amun tossed and turned. He could not sleep at all so concerned as he about his Granddaughter and her broken heart. He could completely understand her love of Nehemiah, he was a good man, a once in a lifetime, type of good man. If he had come from this world, Amun would have embraced him as a son and had them both married off in double quick time. But he didn't! There was no way round the issues involved. Abha had no place in his world. She would not survive out there. Amun thought of himself as a man of the world and had spent a considerable amount of time with Mr. Toshimoto. He had seen things that had confused and delighted him, but he had also seen things that shocked him and frightened him to his core. His beautiful Granddaughter, was quite innocent and thankfully saw the best in everyone she met. The cruelty and the sheer scale of 'Man's Inhumanity to Man' that took place in Nehemiah's world, took his breath away.

He hoped that she would never have to witness such atrocities, as he had seen on some of his visits to Mr. Toshimoto's world. Nehemiah's world. No! It could not be! He would not allow it! He sat up in bed. This required a plan, a cunning and audacious plan and there was nobody in this world that was more cunning an audacious than Amun! He chuckled to himself, "If anyone can do this, I can! What I need is a list of all of the beautiful, eligible, bachelors in the Rich Quadrant, that are not too drunk and not too stupid and can hold Abha's attention for any length of time. Then I just have to make sure that she keeps meeting them until she forgets about Nehemiah." That last thought sobered him up considerably. He wasn't the sort of man you forgot, however, if he could create a diversion long enough for Nehemiah to complete his task and go home, back to his world, she would have no choice but to forget him and find someone else that she could spend the rest of her life with. The whole plan left a bad taste in his mouth, but he could see no way round the problem and it was the only solution he had.

"It will have to do!" He said to himself.

Chapter Fourteen

"If I could just have everyone's attention, please?" Nehemiah said in a loud voice, "We have a lot to get through today, and time is not on our side. In a very short time, there will be pictures arriving through the door. There are two things you need to know about these pictures, firstly, they are original paintings and the most of them are of very poor quality. As a result, we are expecting all of these paintings to be diverted to Amun and from him, to us. However, nothing is guaranteed and as you know, a lot will depend on what mood the Pharaoh is in. So, this will be a very tricky operation. You may be wondering why we need the original paintings, in our current programme. This is where the second factor comes in. They are not actually just paintings. The paintings have been used as a cover to bring through Electronic Equipment, that we need in order to erect the shelters that will be coming through shortly. I understand that you will not know what Electronic Equipment is, and I am unable to give you an answer to this question as it will take too much time. Needless to say, the things that are coming through today disguised as paintings, are not of this world and they should not be in this world. They will be here for a limited time, to facilitate the construction of shelters for everyone that needs them. They will then be returned back to my world, in their entirety. It is essential that no piece of equipment is left behind, and no trace of their existence is found here after the job is completed. As a result of this fact, we are going to have to place guards around the area that they are being stored in to ensure nobody has access to them, who will not be working with them.

Myself, Amun and Zaph, will be with the Pharaoh the entire time that the paintings are being delivered. It will be our job to ensure that all of the paintings that are meant to be here, arrive here. So, we will not be available for any other tasks, until this part of the delivery is complete. Is there anything I need to do now before we head off?"

The room completely erupted, and hands shot in the air as everyone demanded Nehemiah's he needed attention.

"Wait everyone, please! One at a time and only urgent requests, please!" Nehemiah shouted.

The urgent requests took some time to be dealt with, but eventually Nehemiah, Amun and Zaph were striding towards the Pharaoh's Audience Chamber to start work diverting the solar panels that had been disguise as paintings. Nehemiah was very nervous. So much hinged on the smooth diversion of the panels, to the warehouse. Without them there would be no power and they would be unable to inflate the concrete tents, in preparation for the water soaking of the concrete embedded canvas. He was also a very nervous at having so much equipment here in this world, that didn't belong. He was very grateful to Rachid for his offer of trustworthy guards, to ensure their safety. It would not do for the Pharaoh to discover their true purpose and he could not afford any pieces to disappear. Who knows what a difference that would make, to the society that he was now living in. It was important not to change the course of the natural development, their natural learning, the social evolution of the people. He became aware that he was striding ahead of the party and that Amun and Zaph were struggling to keep up with him. He slowed down and waited for them to catch up, apologising profusely when they reached him.

"Not everyone is blessed with longlegs!" He laughed

Amun just grunted and continued walking. He thought that he didn't seem to be in the best of humour, today and Nehemiah was worried about him.

"Are you alright, my friend?" He asked, "You seem very quiet today. It is not like you to be so lacking in smiles!"

"I have much on my mind and none of it is very humorous. I apologise." Amun said, but he kept his eyes averted and continued walking towards the Pharaoh's quarters.

Nehemiah frowned. It was very unusual for Amun to be in such ill humour. He hoped to it would not create any complications, for the very tricky negotiations that were about to ensue.

"I think we are all somewhat nervous, of the task at hand, today." Said Zaph, "It is so important that all goes well, and the Pharaoh can be so fickle. Our fate is in your hands I fear, Amun. You are so good with your words and are able to smooth ruffled, feathers in most situations, where that young man is concerned."

"I am sorry, my friends. I will do my very best to make sure that everything runs smoothly, today and without wasting too much time, I hope." Said Amun, holding out his hands in a placating fashion.

"Let us stay positive. We do not need to court disaster and I am sure that Yoshi has everything arranged perfectly. The Young Pharaoh, will be astounded at the quality of his gifts and will have no time or attention to spare for the rubbish, that will be thrown our way." Said Nehemiah.

"Absolutely!" Agreed Zaph.

They hurried onwards and arrived at the Pharaoh's Audience Chamber just as the first of the paintings were being presented for inspection. The first of which was a huge tapestry made in many different coloured silks, the detail of which took one's breath away. The Young King's eyes grew wide and he could not help but to rise from his throne, hand outstretched and approach the beautiful picture, touching it gently. The picture portrayed a landscape in Egypt taking in the turquoise waters of the Nile flowing through the many layered sands and terraced olive groves of silvery green. It was truly an astounding work of art and nothing else was accomplished for some time as the Pharaoh's attention was fully absorbed by its beauty. One by one the paintings were presented to the young man for his attention, that Nehemiah noticed that his eyes were constantly drawn back to the beautiful tapestry. This was good news!

In a very short time, it became obvious that the standard of art work was deteriorating considerably. The Pharaoh started to look aggravated at the poor quality of work. He waved it away with disgust and lowered his brows with annoyance.

"What is the meaning of this rubbish that is being presented to me!" He shouted, "This is an insult and I will not tolerate it for one more second! Return this is nonsense immediately from where it came!"

Nehemiah's heart missed a beat! And his eyes shot towards Mortimer who was standing in the doorway organizing of the disguised solar panels.

"Your Majesty!" Mortimer said as he approached the throne, "I absolutely agree that the standard of work that is now being delivered is below your immaculate taste but please allow me to explain the motivation behind such shoddy workmanship."

The Pharaoh looked towards Mortimer slightly appeased by his tone of voice.

"Proceed!" He said, waiting for Mortimer's explanation.

"As an expression of your wonderful magnanimity, it was decided that several works of art would be allowed to be given, for the benefit of the common people. This would be an education for them and a wonderful example of your kindness and your gentle rule. The people could not possibly know that the quality of our work is poor as they do not have your amazing perception of beauty. They will only see your generosity of spirit and may indeed, in their own way, learn something from these so-called works of art."

He bowed very low while delivering this short speech, and when he straightened he looked the young Pharaoh straight in the eye and held his attention.

"Of course, if this does not please Your Majesty, I shall return them immediately from whence they came." He said in a disapproving voice.

"I think your idea is just splendid!" The young man, said trying to appease Mortimer and smooth over any perceived insult to him. "You have for such an insight for the skill of Kingship, and the necessity of sacrifice for one's people." He waved the works of art towards Amun and sat back on his throne, with a large smile on his face. Nehemiah, Amun and Zaph were so grateful that they almost fell to their knees with relief. They quickly organized removal of the paintings while Mortimer was busy talking with the Pharaoh. A short while later, it became obvious that all of their solar panels had indeed been delivered and they could remove themselves from the audience chamber, with the permission of the young ruler. One by one they excused themselves and left Mortimer to deal with the rest of the deliveries, and the handling of the young King.

When they finally exited the pavilion, Nehemiah couldn't stop himself from throwing himself on to the ground with relief.

"Thank You, thank you, thank you, thank you, thank you!" If he shouted to the blue sky above him, "And Thank You!"

Amun and Zaph collapse beside him laughing.

"That was a close thing, my friend! I actually thought my heart would stop beating! And yet, that Mortimer can certainly speak with a silver tongue. He puts even me, to shame." Said Amun, with a big smile on his face.

"I just about, collapsed with fright when he decided to send them all back. I don't know what we would have done, had it not been for Mortimer, well... That and the young Pharaoh's need for a new best friend!" Zaph added, and they all started laughing again.

By the time they had returned to the warehouse they were ready for refreshments. Nehemiah had never felt so hungry in many days and he devoured the food presented to him, enthusiastically. The other two, kept pace with him mouthful, to mouthful, and in no time at all they had recovered their vigour and were ready for the rest of the day's events.

Zaph headed off for the fitting rooms, leaving Nehemiah and Amun alone in his office.

"Well, I wish I could stay and help you with the rest of the work needed to be done, but I need to leave now." Amun said.

"Where are you off to, in such a hurry?" Nehemiah asked curiously. "I haven't seen you so out of sorts since I have arrived. Is there anything I can help with?"

"No, my friend. This is private, family business and is something the only I can handle. Do not worry yourself on my behalf, I have everything well in hand. If there is one thing I really know how to do, it is to look after my family."

"Then proceed with all haste, Amun, and hurry back to us soon." Nehemiah stood and held out his hand to shake but for some reason Amun did not appear to see it and he turned and left with all haste.

"How strange!" Thought Nehemiah shaking his head. He made his way round the desk and headed out into the warehouse towards the door. He had a very important meeting with Rachid and it could not wait. Now, it was time to secure the precious equipment they had been so fortunate in procuring, which was at this very moment being stored in one of the slaves sleeping huts. He hurried out, taking long strides making his way to the sleeping huts as quickly as possible, where he found Rachid waiting for him.

"Nehemiah! What is on the secrecy surrounding these pictures?" Rashid asked, "From what I can see they look pretty rubbish and I certainly wouldn't think they needed to be guarded from anyone! In fact, if anything I would say they need to be fed to the bonfire!"

"I really wished I could tell you what was going on Rachid, but I'm afraid in this, you are just going to have to trust me. I cannot tell you why I need these paintings. All I can say is that without them there will be no Accountability. None whatsoever! It is absolutely essential to make sure that nobody enters this building, while these paintings are here, unless they are accompanied by myself, Amun or Zaph. What is in this room is for no one else's eyes and the entire survival of the society, is dependent upon that." Nehemiah said seriously, looking Rachid straight in the eyes, to emphasise the importance of what he was saying.

"Phew! That is serious!" Rashid pulled his hand across his forehead shaking his head slowly. "I can promise you this Nehemiah, I will guard this building with my life! I will have only the most trustworthy guards here at any time and I'll make such threats to them that they will be frightened even to blink, in case they miss something!"

"Thank You, Rachid! I knew I could count on your help!" Nehemiah clapped him on the shoulder and then turning the handle entered the sleeping hut to check the condition of the solar panels and to ensure that all the necessary leads had arrived. The room had a very surreal feel to it, with paintings propped up against the walls, like some obscure gallery. The windows were so small that very little light was able to enter the room and yet even in the dim surroundings, Nehemiah could see that the quality of paintings was extremely bad. It was obvious that Mr. Toshimoto it had taken no chances in these panels been diverted to him.

"Thank You, Yoshi!" He said quietly.

He went methodically from painting the painting, checking each panel to see that it was intact, and no damage had been done in the delivery. Once he had completed all the preliminary checks and found them all in good working order, he then started at the beginning again this time checking all the leads. All he had to do now, was wait for the batteries to arrive and they could start charging. He stood brushing the dust off his knees when he became aware of a disturbance outside the door. He stood stock still and listened to what was happening outside. He could hear very clearly, Rashid voice refusing somebody entry and it sounded as if the person being refused, was not going away. Curious, he headed for the door, pulling it open to confront the person. There, to his surprise, was Abha, looking furious!

"How dare you!" She shouted at Rashid, "I need to speak to Nehemiah urgently, you have no right to stop me. You know who I am, you know I will cause no problems and that I can be trusted."

Nehemiah's heart skipped a beat at the sight of her, and moved to interrupt the flow of the tirade, and rescue poor Rashid from her wrath.

"I am afraid that is my fault!" He said, as Abha swung round to see who was talking. He was shocked when he saw her. Her face was all blotchy and red and it was obvious that she had spent some time crying.

"Abha what is wrong? Are you ill?" he said in a concerned voice. Upon hearing his voice, she fell into his arms and sobbed. Rachid looked away embarrassed by the outpouring of such raw emotion and Nehemiah just stood with his arms wrapped around her, wondering how she was not being deafened, by the thumping in his chest. They stood that way for some time, until she had cried herself out and then she pushed away from his chest and he let her go.

"I am sorry, Nehemiah." She said embarrassed, "I should not have come here."

"Well, you did and now that you are here you must tell me what is wrong. Maybe I can help, in some way?" he said kindly.

"You cannot help me! No one can help me!"

"I am sure that is not true. Come, we will sit in here," and he pointed to the door he had just come out of, "And we will not be disturbed by anyone and you can tell me all about what is happening."

She nodded at his suggestion and made her way into the building, head bowed, shoulders slumped. Once inside, Nehemiah squatted on his heels, back against the wall and waited for her to start. She paced up and down, wringing her hands.

"It is awful! I have had a big falling out with Grandfather and I am just so upset!"

"Tell me what happened?" Nehemiah said quietly.

Abha just stopped and looked down at him sitting by the wall. She had no words to tell him of the conversation she had had with Amun, the previous night. How could she explain what she had said without first telling him how she felt about him and how could she tell him that, with no indication about how he felt about her? So, she stood and looked at him, speechless.

"Can I ask you something?" she asked

"Of course! Anything."

"I may seem forward, but I have no way of explaining what is happening to me without first appearing forward." She said.

"Abha, you can ask me anything you want. I will not be offended. It is not possible for you to offend me. "Nehemiah answered, "Ask away!"

She took a deep breath and looked straight into his eyes. "What do you think about me?"

Despite his earlier protestations, he was taken aback by her question and was not at all sure that he should be forthright about the answer but when he looked into those beautiful eyes that were looking straight at him, he knew that he could only tell her the truth.

"I think you are wonderful, Abha!" was all he could say, his heart thumping fit to burst.

She just looked at his and then, slowly her face broke out into a huge smile.

"Thank you!" she said gently, "You have restored my broken heart and brought me hope where there was none!" She bent down and gently took his hands in hers and looking into his eyes began to tell him what had happened with her Grandfather. Nehemiah was acutely aware of her hands in his, of her eyes on his. He listened intently to everything that she was saying, he needed to know the whole story, he needed to understand what had caused her such pain. And as he listened to her, his heart broke and a tear escaped his eye running down his cheek, slowly. Still he didn't interrupt but let her finish. He needed to know everything. Eventually her speaking slowed and stopped, and she sat in front of him waiting for him to save her, to mend her broken heart and to make it all better. The fact that there was such hope in her eyes, made it so much worse for Nehemiah, he couldn't bear it! He couldn't bear, to see such beauty and innocence hurt so badly and he knew she would be hurt so badly, because he was. She waited for his response patiently, not moving not wanting to disturb his reverie, everything hanging on his decision.

"Your grandfather is right." He said quietly and was pained to hear her gasp, to feel her snatch her hands away from him, in horror. She jumped up and took a step back, staring at him, unbelievingly.

He slowly climbed to his feet and walked towards her hands outstretched, gently enfolding her small fingers in his.

“Hear me out, Abha. Just because the things your grandfather said were true, does not mean that I approve of them. However, his analogy is very appropriate. There are things in my world Abha, that are shocking and horrific, just as in your world the same can be said. The truth is that I am delighted to have met you and I think you are truly a wonder and I have never known loneliness, before meeting you. The way I feel when you leave the room and walk away, leaves me the loneliest I have ever been in my life. I would like nothing more than to spend the rest of my life, being in the same room with you. Yet, I need to go home and even though I know that will cause me such pain, I still have to do it.” Another tear slid down his cheek as he spoke to her, seeing the pain that he was creating in her heart.

“But there must be good things in your world, Nehemiah. After all, it is where you came from.”

“As there are beautiful, wonderful things in this world.” He said as he gently cupped her cheek with his hand, “but asking you to come and live in my world, would be as difficult as me asking you to live on the Moon.”

“Don’t be ridiculous!” She laughed, “You cannot go to the Moon! No one can go to the Moon!”

“Abha, in my world, we have!” Nehemiah said gently.

She gasped and pulled her hands away from his. “What kind of place it is it that you live in?”

“As I have been trying to explain, it is a very alien place compared to your home. There is very little to compare between the two worlds. So, in this, your Grandfather is right.”
“But what am I to do? What is to become of me? I will be alone forever! There is no one else like you in my world, Nehemiah! No one!”

"And no one in my world like you, either, Abha." He stood with his hands hanging loosely at his side, in despair. There was nothing he could say or do to make the situation better. There was no solution, for this problem. Indeed, Amun's story about the fish and the bird was exactly how it was for them. Nehemiah knew that this had to end, now. He knew that the longer it went on, the more difficult it would be for both of them, when the time came for him to go home. And even though it was hard, he did not want it to be any harder for Abha.

"This has to end now, Abha. We cannot torture ourselves or each other in this way, knowing that soon it will end, regardless of how we feel about each other and what we would like to happen." Another tear rolled down the side of his face. He saw the same was true for Abha.

"Nehemiah," she whispered, "Please kiss me. If this is all there is, at least let me have that to remember."

He took her into his arms and bent his head, bringing his lips to hers, gently and reverentially. The taste of her was warm and exotic, mingling with the salt of their tears. He knew he would never taste anything as wonderful again. His heart pounded in his chest and his knees felt weak, as though his legs would not be able to support him for much longer. Very gently, he released her and stroking the side of her lovely face he slowly moved away from her.

"Goodbye my beautiful Abha." He said gently.

"Goodbye my handsome Nehemiah." She replied sadly dropping her head in despair and walking towards the door. She did not look back but gently closed the door behind her and left.

Nehemiah sank to the floor and putting his head in his hands, sobbed uncontrollably and that is where Amun found him an hour later, sitting on the floor, his hands in his lap, staring at his knees, despair written all over his face.

"Oh, my friend!" I am so sorry for your despair!" Amun lowered himself to the floor and put his arm around Nehemiah's shoulders. "If it is any consolation, if there was anyone in this world that I would consider suitable for my beautiful Granddaughter, it is you."

"Thank you, Amun. You are very kind."

"Not kind, my friend, just honest. Come you cannot sit on the floor like this, for the rest of the day. Let us go to your office and I will have food brought in to us. Abha has gone home and the work she is doing with Zaph has been moved to another area. It will be too painful for you both to work together, at this time. Come." He got to his feet and helped the young man stand, steering him to the door by his elbow.

Nehemiah knew that Amun's words were true. The very sound of her name had made his stomach flip and he knew that if he saw her right now, he would just breakdown, in front of everyone. He could not speak, and he allowed himself to be steered out of the building and into the warehouse, which was strangely quiet and lacking in people. He sat at his desk and stared at the floor. He was no stranger to grief, but his life had known such content for such a long time that he had·forgotten how it could punch him in the stomach and floor him, just when he least expected it. When the food arrived he ate woodenly, putting the food in his mouth, chewing swallowing but all he could see was her face as she left him and all he could taste was their kiss.

"You cannot stay here like this." Amun said. "I am going to take you back to the pavilion. I will make sure that you are not disturbed, and you can rest for a couple of days. You have not done this in a long time and you need this time now, for you." He directed Nehemiah out of his office and walked him back to the pavilion, to the room that had been given to him when he first arrived. To a proper bed and a safe space. Once he had seen the young man settled, he had directed some loyal guards to keep him safe and undisturbed. No one was to be allowed in, not even little Moses.

"He is in retreat!" he said, "He needs this time to rest before we continue with the project. This is important to the Pharaoh's accountability." With that Amun hurried away to see to the other casualty of this disaster, as only a Grandfather could, with many hugs and some lavish gifts!

Nehemiah lay on the huge, comfy, bed with his eyes closed. At first, he cried, allowing the tears to soak into the silk pillows, uncaring. Then once the tears were finished, he just lay thinking about her and how they could never be together. He thought he would be able to work out some clever plan, that would fix the situation but after a while he realized that there was no clever plan. This situation could not be repaired, in a way that they wanted. They were indeed like the bird and the fish. Once he had finally accepted this fact and stopped trying to force a solution, he started to feel a little better. He got off the bed and sat on a chair and meditated for a while, but it was very difficult trying to stay with the present moment, when Abha's sad face kept appearing in his mind. He just paid attention to his breath, entering and leaving his body but he still could not shake the image of her as he had last seen her, crying and in pain. He then turned his attention to the sounds that were going on around him, but the same thing kept happening. It felt agonising to find the person that he really wanted to be with and know that he had to stay away from her. Eventually, he realised that sitting in this room as not going to work. It was just encouraging him to think about the past and he would never be able to start coming to terms with things, if he was constantly thinking about the past. He picked up his heavy boots and put them on lacing them tight to give him good ankle support. He asked the guards if they could organise a water skin and some light food for him and while they were arranging this, he prepared himself for a hike, re-arranging his backpack accordingly. In short order he had everything he needed including his phone's solar battery pack and he headed off, out of the pavilion and into the hills, away from anyone. It was time to walk! He knew that putting his attention on his surroundings was going to be better for him, than looking at mental pictures in his head.

There was nothing he could do about the situation between himself and Abha. There was no solution, so the only option available to him was to get on with the task in hand and get it finished, as soon as possible. That way he could go home, and she wouldn't have to keep seeing him, and him, her. Then eventually, they could start to properly heal from the grief that they were feeling. There was no point in wasting energy on 'what ifs'! He began striding out, stretching his legs and eating up the miles, all the time looking around him and taking in everything that he could see. In a little while he began to find himself interested in what he was seeing. He began looking at things instead of just seeing them. Then he started to notice the sounds that were going on around him and his attention was captured by that. So, it went on. After a couple of hours, he was feeling much better and also exercised, so he found himself some shade and sat for a while, eating and sipping his water, allowing his phone bank to charge. Looking up at the blue sky, he reminded himself of the reason he was here, of the terrible conditions that most of these people had had to suffer, over the years and how they were relying on him to help them, help themselves out of it.

"Then that is what I shall do!" he said to himself. "I will get this job done and help these people as best I can. I can't change my circumstances, but I can help change theirs!" Despite the sadness still in his heart he understood, on a spiritual level that there were more important things than him and his wants. So, his ability to change the things that he could and let go of the things that he couldn't, was going to help him through this and help him, continue on.

After a while he got up, packed away his things and started heading back to civilisation. He took a slightly different route back down to the pavilion, one that gave him the opportunity to observe the lay of the land, from above. It was difficult to say what the impact of the concrete tents would be on the landscape and even though they would only be here for a few years, he wanted to make sure that they did not upset the equilibrium too much.

He realised that he had a meeting with the Master construction people, the next day and hoped that Amun had not cancelled it. There was just too much to do for him to be moping around, feeling sorry for himself. He was hoping that some of the people that he was meeting, would be more in the vein of engineers than masons. He needed a device known as an Archimedes Screw. It channelled water up hill and, in his world, it was rumoured that it had been used to irrigate the Hanging Gardens of Babylon. It was supposed to have been designed by Archimedes, but this had not been confirmed or proven. As an accountant, Nehemiah had no idea how to carry out the design or build such a thing. All he could do was to draw a picture of it and explain its function and hope that there was someone here, who had enough savvy to make one. He was hoping to use it to draw water from the river, to soak the concrete tents. That was one of the reasons that he had decided to construct the buildings not far from the river. From this angle, it looked to be an ideal place. There was plenty of flat land on either side that spread out for miles, along the water and plenty of dunes on either side to help bury them once they had set.

"This is going to work!" he said to himself as he continued to head down to the pavilion.

Arriving back at his room, he collected the things he would need for the day. He called Moses to him and asked him to ask Zaph to meet him in his office, along with all of the Master builders that they had identified so far. He collected some papyrus that he had left in a heap on the table and sat down to try and draw a likeness of the Archimedes Screw. It took a little time and although he wasn't really very good at drawing, by the end of the exercise, he thought he had a good approximation of what it looked like. Putting this and his other necessities into his backpack, he headed off towards the warehouse, realising that the day was quickly passing and not much light was left. Walking quickly, he made his way on down to the warehouse, noticing the people he passed on his way.

There were only slaves in this area, but you would not realise it by looking at them. Everyone he passed walked with their head held high, smiling and looking fed and healthy. It made his heart sing to see how well people looked. He had to get everything in place, really quickly now, before the Pharaoh had a chance to see what he was seeing and a put a stop to it. He strode into the warehouse just as the sun was starting to set and was pleased to see a large gathering of men and women surrounding Zaph, just inside the door.

"Excellent!" he said, "Thank you all for coming so late in the day. I have a problem that I need solved and I am hoping some of you will be able to help me with it. Before we look at the problem though, I need to show you some things and tell you some things that are going to be very difficult to understand and accept. I also need to make sure that whatever we discuss tonight will not go any further. Not to your friends, your wives, your children, in fact anyone!" He looked at the people individually, eye to eye, holding their gaze until he got a nod of acceptance for the terms he was laying out. He needed to see for himself, how they reacted to what he was saying and to see if anyone had doubts about the commitment that he was asking them to make. "I needn't tell you how bad it would be, for this information to get back to certain ears in high places but suffice to say that it would be the end of everything that we are working so hard to accomplish. So, I want to give you the opportunity to back out now, if you want. There will be no repercussions for you, if you do not want to go any further in this. We still need your help and expertise in many other areas and will not feel any negativity towards you, because of your decision." At this, three men put up their hands and indicated that they didn't want any more to do with this part of the project, two were fairly young men who had young children and were worried about attracting unwanted attention from the 'Powers That Be'. Nehemiah went over to each of them individually and thanked them for their help and told them how much he appreciated their honesty. He said that he hoped they would continue working on the project and they assure him wholeheartedly, that they would. They left smiling and content with their situation and their decision.

The third man stood near to the back of the group and had a scowl on his face. He was somewhat older than the rest and he had benefitted quite a lot from the old regime, thanks to his habit of ingratiating himself upon the guards. However, things were changing and if anyone was suffering from the new changes, it was him! He didn't like this young man one bit!

"I want to know what exactly you are planning before I give my consent, one way or the other young man!" he said.

The rest of the group parted, trying to distance themselves from him and his attitude.

Nehemiah walked over to face him and smiled at him, extending his hand in greeting.

"I am sure you know who I am, but I would like to meet you properly! What is your name, Sir?"

The old man was astounded at his politeness and stuttered his reply, "I have always been called Grunt!" he said.

"I see. So, what is your name, Sir?"

"My name is actually, Mahu but as I said, no one calls me that."

"Would you mind if I called you Mahu?" Nehemiah asked gently, "I cannot call anyone anything that is degrading and as 'Grunt' is not your name, I would like to call you by your actual name. If that is ok to you?"

The old man was speechless. No one had shown him such courtesy since he was a very young man. Always he had been the one at the back, the one everyone made fun of, the one that got bullied and, in his turn, bullied others. He was astounded!

"Yes! You can call me Mahu."

"Thank you, Mahu. Now what was the problem with my proposal?"

Mahu, grunted, "Well, I can't give my consent to be part of something if I don't know what I am consenting to, can I?"
"I understand where you are coming from," Nehemiah looked him straight in the eyes," but what if I assured you that it is nothing bad, nothing illegal and that no harm would come to anyone because of this knowledge."

"Then why is it so secret?"

"Because. Mahu, it is Alien!"

A gasp went up around the room. Nehemiah held up his hands in a placating manner.

"Ladies and Gentlemen, please let me explain. In my world, things are very different, as you have probably guessed. We have devices and pieces of equipment that could build all of Pharaoh's structures and more. We have ways of doing things that make this kind of job, quite straightforward. However, these things do not belong in this world. They would not work within the fabric of this society, so I cannot bring them here and just finish the buildings. My task here is not to finish buildings! That is not why I was brought here! My task is make the Pharaoh, Accountable. That is a different job and I have the tools for that right here." He tapped his head and then his heart, "And here! However, I have some small pieces of equipment that will help, in changing the living conditions of every single slave here and I cannot in all conscience, ignore this fact. So, here is my quandary, Mahu. Do I bring this equipment in and show you all how I intend to use it, trusting in your faith in me and in your loyalty, in order to simply help so many people? Or do I ignore the suffering of so many and sit in my room and do nothing? Which should it be, Mahu?" He turned and looked the old man straight in the eyes.

Mahu was astounded at this young man! He had spent so much time bewailing his own lack of favour with the guards that he had never considered exactly what was happening around him and the cost of it to Nehemiah. He shuffled from foot to foot and looked at the ground. He was starting to realise that if this man carried out his plan, he himself may well benefit greatly, and that was starting to hit home. Beside which, he was a force to be reckoned with and Mahu thought that it might be better for him, if he had him on his side rather than against him. He was not sure how he would cope having Nehemiah against him! He looked up and saw the young man still looking into his eyes, waiting for his answer.

"I am with you!" was all he said. Nehemiah held his gaze for another couple of seconds and then his face broke into a smile and he took Mahu's hand and shook it, clapping him on the shoulder at the same time.

"Thank you, my friend!" he said and Mahu's heart felt like it would burst with pride.

"I want everyone who is with me, back here at sunrise where we will begin a new adventure together." Nehemiah said, spreading his arms out to indicate everyone in the group and with nods of agreement they dispersed and headed home to their families. He walked towards his office at the back of the warehouse, shaking his head in wonder. It never ceased to amaze him, how things happened. Sometimes, he would have an idea in his head, a plan of action and he would strike out to bring it to fruition, but then, something would happen, and he would let go of his original plan and just roll with it to see where it took him, which is what had happened tonight. He hadn't even got around to showing the men and women the drawing that he had done and, yet he had ended up with a tight knit, loyal, group of people who were committed to everything that he was trying to bring about, and that was worth more than any Archimedes Screw!

"Here you are! You have made a rapid recovery, it seems!"

Amun was standing just inside the warehouse door, his arms folded across his chest. Nehemiah dropped his bag and went straight to him enfolding him in a warm embrace, when he reached him.

"You cannot recover from loving someone, Amun! Thank you so much for your kindness this morning. I didn't know what to do with myself and was bereft. You helped me very much and I appreciate it."

"What has happened to you?" Amun said standing back to look at him shocked, "When I left you, you were so distraught, I never thought to see you up and about for days!"

"Come let us go to the office and I will show you how this mind and heart of mine works!" Nehemiah said with a sad smile.

They walked into the office, sat down and he began telling Amun how it was with him.

"I cannot lie around! I have to get to a level of equilibrium, so I meditated, or tried to and when that didn't work, I went for a long walk to think. I realised on my walk that there was nothing I could do about it! No end of crying or thinking or planning would change the situation, so I let it go! Things will be as they will be, Amun and I cannot change this. I have a job to do and maybe the best thing I can do for Abha, is to get on with the job, finish it and then just get out of here and give her a fighting chance to find happiness without me lurking around in the background!"

Amun looked at him, silently and Nehemiah returned the compliment. Eventually, Amun shifted in his seat.

"You are a good man and you are right! This is a situation you both have to live with and cannot change and by making the decision you have, you honour her. Thank you and I apologise for suspecting you of being cold hearted!"

"Never!"

"I know this, My Friend! I went to the pavilion to see if you were alright and Moses told me where you were. I could not believe it! However, I can see how you feel and think, now. Good! So, what is happening and what can I do!"

Nehemiah told Amun what had occurred at the earlier meeting with the Masters and he was astounded about the change of heart in Mahu.

"Truly, you are a miracle worker to achieve such a thing with such a man!" he said.

"People change, Amun, if they are given a chance to, that is! I believe that everyone deserves to be treated with respect, at least initially. After that, it is up to them to earn repeated respect, I guess."

"But, do you trust him? He has been known to inform on people in the past, you know."

"I guessed as much but, you know, we came to an understanding tonight and I think he has realised, that I am a better bet to side with! I hope so anyway, and he has given me his word and I believe him! It is good, Amun!"

"Then alright! When are you meeting tomorrow? I would like to come along, if that is ok and see this miraculous transformation for myself?

"Sunrise and you are always welcome. In fact, I think you should know exactly what is going to happen next!"

"Sunrise it is then! Are you walking back to your room?"

"No, I think I will just catch some sleep here, thanks."

"Then Goodnight, My Friend!" Amun said and started to leave.

"Amun?" Nehemiah stopped him, just as he was about to disappear. "How is she?"

Amun smiled at him. "She will be fine, she will be fine!" and he continued out of the door and heading for home.

As he lay on his makeshift bed, He thought about the happenings of the day, amazed at how much had changed in such a short amount of time and realised that despite everything, he was content with his lot. Of course, he was still upset about losing Abha from his life, but then he realised that it was obviously not meant to be. He also realised that she would always have a place in his heart and that he would never meet anyone like her again, but he would carry on with his life and if he didn't hold onto it too tightly, new things would happen.

"Tomorrow is another adventure!" he said to himself as his eyes closed on the day.

Chapter Fifteen

Nehemiah was awakened to the sound of everyone assembling, at first light. He took a moment to lie still and listen to the noises around him and reflect at all of the good things he had in his life. Of course, this made him instantly think about Abha and the loss of her but instead of focusing on that, he turned his attention to the comfortable bed that he was lying in, to the comfortable temperature of his body and he relaxed into this, feeling grateful. Moses came bolting into the office space and running up to his makeshift bed, started shaking him vigorously.

"Nehemiah! Nehemiah!" he said urgently, "It is time to go! Come!" and once he saw that his eyes were opening the young boy shot off, back to the group of people waiting in the warehouse.

"I'm coming, I'm coming!" he scrambled out of his cot and put on trousers and a relatively clean shirt. He finger-combed his hair but spent some time with the water skin and his toothbrush before heading around the protective barrier, that separated his office from the rest of the warehouse, towards the group of men and women waiting for him. He greeted everyone and made a point of greeting Mahu by name, before he started speaking to the whole group.

"Ok! Thank you very much for coming back. Today is going to be an adventure for all of us! I just want to say before we leave that if anyone has any questions, they must not feel reticent about asking them. There is no such thing as a stupid question and I for one would rather spend a little time explaining something, than have someone leave because they did not understand. Ok?" he waited for their acknowledgement before heading back for his pack. "Alright, follow me everyone, we have to go see some stuff first, before I give you my special request." He headed out of the warehouse and off towards the old sleeping hut that contained the solar panels. On arrival he was surprised to see Rachid himself guarding the entrance.

"Rachid, Good morning!" he said taking his hand and pumping it enthusiastically, "I am surprised to see you here, yourself."

"Good Morning! My son was up for half of the night with tooth pain, so I thought, as I would not be getting any sleep for a while, I would at least let some other poor soul have some! I will be relieved shortly, hopefully."

"Well, I hope you manage to get some sleep and that your little one feels better soon." Nehemiah said, clapping him on the shoulder, "There is nothing worse that tooth pain!"

"That is true! Poor little thing! Why so many visitors today?"

"We have a small project to work on and I need to carry out some training first. I will update the entrance list with you later, when I know exactly who will need everyday access."

"Good. I will come and see you later on once I have sufficiently rested, then." Rachid said, nodding his approval.

"Rest well, when you get there!" Nehemiah let himself into the dimly, lighted, room and closed the door after everyone had entered. He indicated lanterns stacked beside the door and several were lit so that the room was bright enough to see the paintings that stood around the wall.

"You have all probably heard of the paintings that were delivered here yesterday morning, and probably heard of the explanation for them being here. However, you already have an invaluable education so will not be needing to be educated in the arts. At least not by these." He said to start his instruction. "These paintings are going to be the means for us to change the housing situation for everyone here, and indeed all of the rest of the slaves. I warn you now that what you are about to see, will defy explanation to you and I am not even sure that I fully understand exactly how they work, but I will do my best to explain to you what is going to occur."

He looked around the room to make sure that he had everyone's attention and when he saw that they were all looking at him, he walked over to the first of the paintings. "We are going to construct a whole group of buildings and these are just a front for something else, that will enable this to happen." He pulled the first picture away from the wall so that he was holding it upright and after scratching at the edge with his fingernail managed to get a hold of the silicon sheet covering the solar panel. "This is the real treasure!" he announced, peeling the painting away from the front of the glass, to the gasps of everyone watching him. "This panel, when exposed to the sunlight, takes that light and converts it to energy." He said. A hand shot into the air.

"What is energy?"

Nehemiah paused for a moment to try and think of a way to explain the phenomenon.

"When you take a chisel, and hit it with the hammer, you are transferring energy from the hammer to the chisel. When you take a lantern and strike a flint to the wick and it burns, that is energy."

"You mean like life force?"

"Exactly! This panel takes the light from the sun and makes a kind of life force, with it. This goes into a box along these wires." He picked up the leads to show them what a wire was, "and the box stores that energy for when we need to use it."

"But what would we need all that sunlight for?"

Nehemiah took a deep breath. This was going to be harder than he had anticipated. He picked up a stick and started scratching diagrams into the dirt, to show how the energy would be used, starting with a square shape to represent a concrete tent in the bag, the pumps blowing it up to its proper shape and size and then finally the water being poured down on it.

“Then the sun bakes off the water and makes the wet walls of the structure hard, a bit like baked clay.” He finished.

You could have heard a pin drop in the room, as everyone sat looking at the drawings on the ground, some shaking their head in disbelief.

“And this really works?” said one woman, “It will really make homes? What size will they be? How big are these?”

“Each home will sleep fifteen people.” Nehemiah answered, “Enough for families to sleep in, together.” This answer was again greeted by gasps of surprise, before the room erupted into loud conversations as people threw questions at Nehemiah and made loud statements to each other. He sat quietly and let people talk. He knew the whole idea was completely alien to them, but so much hung on them accepting that it could be done and helping in the construction of them. After a time, the conversation started to quieten down and he stood up in front of everyone again.

“I know I am asking you to believe something that to you must seem unbelievable, but I am asking! I know it will work because we have done it in our world! Each of these structures should last about 10 years. That is long enough for all of the Pharaoh’s constructions to be complete and for you all to be able to go and follow your own dreams. It is hoped that during this time, the Pharaoh’s Accountability will help to restore human kindness to every single person who lives in this land and that at the end of this period, you will all have better homes of your own making and design.”

“But you cannot hide these homes! They are too big! The Pharaoh will see them and surely insist on them being torn down. He would never countenance slaves having their own spaces!” There were sounds of agreement to this statement, shouted out from the back of the room.

“One of the great things about these structures is that they can be buried under sand and soil. When we flatten the ground in preparation, we will keep all of the soil and just put it back on top of them when they are dried. From the area of the Pharaoh’s new pavilion, it will look like nothing but dunes.” He answered.

There was shocked silence. “You mean we have to live underground like insects?” someone asked and that started everyone shouting again.

Nehemiah stood stock still and let everyone get out their fears about living underground. When it had become quiet again, he started speaking.
“You will not be living underground, it is just that the structures will be hidden from view, from a certain direction. Look around you.” He pointed around the room they were in. “This room was used to sleep many of you. Can you see the sky from here? No! Is there lots of light? Open air? No! and yet this is not underground. There is no difference!” The silence in the room made him feel as if they had reached some sort of agreement, so he continued. “Now, in order for all of this to come about, I need a piece of equipment made and I have no idea how to make it or the best materials to use. That is your area of expertise.” He reached into his pack and withdrew the drawing he had made earlier. “It has been decided that these buildings will be put up all along both sides of the river so that we can have ready access to the water and the people can have ready access to the amenities they will need without walking for miles every day. Obviously, there will be sewage requirements to take into account, but you are all already familiar with that sort of building planning. I will leave that sort of thing to you people, to put in place. What I actually need is this.” He held up the diagram and people moved closer to get a look at it. “The purpose of this is to draw large amount of water from the river in order to soak the buildings. I would like you all to take this picture, look at it, discuss it and see what you can come up with.

I am entirely at your mercy when it comes to how to make it, what materials to use and what size it will need to be. We do not have much time as the buildings will start being delivered any day now, so please put all of your efforts into this. I really need your help." He handed the drawing to the nearest person and stood back while they gathered round and started pointing at it and discussing it and in a very short time it became obvious that they had forgotten that he even existed, which was exactly what he had hoped for. However, he needed to wrap this up and move on.

"If I can just have your attention!" he said in a raised voice and they all stopped and looked at him. "Can I just remind everyone that everything that has been said in this room must remain a secret between us only. This information is not for sharing with anyone and that includes the diagram that you now have. I need to go and see about the ground preparation, so we will have to leave this building. Please elect a representative to come and see me when you have all worked out a solution." He was pleasantly surprised when they elected Mahu, who solemnly swore to absolute secrecy.

"We will do our best for you, Nehemiah." He said as they started to exit the building.

"I can ask for no more and would expect no less." He answered with a smile.

After everyone had left he stood breathing deeply, relishing the silence. It had not been as bad as he had thought it could be. After all the entire project was completely alien in both equipment and science. However, it spoke volumes of the quality of amazing people that they were, that even though they had no idea what was being asked of them, they had been willing to take on board his requests enthusiastically and without reservation. He let himself out of the building and spoke briefly to the guard on duty, emphasising the necessity to keep people out who were not authorised to enter, before heading back to his office.

He needed to get started on the site preparation on both sides of the river and for that he need Zaph! Once back at the warehouse he couldn't find anyone who knew where either Zaph or Moses was, so he took the opportunity to head down to the river and survey the areas he intended to use, himself. Once he got down to the riverside he found not only Zaph and Moses but Amun, too. There was a lot of pacing and discussion going on and Nehemiah could only laugh at the joy of it all!

"Great minds, think alike!" he said approaching and was then immediately inundated by all three of them talking to him at once about their plans and discoveries. He put up his hands to stem the assault on his ears, lowering them only to ruffle Moses hair. He reached into his pocket and pulled out two boiled sweets, giving one to Moses and putting one into his own mouth.

"Barley sugar!" he said.

"We have been discussing the preparation for the site, my friend." Amun began, "I think that there will be plenty of room for the structures but that it will go along the river much further than we had anticipated." He laid out for Nehemiah the calculations that they had come up with, based on the sizes of the erect structures..."

"I think you have been over generous in your plot sizes, Amun. They do not require large garden areas per structure. That would certainly call down the attention from the Pharaoh! There really only needs to be passage area between each tent. They are after all only temporary structures."

"But, the people would surely like to have some small ground to cultivate, being this close to the river! Cooking vegetables and herbs would be well received and even the Pharaoh cannot complain about such a past time!"

"While that may be true, Amun." Nehemiah answered, "He may very well question the fact that his 'slaves' have the time to potter around in a garden!"

"Ah! True! I hadn't thought of that!"

"We are not building a city here, we are easing a huge humanitarian problem and making the quality of life better, for people. One day, they will be in a position to build their own homes and can have as much garden as they desire but for now, they need somewhere safe that they can rest as family units."

Amun's face dropped and while he nodded his head in agreement he was clearly disappointed in the fact that his idea was without merit in the present circumstance. Nehemiah's heart went out to him.

"You know what?" he said, "In my world, we have areas of ground that we call allotments. The idea is that where people live in spaces that have no garden, they can hire a plot of land separate from their homes, where they can grow vegetables or flowers, if they want to. The other thing that we have in my world is community gardens. An area where the entire community of people can have input into the area, grow things or just sit and enjoy it if they wish. What if we could create something like that?"

Amun brightened. "Where shall we build such a place?"

Zaph spoke up, "It might be an idea to make something down by the sleeping huts. I mean after all, it is an area that every slave has a connection to and if we are going to use this area for communal cooking and eating then it would be an ideal place to put it. Also, it would be well away from prying eyes, so that people who are on their rest days could be there and the Pharaoh wouldn't notice they were not working."

"Zaph! That is an excellent idea. Do you know who to talk to about getting that started?" Nehemiah asked.

"Leave it to me!" was the reply and Zaph took off jogging towards the sleeping hut area, Moses in tow.

Once they were alone, they started to walk at a more leisurely pace along the river bank.

"How did it go, this morning?" Amun asked. "I was held up and was unable to make the start, so rather than interrupt, I thought we could catch up now. I am very keen to hear about it."

"It was harder than I imagined! Some of the concepts that I was trying to get across are so alien to anything that is happening here that I could hardly find the words to say what I needed to express! However, everyone was amazing! They have taken my request and are going to see what they can design."

"That is very good, my friend! So, tell me, how does all of this picture thing work?"

Nehemiah began explaining the idea of the solar panels to Amun and although he had had much contact with the world through Mr. Toshimoto, he had been kept very much in the dark when it came to technology. As a result, it took quite some time for Nehemiah to get across what he needed him to know. Eventually, they came to an agreement that regardless of how it worked, it would work and decided that food was more important than anything else, at that point! They headed back to eat, discussing ground works as they went.

"We need to get the area prepared as soon as possible." Nehemiah said, "I am expecting the tents to start coming through any day now and the sooner we start constructing, the quicker we will be done. The batteries will be here today or tomorrow, and we can get the panels out straight away and the charging can begin."

"Where are you going to put them?

“I think behind the sleeping huts. We will have to mark out an area and construct some kind of make-shift barrier. The setting up will have to be down to the small group that I spoke to today but is simple enough and we will have to call upon Rachid’s, guards to keep people out while the panels are in the sun.”

“I have a team of men who can erect barriers today, if you want?” Amun said, “I just need the measurements of the area and I can get them started.

Nehemiah turned to look at him. “Amun, that would be amazing. I will show you exactly the place I need.”

“Then consider it done, my friend!”

“You are a wonder, Amun! I don’t know how any of this would have been possible without your help.” Nehemiah said, sincerely.

“I think the same could be said for you, my friend!” replied Amun chuckling.

As predicted the batteries arrived not long after they had finished lunch and were placed in the same hut as the panels. Amun rushed off to get together a team and by the end of the day, a large area had been barricaded in preparation for the solar panels being set up. The Master builders all arrived in the warehouse as the sun was heading towards the horizon and Nehemiah, Zaph and Amun directed the set-up of the panels with the help of lots of lanterns. Rachid had a team of guards who stood all night long, guarding the entrance to the enclosure and patrolling around the barricades throughout the night. Nehemiah managed to grab a couple of hours sleep before heading out to watch the sunrise and the start of the charging that would go on all day and the following day. It was such a massive and alien task and he wanted to be sure that it all went smoothly. After this phase of the task, he would certainly be a little more at ease.

He stopped to chat to the guards on his way to the entrance, taking his time to show his appreciation of all their efforts. He was surprised to find Zaph at the entrance and also Mahu, both eager to see the phenomenon of charging solar panels. Nehemiah hadn't the heart to tell them that there would be nothing to see, so he just stood and joined them in watching the sunrise, knowing that things were truly getting underway. It made him feel very proud of all of the effort that had gone into making things better to see the sunlight hit the first panels and to watch as the others were slowly folded into its embrace. He waited until he could see the entire enclosure filled with the beautiful golden light and then decided to head up to the pavilion. He was going to see if the promise of Wi-Fi would be available yet, in his old room. He had a rather large event to plan and thought that, as event planning was not part of his expertise, the Internet was the place to start.

Over the next two days the panels charged the batteries until it was decided that they had more than enough power to get the concrete tents inflated, when they arrived. The panels were loaded onto carts and covered with canvas, during the night and driven back up to the door. Rachid managed the protection of the panels and availability of the door so that in one night all off the panels were returned, along with the leads, leaving only the batteries sitting in the old sleeping hut. It was still heavily guarded but anyone breaking into it would find only large wooden. boxes surrounded by old sacks of grain and nuts and it all looked very innocent. Nehemiah had asked that the fencing surrounding the charging area be left intact. This was going to become the community garden that he had talked to Zaph and Amun about. There was no point in wasting the fencing and now that it was up, people could start planning its layout and using it and as it was not going to cost the Pharaoh anything, there would be no problem. Once again, the people had helped themselves out of a situation with an excellent long-term plan.

Nehemiah awoke with a sore head and heavy eyes. He had been working all night and had had very little sleep. In fact, the last few days of activities had left him needing to catch up on rest. He wondered why he had woken so early, yet still so tired. Then the noise started again! There was such a banging and clattering and people shouting. Obviously, something important was going on and he sat up in bed, determined to find out what was happening. The noise was somewhat distant, which worried him as he didn't know what direction it was coming from. Instead of sitting in bed worrying about it, he got up and quickly drew on some clothes, making his way hastily outside to see what was happening. He stood alone outside of the pavilion, which in itself was really strange, as there were usually people going about the Pharaoh's business. He listened again to try and determine which direction the sound was coming from. It really was a cacophony. He slowly started walking towards the noise. It seemed to be coming from an area near the Rich Quadrant and this worried him, so he picked up the pace. He walked for a good ten minutes before he could see a lot of movement in the distance and what looked like a very large area covered in white. Hurrying on, he followed the noise down into large dip in to surroundings. It stood next to a large oasis and was very beautiful. He couldn't believe that he had not been this way before. There sitting underneath the shad of two large palm trees, was the Pharaoh himself looking absolutely delighted. In front of him where literally hundreds of people working at the construction of an enormous structure that, so far looked like a giant tent! It looked as though the people working on the construction were not locals but actually looked as if they had come from Nehemiah's world. They looked a bit out of place in the strange local dress but wearing hard hats! He just stood and watched from a distance, trying to get his brain to process just exactly what was happening and just why it had to be so noisy. Then it hit him! This was the diversion to enable them to erect the concrete tents. He turned and ran as fast as he could back to the door, his heart pounding in anticipation of the next few days' events.

He hoped beyond hope that Amun and Zaph were more together and organised than he felt at that very moment. They wouldn't have long! Maybe a week and would need every single person on standby to work day and night.
As the door came into view he breathed a sigh of relief. There were a group of people, among them he could make out Zaph, Amun and Rachid and pouring out of the door were very large square canvas bags. They had not even wasted time on disguising them! The only emphasise was on getting them in and away to the site. A chain of carts stood ready to accept their burden and once loaded the made off with all speed, only to join the back of the long queue once they had divested themselves of their load.

"Ah! You got up eventually!" Rachid said, as Nehemiah arrived, bending over to help get his breath back.

"What… what… is going on?" he panted.

"Ha! I would have thought that was obvious! The diversion is created, and the tents have started to arrive. We have to work fast! We have not much time and there is much to accomplish!" Rachid looked at Nehemiah as if he must be stupid and indeed at that very moment and he did feel stupid. "We got word sometime during the night and that the tents would be arriving today, and that the diversion would be starting at first light. You were busy working all night and then when we came to find you, you were asleep. So, we decided to take control of our own destiny and just deal with it! What do you think?"

Nehemiah looked from Rachid to Amun and then Zaph, a huge smile starting to appear on his face!

"I think that is exactly as it should be!" he answered. "You people amaze me every single day! So, what do you need from me? I will not get any more sleep now and I can be of some use."

"You must be careful with this body, young man!" Amun said, resting his hand upon Nehemiah's shoulder. "You have had very little rest for many days and you do not look at your best. I have sent Moses on with a message and he is seeing to the preparation of food for you. Go to the warehouse! Eat, then and only then, head down to the site. You will see the place to go owing to this very large screw like contraption standing beside the river!"

Nehemiah's eyes opened wide. "They built it? They actually built it? Amazing! You people are amazing!"

The three men watching him burst out laughing and Amun waved him on, pointing in the direction of the warehouse.

"We will contact you if there are any problems. Send Moses back as soon as you can. We will have need of his fast legs." He said.

Nehemiah took the opportunity to jog down to the warehouse, grinning all of the way. It never ceased to amaze him how some people, whose lives were so downtrodden could rise from the ashes, so easily and take on the mantle of a bright new life, when offered the right sort of help. In a way, it was true that people did not want charity, but what that really meant was that they didn't want someone to come along to do it all for them. They actually wanted the opportunity to carve out their own life, to create their own successes, to take control of their own situation and develop it into something that would make them feel fulfilled and content. To be the Masters of their own destiny! In this, they would then discover, that nothing was more important than that they felt good about their lives and themselves. The truth was, that they would never be the same again! They would take what they had learned from the horrible conditions that they had been forced to live with, and they would use them to mould a new and better experience, that would bring them joy, and that was exactly how it should be!

He arrived at the warehouse, sweating and breathless but feeling exhilarated by his run. He headed for his office to retrieve his water skin and found Moses, moving things to make space for the plates of food that he had set, temporarily on his cot. Draining his water skin, he plumped down into his seat, ruffling Moses hair on the way.

"Thank you, my amazing assistant, without whom, I don't know what I would do!" he said to him, causing a huge smile to appear on Moses face. "You need to be back at the door as soon as possible. They have great need of your speed today, young man. Fastest Legs, Moses! Fastest Legs!" He laughed as Moses took off around the makeshift wall of his office and made a start on the wonderful food waiting for him.

Once he was replenished, he headed off towards the sleeping hut that was being used as storage. On arrival he spoke to the guard and got his advice as to where he might find some transport for the batteries that were waiting to be used inside and in short order had a small, but capable team of strong armed men, lifting the heavy boxes onto a cart which he directed to the site. He didn't take all of the boxes, just enough that they could get started. He needed to show them all how to construct the tents and to see what the Master builders had constructed for the water part of the task. He walked behind the cart, chatting to the men he had brought along. Asking them about their skills and their families. He was amazed to discover how grateful everyone was for his skills audit. He realised that as people's talents had been identified, they had been directed to the sort of job that they were both suited to and enjoyed. This had greatly improved the quality of their working time, which was still long but was so much more fulfilling now they were doing something they liked. They headed down to the site, talking, all of the way and Nehemiah was again amazed at these wonderful, robust people. At the site he saw that the tents were being placed along the river, each with its own space, to allow walkways between each construction. They were laid five deep, which was the maximum amount of distance that the piping would reach from the Archimedes Screw.

The contraption was a sight to be seen and Nehemiah headed straight over to it, towering over everyone, standing beside the water. It was beautifully constructed from wood and was built on a sturdy wooden platform, which itself was mounted upon wheels so that it could be moved up and down. It had gears which led to a turn-handle that enabled someone to turn the device and draw the water up from the river. The bottom end, could not be seen as it was submerged but the rest of it looked as if it was of good construction. Beside the machine, on similar wooden frames were half pipes that angled slightly downwards. These were also on wheels and could be placed in front of the Archimedes Screw, to take the water that had been scooped up from the river and allow it to run in a particular direction. It was ingenious! Several of these stood waiting to be put into place, as and when needed, each starting from a slightly lower elevation. Nehemiah was completely delighted and laughed out loud with joy. He went among the Masters pumping hands enthusiastically, in congratulations at their amazing work. It looked like something out of an old TV program, recently revived on his world, called The Crystal Maze, but it would really work and that was all that mattered.

He gathered all of the Masters together and the moved over to the first tent. He waved to cart with the batteries over and learning began in earnest. The opened up the first box containing the batteries. Nehemiah made sure that they all understood that they were now working with a resource that was limited and could not be replaced. If the batteries ran out, the building would stop before everyone had a home constructed and there was nothing to be done for it. They all nodded seriously. They were used to living and working with a limited supply of resources and knew to be careful of things they did not know. Then, he unzipped the large canvas bag and attached the pump to the tent at one end, showing them all how it was done. After they all had seen and understood how it was done, he attached the other end to the pump, making sure they all saw and understood how it should be done. After ensuring their full attention, he then explained that the noise would be very loud and unlike anything they had experienced before.

He also explained that it was just noise and could not hurt them and that if it bothered them, they could put their fingers in their ears till they got used to it, but that they would have to get used to it if they were going to work with the tents. Obtaining their agreement, he turned on the pumps and watched as the concrete tent emerged from the canvas bag. He was amazed at the size of structure that came out of each bag and turned to comment to the group of people with him. They stood, jaws dropped in amazement, not a few of them shaking in fear, most of them white as a sheet, all of them still with shock. Once it was fully inflated, he waited a moment after turning off the pump for them to come to their senses, but they didn't!

"Chop, chop!" he shouted, clapping his hands "Where is the water?"

The Masters jumped and immediately sprang into action with the water drawing machine. Nehemiah emphasized the importance of keeping the water and the batteries and pumps well apart. In the end, they decided to keep the batteries and pumps on the carts they had arrived in, so they could be removed easily and replaced by the Archimedes Screw. Once they had the logistics sorted out, the handles were turned, and the erect tent was soaked in water for the required amount of time. Then they all stood back and looked at it.

"One down, several hundred to go!" he said, and they started towards the next bag. Several hours later and he found himself watching as they got on with the task. They had set things up with the battery carts so that they could actually pump two at a time and things were progressing well enough without him, that he began to think about the little cot in his office. After ensuring that they felt confident enough to continue without his presence and after having a word with some of the guards about keeping a lookout for any attention coming from the direction of the pavilion, he tiredly started walking back towards the warehouse, hands in his pockets, eyes on the ground.

So, he didn't see her until he was almost upon her. In fact, what he saw were her slippered feet and he looked up quickly so as not to run over the person wearing them, only to find himself staring into the beautiful eyes of Abha. He gasped.

"Abha!" he said, and he couldn't help himself but to enfold her into his arms. There they stood, quietly, until she moved away from him, sadly.

"Hello, Nehemiah." Her voice was like cool water to a thirsty man. "Grandfather said he was worried about you and I had to come and see for myself. You look terrible!"

He looked at the ground as if he had been thoroughly admonished, which he had!

"I am sorry! It has just been so busy and there is so much to do and…." he tailed off lamely, excuses dwindling to nothing.

"It is alright. Come, I will walk you back to your office!" She linked arms with him and they walked towards the warehouse, Nehemiah acutely aware of her hand on his arm.

"If only I wasn't so tired!" he thought.

She deftly led him back to his space and handed him a water skin, so that he could quench his thirst and then led him to his cot where she pushed him down, not unkindly.

"You must rest now, Nehemiah," she said in a voice that would brook no nonsense. "You are very low in energy and you will not be able to function if you do not replenish yourself."

"I am very tired, but I cannot sleep with you here. That would be rude and inconsiderate, and my heart would never slow down enough for me to start resting." He said smiling up at her. She laughed, "And if I leave you will go back to work! No, you don't! I will just sit here and talk to you until you are bored to sleep!"

“That is never going to happen,” he replied snorting.

Abha sat on a small stool at his head and gently stroked his forehead as she started talking to him in a quiet voice. She didn’t talk about anything important, just everyday things that were going on in the Rich Quadrant and little stories from home, all of it inconsequential and all of it delivered in a soft monotone. The truth was a very different thing and her heart was pounding out of her chest and her hand was trembling as she stroked him to sleep, much as she would a small child, which he was in a way. She looked up and put her finger to her lips as she noticed someone coming into his office. The woman put up her hands and pointed to indicate the dirty dishes on his desk and Abha just shook her head gently to indicate that she would deal with it later and the woman left. She carried on in much the same fashion for another five minutes, until she heard a soft snoring sound coming from him and then she stopped stroking and just looked at him. He really was beautiful to look at! As handsome in repose as he was in animation. She felt a pang of loss at her inability to have him but instead turned her attention to the one kiss they had shared and sighed softly at the memory. That kiss alone would be enough to keep her warm for a long time.

“Time enough to come up with a solution.” She thought to herself and smiled gently.

Abha stayed with him for the rest of the day, watching him sleep and making sure that he was not disturbed. She only left his side when Moses arrived, rubbing his eyes after his newly wakened rest, to take over the helm and then she headed home, promising to return in the morning, in time to serve him breakfast and warned of dire consequences should his rest be disturbed by anything or anyone that wasn’t as serious as the End of The World.! Moses nodded agreement, seriously and took his seat at the entrance of the office, making sure that he moved his little stool so that he could also see Nehemiah, sleeping.

When he finally stirred, Nehemiah looked around, disorientated to see Abha, still sitting beside him. With the very little light indication that he had in his office, he had no idea of the time and although he felt rested, thought he had maybe slept for a couple of hours. The only thing that made him suspicious that it might be longer was his bladder, straining fit to burst!

"Hello!" he said to Abha, smiling warmly, "What time is it?"
"Two hours after sunrise." She replied returning his smile.

"WHAT!" he said, sitting up sharply, "Have you been sitting her all night? Why did you let me sleep so long? There is so much to do?" He struggled to get out of his bed.

"Easy, Nehemiah! No, I have not been here all night, we took it in turns." She laughed at his agonised groan that he should be so babysat, "Secondly, you needed the rest and I was not going anywhere until you got it and thirdly, things will wait until you are fed." She picked up a bowl piled high with delicious looking food and handed it to him.

"I hate to be rude, but I have to deal with my other bodily functions first or else I might burst." He said to her, making her laugh and after promising to come straight back he hurried out to relieve himself.

A short time later he was back and getting stuck into the food she had brought him, prepared by her own hands he discovered. She had promised him that she would bring him up to speed as he ate, and she did, telling him that all of the tents had been delivered and were now in position at both sites. She also said that the Masters had continued to work on erecting the tents, throughout the rest of the day and by lamplight, during the night. As a result, the tents were well on their way to being completed.

"You however, are not going to go and see them until you have bathed!" she said to Nehemiah, sternly, "You are quite odious after all your exertion yesterday! I have brought you some clean clothing and while it is not of your style, is cool and clean and I think you might look quite fetching in it!"

He humbly took her instructions and while be very keen to go and see what was happening, was very aware that the people who he had left on site were more than capable of getting the job done. Besides which, he really was having a wonderful time in her company! He accepted the clothes off her and took the time to look at them appreciatively and to feel the quality of the cloth and neatness of the stitches. It turns out that she had made them herself, guessing at his sizes and from his eyes, she had done a very good job of that estimation. That she had gone to such lengths to present him with such a fine gift, moved him deeply and he said so, with sincerity, tears in his eyes.

She looked down, embarrassed. "It is nothing, Nehemiah! Just some clothes. Compared to what you have given me and my people, it is truly nothing."

He put the clothes beside him and took her hands in his. "It is everything!" he said looking into her eyes, "And I will always treasure them as the beautiful gift that they are. Thank you."

They sat like that for a short while until she could bear it no more and let go.
"Come you, smelly man!" Bath time!" and she turned away from him and started heading towards the warehouse door while he scrambled to collect what he needed and follow her.

They walked amiably down to the river, away from the building projects, so that he could bathe in peace. They walked in silence, the company of each other enough to make them feel relaxed and at ease, warring with the proximity of each other that had an entirely different effect on both of them!

Once beside the water, Nehemiah found an area sheltered by reeds and hiding behind it divested himself of his clothes and dove in, while Abha sat giving him the privacy he needed, only occasionally sneaking a peek at his lithe form, appreciatively. He took some time to clean himself, even making an effort to thoroughly washing his hair, which he noticed had lightened considerably since he had been exposed to so much sunlight. Once he was satisfied that he was clean enough, he pulled his heavy body out of the water, reconnecting with the gravity of land and dried himself off, using his deodorant stone before donning his new clothes. They felt so light and very cool and covered all of him, protecting him from the suns harsh rays. He felt as though he had just put on his 'Sunday Best'!

"Well here I am!" he said walking around the bushes to stand in front of her, for her perusal! She gasped in surprise before jumping up and checking the fit on his shoulders and back, making sure the sleeves were long enough and basically taking any and every opportunity to touch this wonderful handsome man. He soaked in every second and was about to pull her into a warm embrace when he heard Moses shouting for him and there was something about the sound of his voice that brought him fully alert.

"Nehemiah! Come quickly! The Pharaoh is demanding your presence! Now!" Moses panted and immediately turned and headed back the way he had come.

"Moses!"

The young boy stopped, looking hot and miserable.

"Come here! Now just breathe and drink some water. Here!" Nehemiah handed him the water skin and let him drink his fill and waited until he had recovered. "Good! Now I will come with you and you can tell me what is happening, as we walk."With a shrug to Abha, he turned away and started heading towards the direction of the Pharaoh's new pavilion.

"No! It is this way! He is at the new concrete tent site and he is not happy!" Moses said tugging at his arm.

Nehemiah's stomach sank. This was the very thing that he did not want!

"How?" he asked, "What made him come all of the way down here? He hates it down here!"

"Something we did not think about. He decided to be kind and come and give some small gifts to his people!"

"For goodness sake!" Nehemiah said in exasperation!

They hurried towards the site, in trepidation, not knowing what they would find. He had missed out on so much by sleeping but felt much better for it and much more able to deal with a recalcitrant young King. This would take smooth talking!

As he approached the site, he could see the Pharaoh sitting with his back to the concrete tents, arms folded over his chest, foot tapping in impatience.

"There you are!" he said, standing as they approached. "I have been waiting for a long time, Nehemiah and I don't like to be kept waiting!"

"Your Majesty, I am very sorry that I have kept you waiting. How can I be of service to you?"

"I have thought to bring some little trinkets to the slaves to give them, demonstrating my magnanimity! However, when I get there, I can find hardly anyone where I thought they would be and lots of people here doing goodness know what, with some giant contraption. I suspect this has something to do with you! Explain!"

Mentally, Nehemiah breathed a sigh of relief! It appeared as though the Pharaoh had not even noticed the concrete tents or thought them worthy of comment. If he could get him out of here, quickly, he might save the situation.

"Your Highness! We are all working so hard on your Accountability. Sometimes this requires us to be innovative and develop new ideas to try and make everything quicker and easier to implement. I can assure you that work is progressing very quickly, and it is costing the Pharaoh nothing." He looked at the young man's face to try and gauge his reaction, and so far, it looked quite favourable. "I have heard about your beautiful new home being constructed. May I humbly make a suggestion?"

The young King nodded, starting to look bored.

"It would be a wonderful thing for the common slaves to see you in your grandeur, with your beautiful and sumptuous home around you. Would it not be a grand gesture to hand out these trinkets as a way of opening your new palace, officially? A gift to celebrate a gift, so to speak?" He could see the Pharaoh thinking about his words.

"I could do that! In fact, I was going to do that anyway! It is obvious that this is not the place to carry out such a grand gesture. But where is everyone? Where are all my slaves?"

"We have rearranged things a little in order to get the most out of the people available, as a result not everyone is in the same place all of the time, but the work is definitely being done much more efficiently and new methods are being investigated all of the time, too." He pointed towards the Archimedes Screw, now standing idle due to the operators lying flat on the ground, prostrating themselves in obedience.

"Well I suppose, I will just have to trust you, Nehemiah. Why not come back and see my beautiful home? I haven't seen you for days and I know you will love it! I need someone to share that with!

"Of, Course, Your Majesty." Nehemiah said, bowing low and hiding a sense of relief clearly showing on his face, "I would be most honoured."

With that, the Pharaoh clapped his hands to get the attention of the canopied chair carriers and looked away from the site.

"Come then! As I said, I don't like to be kept waiting!" he said as the chair was carried away and back towards the pavilion construction.

Nehemiah walked behind with Moses at his side, holding his breath, hoping the Pharaoh would not see anything else that might grab his attention and make him stop. He wanted him as far away from here as he could.

"Phew!" said Moses quietly.

"Exactly my thoughts!" he replied.

Chapter Sixteen

They stood together, 'The Motley Crew' as Nehemiah had come to think of them, Amun, Zaph, himself and Moses, looking around the vast hall being presented to them. He had never seen such a sumptuous room before, and he had seen quite a few! It was large enough for a party of three hundred people, they were being told with facilities at either end and a large semi-circular stage in the middle of the room along the left-hand wall. Amun was dealing with the very ostentatiously dressed, obsequious gentleman who was trying to rent it to them at an exorbitant price. He watched Amun's face as he was speaking to the man.

"Good luck, with that!" he thought.

They were looking for a venue to launch their training scheme, the idea being that the people from the Rick Quadrant would pay good many to be trained with new skills, thereby giving them a sense of purpose to their lives. They would not know, of course, that the very people who were training them, were the Pharaoh's own slaves! The important thing is that they would pay good money, thereby freeing up the Pharaoh's funds. Part of the training would involve internships, where they would have to pay to go onto practical implementation of their knowledge, and in so doing would be paying to build the Pharaoh's structures. Nehemiah thought it was an excellent idea and one based upon his own world's way of doing things. While he did not agree with the system as it worked in his society, here it would balance out the economy and the social injustice being forced upon so many people. It would make the people in the Rich Quadrant responsible for their lives and make them contributing members of society and it would make them accountable for their actions, while also giving the slave population the opportunity to use their skills, for the betterment of themselves and their fellow man. It was all part of the plan to make the Pharaoh Accountable.

He could hear raised voices behind him, one of them Amun's and realised that the bargaining must be about to come to a conclusion. He didn't have to listen to how much this was going to cost. No one could haggle like Amun! The room would be perfect for the event they had in mind, he just had to make sure that all of the other bits came together; the right teachers, the costumes, the mocktails and most importantly the old pavilion which he so desperately needed to turn into a college. In fact, that was his job, once they had finished here. He saw a shaking of hands out of the corner of his eye and knew a deal had been struck and turned to Amun and Zaph.

"Well? How did that go?" he said watching the ostentatiously dressed gentleman departing with a disgruntled look on his face.

"Very well, my friend!" said Amun beaming satisfaction. "We will have to use of if for a whole week, which will give us time to set everything up and to prepare for the actual weekend. Do you have someone to sort out these Mocktails you keep talking about?"

"No, but I am open to suggestions? I need someone who is really good with food. I have recipes for them but have no idea how available the ingredients will be here. I need someone who can look at them and come up with their own version."

"I know just the person!" interrupted Zaph, "She has been working with the slaves, food since the project started and just lives and breathes food! I can speak to her if you like?"

"I would like that Zaph, Thank you.!"

They sat for some time discussing the sorts of courses they would be selling and what they should be charging for each. It was decided that there must be samples of work available, some really good quality examples that they would be able to see and appreciate.

They also decided that although Nehemiah would do a speech, of sorts, the selling should really be Amun's job, as it was his area of expertise. Much more discussion continued until Nehemiah stood up and brushed off his trousers.

"I really can't put it off any more! Wish me luck and hopefully when I see you next, we will have our college. If not, assume I have been thrown in prison and someone come and rescue me please?!"

They laughed as he headed out of the door and he could hear the conversation continuing without him. As he walked to the Pharaoh's new home it occurred to him that everyone around him was becoming accountable except the Young King. In fact, he seemed to be coming more and more spoiled and irresponsible every time they met, and Nehemiah knew in his heart that this would have to be dealt with, before he could go back to his own world but, right now, he had no idea how that was going to be accomplished. There was no point in worrying about it and he knew that something would arrive that would enable him to deal with the issue, exactly as it was meant to be dealt with. He wasn't even sure how he was going to get the Pharaoh to give him the old pavilion, for him to use as a college. He would just do the same as always, namely, go with the flow and see where it takes him and hopefully that would not be in a dungeon somewhere!

The walk was much shorter coming from the Rich Quadrant and he arrived in no time, still ill prepared. The Pharaoh's new quarters were quite spectacular to see. He had been shocked by the scale of the structure when he had come with the Pharaoh before. There were many more rooms than the old base but not only that, each room was much bigger than before. Each was furnished with the most exquisite pieces of furniture, all crafted by the very best at their trade. The pieces of art work that were decorating the place were spectacular. Everywhere he looked, Nehemiah could see gold and turquoise and coral, rubies and emeralds and sapphires, topaz and opals.

Construction was still going on, so the noise was still very intrusive, but he knew that the builders would be finished and out of this world within the next two days. He knew that because that was how long it was going to take to finish the concrete tents. Crews of people were busy burying them in sand and now, when you looked down at the river, it looked like dunes on either side. He had been so shocked to see the Pharaoh on the site and was convinced that he would shut it down but to his astonishment he had not even noticed what they were doing, so self-absorbed was he. He should have known, that was how it would be but in his naivety, he thought the Young King would be angry when the truth was he just didn't care, at all. Not about anyone but himself and his own situation. That was fine with Nehemiah! People were already starting to move into the finished structures in family groups with plenty of space and privacy for them. The old sleeping huts had been painted with a sort of whitewash and were being converted into cooking areas, dining areas and one hut had been given over to handle the storage of the things needed for the communal garden. The last three huts had been turned into school buildings for the children, with all three being used in the evening for adults who wished to learn to read or do numbers. Nehemiah had seen Rachid there every night, since it had begun. The Pharaoh's constructions were still ongoing of course, as they had been since he arrived, but it looked very different now and more was being achieved there, every day both because the people on the site were properly fed and rested but also because they were happy, and now had a pride about their work. He was very aware that the final part of his job here, would be about ensuring that these people could develop from the place they now found themselves in, and not be forced back into slavery. He hoped that the changes had been far reaching enough to ensure they stayed but at the end of the day the book stopped with the Pharaoh! It was, after all, His Accountability that Nehemiah was here to fix.

Once he arrived at the new structure, he was told by the guards that the Pharaoh had retired to the old pavilion due to the noise and had been gone for some time, so he set off in that direction, striding out in the heat, which he had become very used to. It was going to be chilly when he got home, he suspected, for a while, until he re-acclimatised himself to it again. Once he reached the old pavilion, he was shown straight in to the room that the Young King was in and as soon as he entered he bowed low, in respect.

"Your Majesty." He said.

When he stood again, he could see that the Pharaoh had not even noticed that he had entered the room. He was moving slowly around the room, which was full of beautiful and expensive objects that Yoshi had sent through and he was stroking them reverently, picking them up and admiring them, one at a time. The room was large, and it was full of gifts, Nehemiah could see that it was going to take some time for him to get around to looking and touching them all. He cleared his throat.

"Your Majesty!" he said much louder.

"Hmmm?" was the only response he got. The Young King was totally and completely absorbed. He resigned himself to watching the Pharaoh to see if he could determine what was going on and how best to elicit his attention. He certainly was not going to leave this room without first having spoken to him. The request for quarters was too important to put off any longer and the big event was scheduled to take place in ten days, time. So, he stood quietly, feeling the ground beneath his feet, listening to the sounds that were going on around him and noticing his breathing in his body. When he was centred and very much in the present, mentally, he turned his attention onto the young man in front of him and watched him carefully. He noticed his eyes, wide and totally fixated on the object of his attention. He noticed his mouth, turned into a slight smile which widened or relaxed according to the object that was being examined. His jaw was relaxed but there was an overall tension to his face and his body.

Nehemiah tried to put a name to the emotion that he was seeing all too clearly displayed by the Pharaoh, but it eluded him for a little while. He continued to watch and learn, until it came to him. Avarice! The young man was completely and absolutely absorbed in his new possessions! Totally and utterly and the look on his face showed a very unhealthy obsession, developing. This did not bode well for the forthcoming conversation that needed to take place. He needed to take control of this situation and begin the arduous task of making the Pharaoh Accountable.

He walked over to a pile of things that were just to the right of the Young King, meaning that he would reach them in the next few minutes, and keeping him in sight out of the corner of his eye, he picked up one of them and started to look at it with feigned interest. He heard a gasp from over his shoulder and heard a rapid approach, seeing just in time a raised hand coming for him on his left. He whipped round and grabbed the arm by the wrist where he held it firmly but not tightly.

"Don't!" he said in a stern voice, "You will never raise your hand to me again! Do you understand?"

The Pharaoh was completely taken aback and with his mouth hanging open, nodded dumbly. Nehemiah slowly and calmly let go of his wrist and stood facing him, looking him straight in the eyes.

"As, I said before, Your Majesty." He bowed again, this time having the full attention of the King. "I have come to talk to you about important matters and we need to be in conversation for some time."

Having recovered his equilibrium a little after seeing Nehemiah bow, he straightened up and put on a superior, blank face. "I am Pharaoh and therefore, I decide who I will talk to and when!"

"That is true, but if we do not have this conversation, now, I am no longer responsible for what will happen here, and I will leave immediately!"

"You cannot do that!" Pharaoh said in outrage, "You are here to make me accountable and I will not release you, until that is done!"

"Firstly, I can and secondly, I will, if I choose!"

The King was flabbergasted! No one had ever spoken to him in this fashion and he had no idea what was going on or how to react to it, let alone deal with it.

"The truth of the matter is that we can only control ourselves, Your Highness! You can say anything, and you can do anything to me, but at the end of the day, only I control what happens in my mind and body, my heart and soul and you cannot do anything about that. You can hurt this body, even kill it if you wish but you will never change my mind or my heart. Only I can do that!" Nehemiah said, directly. "Come let us sit and be comfortable. We are going to be here for some time. I will get the guards to bring you refreshments to make you more comfortable, but we are going to talk. Now!" he walked to the door and gave quiet instructions to the guard, which also included something about not being disturbed, regardless of what was happening. Then he picked up two stools and carried them to the furthest point from the doorway and indicated the one closest to the inside, to the Pharaoh. The other he took himself, thereby placing himself between the Pharaoh and the door. He meant business this day!

"Things are good!" he started, looking at the Pharaoh to make sure that he had his full attention, holding his attention with his eyes." Things are fine! We need things and it is nice to have them. We like to look at them, hold them, use them. However, they are just things! Just objects! They cannot give us anything! They cannot make us sad or happy, only we can do that. They are just inanimate objects.'

‘That is all they are! Now, people are not objects, they are living and breathing human beings the same as you and the same as me. They think, feel, communicate, love, hate, laugh, cry and breathe. You cannot own people! They cannot belong to anyone person! They are not objects! It is not possible.”

The Pharaoh gave a snort of derision! “That is nonsense! I own lots of people! It is my job as Pharaoh, they have to do what I tell them! I own their lives, their food, their homes, everything! I own them!”

“No! You do not! I know you are not a stupid man, but you are ill informed, and I need you to think about this, seriously, now. Just as I said before, you cannot own a person. They have their own likes and dislikes. Their own considerations, about what is happening. Let me give you an example; If a person decided that they would no longer work for you, could you make them? Could you force them to work for you?”

“Yes, of course!”

“How?”

“Well, I would beat them until they got up and worked!”

“What if they decided that they would rather be beaten to death than work for you?”

“Then I would beat them to death!”

“But then, they would have won! Because they would still not be working for you!”

The Pharaoh sat stunned! “But they would be dead!”

“Exactly, but maybe for that person, being dead is better than working for you! The fact is that in the end, it was the other person’s choice to make and not yours!’

'You did not own his decision, you could not force him to do something that he did not want to do! He won!" Nehemiah sat back and watched the young man take his theory on board, watched him struggle with the concept, until he finally accepted it.

"So!" he continued, "People cannot be owned or even controlled. As you pointed out, you are the Pharaoh, and these are indeed, your people but not because you own them. Not because you tell them what to do and certainly not because you own their houses and food! They are your people because you have responsibilities to them!"

"What!? I have responsibilities to no one! I rule this land!"

"Ok! So, what if all the people decided that they didn't like you and just left?"

"What!? That couldn't happen!"

"Why not?"

"Because I would get the guards to stop them!"

"OK! What if the guards didn't like you either and they left too? Then you would be King of nothing land!"

The Pharaoh clearly felt uncomfortable! No one had threatened his rule so calmly and clearly and non-violently, than the man that sat opposite him now. He had nothing to say! He had no answers to the challenging statements being made to him! He was at a loss.

"I would give them all beautiful presents to make them love me and want to stay!" he said, thinking that he had figured it out.

"Ok! So, we are back to the beginning! Objects are nice, but they are just things. They cannot do anything!'

‘They cannot make us change our minds or feel anything! Only we can do that and that cannot be controlled by someone else! You may give people presents, and they may decide to stay because they want the things you are offering, but that will not make them love you. It will only make them stay and take your gifts.”

“But that is not true! I have many servants who love me!”

“OK! Let us leave that for the moment. Let me ask you a question about you being the ruler of this land. What does it mean to be the Pharaoh? What does that entail? What does that look like?”

“I am like a God to these people! I give them what they need, and they adore me! That adoration is like food and water to me! Without it, I would be as nothing! It is my job to rule them, make decisions for them, when they are not able, instruct them, direct them and teach them to do my bidding!”

“Yes, but to what end? Why? What is the point of it all? What are you trying to achieve?”

“I am trying to build the greatest monuments so that everyone in the world will look at them and see my greatness! You know this! It is why you are here!”

Nehemiah shook his head and took a deep breath. It was clear that he was definitely dealing with a Bronze Age mentality but that didn’t change the fact that he had to get this young man thinking and feeling! Give him Accountability, for his actions! How to do it was the problem. He sat quiet for a moment gathering his thoughts and his examples and got to thinking about when he was at Uni and his weekend job that drove him to despair. He had stuck it for a couple of years but ended up so frustrated, that going to work had become more of a hassle than the financial reward. He had quit! Left politely, of course but he had never been so relieved to walk out of that place and the reasons for that frustration were the very same reasons that were causing the issues, here.

“In my world,” he began, “You have people that control businesses, not unlike the way the Pharaoh controls his land. Their job is to make sure that the business is running smoothly and increasing in wealth and is stable. They are called Managers, because they manage the business or company. Now, as I see it, the problems start arising when the Managers see their job as a position of privilege, as opposed to a position or responsibility. For example, the workers might see a problem occurring. Now, they can go and tell the Manager, who may instruct the workers to deal with the problem and walk away. They would be within their right to do so as they are managers, not workers but then the workers gradually build up a resentment for the attitude of the manager. They feel that they lack support, when they need it and while the Manager is not obstructing them, he is not assisting them either, and he is burdening them in a way that is unnecessary. So, next time there is a problem, they will not be so quick to talk to him about it, because it will mean extra work for them. So, they may hide it or blame someone else. Eventually this will increase to such a point where everyone is just busy coping with things because there are so many undealt with problems and then they will feel stressed and pretty soon will realise that the effort they are putting in is more than the money they are getting out and they will quit. This then, causes a shortage of workers which means that everyone has to cope with that and cover it and that causes problems and there we go around again!”

“Already, I feel sorry for the lot of these Managers!”

“Ah! Well that is where we differ! Let us look at it a different way. What if this Manager felt that his job was a position of responsibility and not privilege. What if he felt that his job was to train and assist the workers, to look after them so that they felt as though they were contributing and helping him? He would walk around, and someone would tell him about a problem and he would roll up his sleeves and go take a look. Then he would help to put it right.’

‘The workers feel as if he has their best interests at heart and start to feel appreciated. They also know that he is looking out for them and will be supportive when there are problems. Next time there is an issue, they will take it straight to him and the wheels are kept running smoothly.”

“That is not right! Very soon they would all be running to him with silly little quibbles and he would not be able to do his important job!”

“That may happen at first, but if he is a responsible manager, he will make sure that training is given to those who work in area that keeps creating problems. Then those people will be able to handle the issues as they arise and also feel that he has their best interests at heart, which he does. He could then just keep an eye on everything and get on with his own job, with a higher degree of confidence. Realising that he has a responsibility to his work force means that he works hard! Harder than the rest, always the first to arrive and the last to leave, but that business will thrive with a respected group of workers who enjoy their job and want to give of their best because they know they are supported and respected in return.”
The Pharaoh looked at Nehemiah as if he was truly insane! The idea that he should be working for the good of his slaves instead of the other way around was lunacy to him and he could not, for a minute see the benefit of it. He just looked at Nehemiah blankly, in silence, unable to agree with him at all.
The young accountant took a breath and looking at the young ruler’s face, realised that he had lost him! There was no reality whatsoever, in anything that he had just been saying. He was just incapable of understanding any sense of responsibility to his land and his people.

“So be it!” he thought but still intent on rescuing the situation if at all possible.

“It is with regard to this training, that I came to speak with you today.”

“You want me to start training? Me? The Pharaoh?”

"No, Your Highness! I think you have had plenty of training already." He said unable to resist that small sarcastic comment and immediately feeling guilty for it. "I have a need to open a school for adults to learn different skills."

"Where did this need come from? How is it going to help me?"

"Well, if I can train more people up then they can work on your construction, and it will be completed sooner. Also, these people will pay for the training that will be given them in the school and that will help the revenue problems that you have with the buildings."

"Really?" Pharaoh said aghast, "You think that people will pay to go to school?"

"Absolutely! They will pay, and they will learn the value of education and they will find a purpose in life that will help themselves and contribute to the rest of this society, positively."

"Why that sounds amazing! Why did you not say this earlier and save me the rest of the drivel about responsibility!"

"There is only one problem and that is that I have nowhere to carry out this teaching. You now have an amazing new home and I would like to use this old one for my college." Nehemiah said.

"Absolutely not!" Was the Pharaoh's response. "Do you think I am stupid or something that I would just hand over such a structure? For nothing? And you cannot afford to buy it from me. You have nothing!"

"I would like to say a word about generosity, if I may." Nehemiah pushed on, indicating all of the beautiful things in the room, "You have been given so many beautiful things from Mr. Toshimoto, I thought you might like to take an example from him and demonstrate, to me, some generosity of spirit?"

"Absolutely not! This is mine and you cannot have it. So is everything in this room! It was given to me and not you and you can't have it!"

"I guess I will just have to have a word with Mr. Toshimoto then."

"What do you mean? About what?"

"Well, as you so rightly pointed out, I have nothing, but in order to make you Accountable, I have to start this training school. It is imperative to everything I have done so far and will make a huge difference to everything that is happening here. So, my only option will be to ask Mr. Toshimoto for help."

"Ask him if you must. That is nothing to do with me."

"True!" said Nehemiah, cunningly, "But that may mean that you will get no more gifts from him, as he will be busy sending things for the school. His funds are not endless, you know, and he will always support the cause for the greatest good to the greatest number of people." He stood as if about to leave, "But, not to worry. You have all of this which is plenty, I am sure."

"Wait!" the Pharaoh also stood, a worried look now forming on his face, "Maybe we can come to some agreement?"

"I am listening."

"What if I was to rent it to you?"

"Well that wouldn't work. As you so rightly said I have nothing."

"But as the Pharaoh surely I should get some benefit out of it?" he asked slyly.

"But you are Your Highness! You are getting your monuments completed! In your life time!"

The Pharaoh sat down again looking at Nehemiah's face, stroking his chin in thought, balancing out the best option to fulfill his need; his greed. Nehemiah just stood with a straight face, fingers crossed behind his back. The pause seemed to go on for a long time and he resisted the urge to break eye contact and start fidgeting. Eventually the young king stood and held out his hand.

"You may have it but only on loan! You may have the use of it!"

"That is all I need, Your Majesty," he said and shook hands on the deal.

An hour later he couldn't resist a fist pump into the air, as he exited the pavilion and started back to the warehouse to progress their plans and tell everyone what had happened.

Nehemiah looked down on the three exquisite outfits laid out before him. As it was to be a three-day event, Amun had insisted that he should have a different outfit for each one. He had never felt comfortable in the short, belted kilt that many of the men and women wore, so had given Amun a rough sketch of a modern man's Egyptian wear, namely a long-sleeved, tunic and loose trousers, quite some time ago. This was what Abha had based the outfit she had made him, on, and because he was foreign to the land, he could get away with wearing different clothes. Now, here before him lay another three outfits made of white silk with beautiful decoration around the neck and sleeves. They looked very fine indeed. By now, his hair was quite long, and he didn't trust the excellent barbers with cutting it. Many of the people here just shaved their head and wore wigs as a way of keeping their head covered from the sun. He liked his hair, which was now very blonde and, so he had managed to tie it back into a small ponytail at the nape of his neck, which would keep it tidy until such times as he could get a better haircut, once he returned home.

He sighed. The thought of returning home made him uncomfortable, on so many levels. He had been very disturbed, after leaving the pharaoh last time despite the fact that he had been successful in securing the pavilion so that they could use it for a college. He was deeply concerned about the Pharaoh's complete lack of responsibility, for his people and the plight that they were in. He had displayed no understanding of human suffering or indeed, his responsibility for creating it. He displayed a complete lack of compassion towards to his fellow man and Nehemiah had no knowledge of how to proceed in such a situation. He had never met anyone so and selfish and greedy, in his entire life. This gave huge repercussions to the people in the land who had worked so hard to improve their lot. He was very concerned as to how things would go, when he left. It would be dire if things deteriorated back to the way they were when he first arrived, after all the hard work that everyone had put in, and all hope that everyone had gathered to themselves. They had improved their lives so much by working hard at the merest suggestion of that improvement, that it would indeed be a crime if the Pharaoh were to take that away from them. So, he had gone to speak to the only person that he trusted, to ensure the survival of the project after he had left, that was Rachid.

He had found him at home just before sunset, working with a huge sheet of papyrus, doing sums. He was ecstatic to see him! “Nehemiah!” He boomed. “How nice of you to come and see me! I am working on some homework and am please reports that my numbers are coming on greatly! I am enjoying this so much, let me tell you.” He carefully removed the papyrus so that he wouldn’t get damaged and pulled over a seat so that Nehemiah could join him. His wife bought them both a drink and left the room, with two children in tow.

“Your wife is looking very healthy! She’s positively blooming!” Nehemiah said to Rashid, sitting himself down beside him.

"She is! She does very well at this time! It is good. It bodes well for my new heir." Rachid replied. "But I suspect you haven't come here to discuss the health of my wife. What is troubling you?"

"I am not sure where to begin." Nehemiah said thoughtfully. "I have great doubts as to the success of the project."

"How can you say that! It is a huge success. People have homes, are enjoying their work, have plenty to eat, and even the guards are smiling at each other!"

"That's true, but will it remain that way once I have left?"

"Ah. I understand. I can't answer that I am afraid, it will be a very tricky situation. What are you thinking?"

"I am not sure." Said Nehemiah scratching his head, "I have been to see the Pharaoh and now I am deeply worried. He does not understand his responsibility to the people, of this land. He does not understand the plight of the people, that have been working for him. And try as I might, I cannot get him to understand how important it is that he looks after them. This worries me greatly. So, I thought I would come and speak to you, to see if there was anything we could do, to ensure that the improvements that have been made, remain steady. That the progress, that the people have made with their lives, continues."

"What makes you think that there is anything that I can do about it? I am a nobody in this land. And just a guard, Nehemiah."

"You are so much more than that, Rachid! You are a man who has changed his life in the face of adversity. Not only have you turned your life around, you have helped a huge amount of people to do the same for themselves. People respect you, they look up to you."

He thought for a moment, choosing his words carefully, "And, you have the might of the guards behind you. No other person has such power in this land, not even the Pharaoh."

There was silence. Rachid was completely shocked, and while the statement that Nehemiah made was true, he had never thought about it before.

"That's not entirely true. The inner guard are very close to the Pharaoh."

"Are they still part of your remit?"

"What you mean?"

"I mean are you still their boss? Do you supervise them? Is it your job to see to their rotas? If they have a problem with their work, do they come to you?"

"Well, yes. I am their boss."

"Do the Inner Guards, always work in that position? I mean do they ever come down and work with the rest of the people?"

"Well, occasionally, but mainly their duties are linked to the palace. It saves disruption and they know the job. Keeps them happy, if you like."

"Then, I think we may have a solution." Nehemiah said, smiling at Rashid. "And I think it starts with the changing of the guards."

"How do you mean?"

"If the Inner Guards were to be removed from the Pharaoh, just a couple at a time, and worked with the people here, they would have more reality on what we are achieving here, on what it means to everyone."

Rachid thought about it. “They know what has been happening. I mean they can hardly not know! They live here! Some of them won’t like to be moved. They think of themselves as a bit better than the other guards.”

“And are they?” Nehemiah asked, “I mean are they paid more? Do they have extra training?”

“No! Not at all!”

“OK then! So, if you move them and change them with guards that are more likely to agree with the transition that has been happening here, it will give them the opportunity to come to a personal understanding of the changes that have occurred, and how important they are.”

“Some of them won’t like it! It is a bit of a cushy number, sometimes!”

Nehemiah laughed, “Come on, Rachid, you can deal with that! Or have you gone soft in your old age?”

Rachid grumbled under his breath, “Never! I can keep them in line! It is how I got my job! There is nothing like a few days down at the cess pits to knock them into shape! But what is the point? What good will it do?”

“Without any law enforcement, what can the Pharaoh do? He might shout and curse but, essentially, he has no physical force? He cannot enforce any changes he may want to make. He becomes toothless.”

Rachid’s eye opened wide as the implications of what Nehemiah was saying, hit home. “You truly are worried, aren’t you? What you are suggesting is almost treason!”

“No! I am not suggesting anyone take any action against the Pharaoh. That would be wrong. What I am suggesting, is inaction!”

Rachid shook his head and stroked his chin. “I am not sure, Nehemiah. I will have to think about the implications, not just for me but for my men. What I can say, is that I will start changing the guard, but only because I think that your idea of them all being equal has merit. They should all get a turn down here and up there. But, beyond that, I cannot say.”

“You are very wise and definitely good at your job! Your men are very lucky to have someone who is so responsible. Can you promise me one thing, please? When the time comes, get me home? No matter what?”

“You think he will try to keep you here, against your will?”

“Maybe. I don’t know, but I need someone to have my back on this. I need to make sure that I can get back.”

“Rachid looked him in the eyes, sincerely, “You have my word. I will get you back, when the time comes.”

“Thank you, Rachid.”

That had been days ago, and Nehemiah had heard no more from him, so was unsure about his position with regard to his suggestions. He had been true to his word about the changing of the guard though and new faces were appearing around the Pharaoh’s quarters. He had been there every day since the conversation with the Young King, making sure that they old pavilion was being emptied and setting up new spaces. It had been long days and sometimes long nights too, but they were almost ready to start training courses. Another couple of days and they would be able to go. The new quarters for the Pharaoh still had quite a bit of sorting out to do but the good thing was that it was keeping him busy and out of harms, way. He had a lot of things to position around his new home and he wanted it ‘just so’! The gifts had stopped arriving, the construction men had gone back and even the equipment that had been needed for the concrete tent construction had been returned, during the quiet of night.

Now, was the time to finish the project and go home, the thought of which always left a pang of sadness, because of leaving Abha. Losing her from his life was going to be the hardest thing he had ever experienced. She was such a joy and as he looked down at the beautiful clothes in front of him, he could see her hand in every stitch.

"Time to get ready, Nehemiah!" he said to himself and started to prepare for the first night of his Big Event.

The whole thing was supposed to kick off just before sunset but there was no one waiting when they opened the doors. An hour later and Nehemiah was pacing the floor alone in a state of nervous anxiety.

"I have told you, my friend, no one will come this early. They will have to get thoroughly drunk first." Amun said, trying to calm his friend. All around the room people sat on stools next to tables which held things that they had made. The people were previous slaves but to see them you would not know it, bedecked in finery, as they were. Everyone had been instructed to keep talk based on their skills and not on themselves. The tables were full of all sorts of goods, from clothes to the finest foods. There were demonstrations of exquisite masonry and carpentry, rug making and weaving, painting and sculpting. Any skill possible was demonstrated at the event. The tailors had done an amazing job at clothing everyone and Nehemiah did not recognise Zaph when he first came up to speak to him. He looked amazing. They all did. At either end of the room, tables were full of free Mocktails and although it looked like a very sumptuous party, not a drop of alcohol was present in the room. Amun had brought in his four sons to help sell the courses, all expert salesmen with skills in haggling almost as good as their father. Indeed, the only thing missing were the people they needed to sell the courses too.

After another hour people started arriving in dribs and drabs. They staggered in and make straight for the drinks tables, helping themselves to the free drinks and food.

Eventually those people had to make way for new people coming and start to make their way around the room. At first, they tried to buy the things at the tables, but it had been suggested that they be refused, at first, with selling only happening only on the last day, as they would need the items displayed to encourage people to sign up for the courses. So instead people were saying;

“I cannot sell you this, but I can teach you how to make it for yourself?”

In the case of consumables on display, people were instead suggesting;

“If you find this tasty, I can teach you to make it yourself.” In this way there would always be an encouragement to learn.

Soon the room was bursting to capacity with many wanting to get in but not being able to, because of the lack of space. They opened another door to allow people to circle round and thereby allow more people in, directing everyone in a ‘one way’ flow.

“It is a good job they don’t have fire regulations!” Nehemiah thought.

Something caught his eye and he looked up. What he saw made his heart almost stop! There in the doorway stood Abha dressed in a figure hugging white dress with wide straps on the shoulders, it was covered in a silk gossamer that softened it and topped off with a beautiful turquoise and coral decorated collar. She looked absolutely stunning and Nehemiah had to remind himself to breathe. He could not go to her, as that was moving against the flow of people, so he found a place near the wall to stop, waiting for her to come to him and enjoyed watching her approach slowly. To his horror he saw a drunk young man approach her smiling lasciviously, and she jumped as though she had been touched inappropriately, her face registering her displeasure and shock.

He started to push against the people to try and reach her but there was no way to do it and as he saw, no need. She grabbed the man's arm and whipped it around, so she held it up his back and swiftly threw him face down to the ground. She stood with her foot against his shoulders and said something to him. Once she let him up he looked very ashamed and shuffled quickly away and out of the building. She looked up at Nehemiah smiling, and swept her palms against each other, brushing off imaginary dust, and winked at him. He burst out laughing and waited for her to reach him.

"You don't grow up in the Rich Quadrant, without learning pretty quickly how to deal with lecherous men!" she said smiling as she approached him, and he pulled her towards him and kissed her! Right there in front of everyone. When he finally let her go, she looked at him with sparkling eyes.

"You be careful, young man." She said laughingly, "You might just find yourself eating dirt if you are not careful!"

He joined in with her laughter. "You look stunning, tonight! That dress is absolutely beautiful. Fit for a Queen!"

She blushed with pride. "Thank you. It is one of my own making and design!"

"Then I hope you have always wanted a career as a teacher! You could teach people how to make and design such lovely clothes in my college."

"That is true, but I am happy with my life and do not need another job, thank you." She replied smiling.

As the night progressed the people started to sober up a little and became more and more interested in what was happening around them, the items on display were like precious artefacts to them, they had never seen such work before, or never been sober enough to notice such things.

The more they heard about the courses and the fact that they too would be able to make such things, the more interested they became. People started to sign up to different courses, slowly at first but more and more towards the end of the night. In the end they had to call a halt to the event but promised that they would open their doors in the morning so that others could come back and join.

Once they had managed to get everyone out of the room and the doors closed for the night, Nehemiah and the others slumped down onto stools and took a moment to enjoy the silence after the night's events.

"That went extremely well, my friend." Amun said with a sigh, "Much better than expected. We have many sign ups already and I suspect that word will spread like the proverbial wildfire and when we open the doors tomorrow, we will be swamped."

Nehemiah nodded his agreement. "I have to agree with you Amun. It went much better than expected and I suspect that the amount of people arriving tomorrow will be many more than we had tonight. How much money did we make today?"

"A lot!"

Nehemiah looked at Amun in shock. "What do you mean, a lot?"

"I mean, my friend, that we will end up with enough money to be able to pay every single slave a wage for their work regardless of whether they're teaching or not. Even the people working on the construction site will receive a wage and on top of that the new students, will of course be working, completely free."

Nehemiah fist pumped the air. "Yes!" He said triumphantly. "I knew this was the rich quadrant, but I guess I hadn't realised just how rich that was!"

Amun chuckled, "Very rich indeed, my friend! More than 85% of the money of this land is in the rich quadrant, and that is an expanding amount. What you have achieved here is indeed monumental the Pharaoh himself could not have made this happen even on his very best of days."

"It was not me, Amun, it was everybody. The majority of the work that has been done here has been done by the people, not by me. I have merely an orchestrated the tools to enable them to do what they wanted to do. These are remarkable people and I am very proud to have been able to work with them and you especially!" He looked at Amun affectionately and patted his arm. "And now, my friend, I am going to help those poor people at the drinks tables clean up as we have a lot to prepare, for an early morning start. And if you don't mind, I might not join in the event until later in the day. It seems to me that you have everything under control and I really could do with some sleep."

Amun moved his hands in a shooing motion, "Go, my friend, and sleep and deep and long, when you get there. My sons and myself will deal with everything here and you can join us when you are fully rested, with no worries." And motioning to his boys he started towards the exit. Abha hung back a little.

"Grandfather, I think I will stay and help with the clean-up, if that is alright with you?"

"Stay, my little one, I know that young man will see you safely home. Make sure you get enough sleep." He said wagging his finger as he walked away.

Nehemiah's heart skipped a beat and his stomach flip flopped as he heard her say she was going to stay. He got stuck in with an urgency knowing that the sooner they were cleared up, the sooner he would get to be alone with Abha.

He felt as though he had been given a new lease of life just thinking about it and began helping with the clean-up enthusiastically, making jokes and buoying up all the people around him, all the time watching her at the other end of the room, out of the corner his eye. In no time at all the job was complete and he was outside the room saying goodbye to all of the people he had been working with that day, and then they were alone. He looked down at her and gently picked up her hand and they started to walk slowly, towards Amun's house. It was dark, and he held a lantern and his other hand so that they could see the way walking together in silence accompanied by the music of the crickets singing background.

"You look truly beautiful tonight, Abha!" He said looking down at her.

"Do I not normally look truly beautiful, Nehemiah?" She said with a cheeky grin looking up at him and meeting his eyes.

"You do! But when I saw you tonight, I thought my heart would stop beating."

"No! That would be awful."

"Figuratively speaking, of course. The dress that you designed and made, is stunning! You have great skill. Actually, you have many great skills!"

She laughed softly beside him. "You have a few yourself, you know."

He chuckled. They continued the walk chatting quietly back and forth ambling slowly towards their destination and when they reached Amun's door, they stopped. He looked down at her and feeling bold, he did not wait for her invitation but took her into his arms and kissed her thoroughly, passionately, and she did not object! When they parted, he knew he had to leave right now, before it was too late!

"I love you, Abha!" He said in a croaky voice and turned around and started heading to the pavilion.

"I love you too, Nehemiah!" He heard her say as she headed into the house.

He awoke very dishevelled after a night of tossing and turning, to discover that it was already early afternoon. His initial panic subsided when he remembered that Amun and his sons would have everything covered. He couldn't believe how well it was all going. He bounded out of bed and took a jog down to the river to bathe his sweaty body. He had to pass the new concrete tents and was pleased to see everyone going about their daily business, with smiles on their faces. They waved and shouted to him as he passed, and it took him a while to get to the water. After a freshen up he headed off to grab some food in the new food serving area. It was looking really good and the food smelt fantastic! He sat among the rest of the people eating and chatted easily about how things were going, catching their easy grins and laughing with them. Life was indeed great!

So, it was that he did not enter the room, that the Event was being staged, at until the early evening and was astounded when he got there. Once again it was packed with people but this time they were mostly sober people, there was a massive queue leading to the building where the Event was being held and he had to join it in order to get in, himself. It took half an hour of standing in line, before he was able to enter the room.

"Good job I live in London and am used to it!" he thought to himself.

Once in the room, he was able to look over most of the heads in the crowd and spot Amun sitting beside some tables, on which were lots of pieces of papyrus and bags of what looked like money. He headed in that direction.

"How is it going?" he asked when he finally arrived, clapping Amun on his shoulder.

"Ah! You have woken! It is going extremely well my friend. People are not even bothering with the Mocktails anymore and are only coming so that they can sign up!"

"Excellent! Would you like one, though? Can I get anything for you?"

"Oh Yes, please!" Amun said, "It has been a little time since I had a break!"

"Do you want me to take over from you?"

"No, my friend, I fear that you are too kind, and your haggling skills leave a lot to be desired! These people need to be handled by someone who knows them well, but you can certainly, obtain refreshments for me. That would be very much appreciated!" Amun said turning back to the person he was haggling with, in a loud voice.

So, Nehemiah spent the rest of the day squirming through a crowd of people, carrying Mocktails and food back and forth, between the refreshment tables and Amun and his sons. Once again it was a very late finish but this time he headed straight home, knowing that tomorrow would be key to finishing the project and that the time for him going home was quickly approaching. It was going to truly break his heart to leave Abha, but in the back of his mind, he knew that Yoshi saw Amun on a regular basis and this gave him a tiny glimmer of hope. He had no idea how long that had been going on, or even how they managed it, but the fact was that it happened and that made him think that maybe he would be able to see her again, one day, somehow.

The next day was frantic down at the Event. It was the last day and so things were going to be sold off. The people who had worked so hard making the demonstration pieces were now going to be able to sell them off, and there was a lot of interest and a few pieces.

Nehemiah had arrived well before sunrise to discuss how they were going to manage it, with Amun and he saw that the queue had already started. As he made his way into the room, he had an idea.

"Amun!" he shouted as he saw him at the other end of the room. "I have a great idea!"

"You usually do, my friend! What is it this time?" he approached and shook his hand in greeting.

"Well everyone wants to buy the pieces that we have been displaying but there are so very few pieces compared to the number of people who want them. I say we hold an open-air auction! That way everyone will be able to bid, and we will make the most money for the people who made the pieces."

"You truly are a wonder, young man! It is an excellent idea. Come, let us speak with the craftsmen and women and ask them what they think."

The discussion was long and hard, mostly because the people who had made the beautiful items were horrified that Nehemiah thought they should keep the money! The whole thing had been set up for the good of the community and that is where the money should go! However, on this, Nehemiah was unshifting.

"What you do with your money, is up to you!" he said loudly, "But you have worked hard to craft the pieces and then sat here for three days to make this all happen. The money will belong to you and that is final! I will have it no other way! If you decide to give that money away, then that is your choice, but it IS your choice to make and not anyone else's!"

Seeing that he was so adamant, everyone eventually conceded, and they started setting up tables outside, so that the auction could begin.

The crowd was massive, and they had to have people to relay the bidding to the people standing at the back. Everyone wanted the pieces that were on display and Nehemiah was astounded at what people were prepared to pay in order to get them. Even the consumables went for a huge amount of money, mostly because people need food and drink, out in the sun and Amun made sure that everyone paid for them, which they did generously and without complaint. The auction went on for most of the day with the bidding going back and forth until finally someone won, after which there would be huge cheering. It was intense but good natured, which was a relief to everyone. It was quite apparent that a weekend of being sober had done the Rich Quadrant the world of good! However, finally they ran out of items to auction and the pieces were collected by their new owners and the debts settled and the relevant money handed out to the craftsmen.

Nehemiah walked back into the room that they had hired and dropped into a seat, exhausted after the day's events. He was pleased to enjoy some peace and quiet after the frantic goings on of the past three days.

"Excuse me, Sir." He heard from just inside the door.

"Nehemiah, please." He said indicating that the older woman should come and join him, pointing to the seat next to him. She came carrying a large bag that contained money but did not sit beside him but fell to her knees in front of him. He was horrified and immediately got up from the chair and joined her on the floor.

"You must have this!" she said, handing him the bag of money, tears starting in her eyes.

"No, I don't have to have it. It is yours and well earned."

"This is more money than I have ever seen in my life and is more than I would need to see me comfortable for the rest of my life. You have nothing and are just starting out. You have given us so much and yet have taken nothing for yourself. You too must be paid for your hard work." She said, tears of gratitude rolling down her face.

He took the money out of her hands and placed it beside her on the floor. Then he took her hands in his.

"I have been paid!" he said gently, "I have been paid in hugs and smiles, kisses and love, experiences and knowledge, friendship and care and all of those things are worth more to me than all of the money in the world." He gently wiped away the tears from her face. "I can never repay all of the kindness that has been shown to me here, and it has been my greatest pleasure to meet and work with such resilient people, who have such huge hearts, who have taken my suggestions on board and made them so much more than I could ever have imagined."

"But truly, I do not need this money!" the lady said insistently.

"Your money is yours to do with as you wish. You earned it. If you are unsure how to proceed with it, speak to Amun. He will help you." He stood and extending his hand helped her off the floor, placing the money securely in her hands.

"You are an amazing person, Nehemiah!" she said before she walked away.

"So are you!" he said after her.

Chapter Seventeen

Nehemiah sighed and continued to try and stuff things into his backpack. He had to be sure not to leave anything behind, that had come from his world. He had to leave things pristine. First thing to go into his bag had been things like the chargers, tablet and phone and then the second thing had been the beautiful outfit that Abha had made for him. His heart was breaking in two and he couldn't stand it. He had not seen her since the night he had walked her home from the event, because he just couldn't bear it. It hurt too much. He had decided just to go. He couldn't say anymore to her than he had already said. He had told her the truth, 'I love you' and there was nothing else that he could say to her to make it better or to make her feel better. So, he would just go, and they could both deal with it in their own way, making the most of their lives, living everyday but never forgetting each other and who knows? He had bought her a small gift that he had asked Yoshi to get for him. It had come through with the concrete tents and he had slipped it in his bag waiting for this day. He had written a small note to her, too. It was not enough but it would have to do. He pulled the box out of his pocket and read the note again, just to make sure that it was right.

> *"My darling Abha,*
>
> *We have talked about this day with tears in our eyes and broken hearts and, yet we continued to love each other because we could do no other. You have been a gift that I had not expected, and I would give everything to be able to spend the rest of my life with you. However, that cannot be. I love you truly, my darling and will never give up hope that somehow, one day, I will see you again, hold you in my arms and feel your body next to mine.*

I have bought this small gift for you, as a token for you to remember me by and to know that my love for you knows no bounds.

Be happy my love.

Nehemiah."

He looked at the beautiful golden bird, in the box, wings outstretched beak pointed towards the sky, beautiful, diamond, eyes searching for the sun. The detail was exquisite. It was precious little to leave her with, but it was something, at least. He called for Moses, gruffly.

"Take this to Abha, please Moses and then come straight back here." He ruffled his hair as he looked at the little boy, a lump forming in his throat. He put his hand into his pocket and pulled out two lumps, he gave one to Moses and put the other into his own mouth.

"Cola cubes" he said in a quiet voice.

"Fastest Legs, Moses. Fastest Legs."

He turned away, so the boy would not see his tears. He had left something for Moses too and now put it on the bed. He had not left a note because Moses couldn't read but he wouldn't need a note. It was a large wooden chest and inside was enough money to see him set up for the rest of his life. Through school and college, to buy his own house, to take his own wife and to start his own family. It was the least that Nehemiah could do for the young man.

He took a last look around the room and swung the heavy backpack onto his shoulder, heading for the door. He took long strides out of the pavilion, keeping his eye on the ground and a determined look on his face, so he didn't see the crowd of people surrounding the doorway to Yoshi's house until he spotted a pair of sandals in front of him and he looked up in surprise.

There making a corridor towards the door way was a huge crowd of people. He stood still, jaw dropping in surprise. Everyone was there, Amun and his sons, his beautiful Abha, Zaph and his family, all of the people who he had been working with since his arrival and Rachid and his family.

“How?” he croaked, his throat tightening with supressed emotion.

Amun walked towards him, hands outstretched. “My friend!” he said “I knew you would be leaving us soon, it was a small matter to set Moses to spy on you, so that we would know when. I am sorry for that, but not for the opportunity to see you one last time. To see you safely home.”

Nehemiah just looked at him, at all of the people around him and at his beautiful Abha, who was now approaching, and a sob escaped him. Tears ran down his cheeks and he just stood, overwhelmed by the grief pouring out from the bottom of his soul. He stood shaking with the force of it until, Abha came to him and put her arms around him and then he could hold it no more and broke down into heart-wrenching sobs. The corridor to the doorway closed as people came to him to help him and to share his grief, one last gift from the people.

“What is going on?” They heard the shouting, but no one moved away from Nehemiah. They were too profoundly, absorbed, by his emotion.

“Get away from there!” this time the voice was louder, and people started moving away. The Pharaoh sat upon his canopied chair with a look of complete rage in his eyes.

“What is going on? Why was I not informed?” he was seething that he was being left out of what was obviously a momentous occasion. Rachid moved away from his family and nodded to some guards standing nearby, who edged closer to the Pharaoh. Nehemiah, released Abha and wiped his eyes with the back of his hand. He sighed that his last moment were to be taken up with the spoilt Pharaoh but was glad of the opportunity to collect himself a little.

"Your Highness." He said in a croaky voice. "I am pleased to see you one last time."

"What do you mean, 'one last time'?"

"I have finished my work here. All is as it should be. Your constructions are well on the way to being completed. It is done."

"But, what about my Accountability?" he demanded rising from his chair.

"You are indeed Accountable for your actions, Your Highness, as are all of your people." Nehemiah could sense the unease starting to ripple among the crowd. He needed to go. He eased the straps on his back pack and made a step towards the doorway. "Thank you for your hospitality and I wish you all the very best for the future." He took another step

"No!" the Pharaoh said, "You shall not go!"

"Your Majesty, we agreed. My work here is complete. I understand how difficult it can be to say goodbye, but I have to leave now." He took another step towards the door.

"I said, no! If you go I will undo everything that you have done while you were here. The people will suffer like never before." The young King shouted in rage.

"I don't think that is going to happen!" Nehemiah said indicating the huge crowd of people who were now looking angry and starting to close in on the Pharaoh.

The young king looked stunned and become very quiet, paling considerably.

"This is what accountability looks like, Your Majesty. As I said in our conversation, it is all about responsibility. Now, I am going home, and you are going to look after your people. They will ensure it." He said indicating the crowd who had stopped and were standing hands on hips. He looked around at all of the people.

“Good bye.” He said and looking at the floor started towards the doorway, Rachid at his shoulder.

He had almost reached the door when he heard a cry and looked around to see the Pharaoh grab a spear in rage and throw it at him.

“RUN!” shouted Amun as he put himself between the spear and Nehemiah. It hit him in the stomach and he fell. There was silence and then several things happened at once. The Guards crossed their spears in front of the Pharaoh in order to stop him taking any more action, one of them pushing him back to the seat and ordering the men to pick up his chair and run. The people were enraged and started shouting, however, they were more concerned for Amun’s welfare than a retreating Pharaoh.

“Grandfather!” shouted Abha and rushed towards him, elbowing people out of the way where necessary.

Nehemiah, turned to go to him.

“I am sorry, but I promised.” said Rachid and he grabbed Nehemiah’s arm, before he could figure out what was going on and swung him, with all his might, into the doorway. It all happened so fast and before he knew what was happening, he was on his knees on a carpet with the noise of a slamming door, in his ears.

“NO! Not like this!” he said jumping up and turning to the door. He grabbed the handle and pulled the door open only to see Yoshi’s hallway, standing there. He slammed the door and opened it again, several times but to no avail. He was home.

He closed the door one last time and fell to his knees. It was gone! He had no idea what was happening to Amun and his beautiful Abha, but he wished more than anything that he could be there to help them at this time. Tears rolled down his cheeks and he knelt on the floor and let them.

A short time later he heard a quiet tap on the door and jumped up to open it. There stood a very sombre looking Yoshi.

“Ah, Nehemiah.” He said

“Yoshi.” Nehemiah didn’t know where to begin and tried to find the words to tell him of his distress.

Yoshi walked into the room and put his arm around his shoulder.

“I know, my friend, I know.” And he quietly led him from the room, closing the door behind them.

To be continued…….

Printed in Great Britain
by Amazon